Teddy Bears
and
Ghostly Lairs

Teddy Bears and Ghostly Lairs

A
**JULES KEENE
GLAMPING MYSTERY**

Heather Weidner

To Stan, thanks for joining me on this wild writing journey.

Praise for the Jules Keene Glamping Mysteries

mysterious strangers—and handsome security guy, Jake Evans. Jules and her loyal pup Bijou are in for a suspense-filled adventure. I love the warm and friendly characters and the twists and turns in this new down-home, mutt-loving series."—Susan Van Kirk, author of The Endurance Mysteries and *A Death at Tippitt Pond*

"Jules Keene is focused on her vintage trailer camping resort, but when a dead guest is discovered in the woods and her aunt is questioned, Jules decides to help catch the killer. She must stop the culprit, keep her guests satisfied, grow her business, run for president of the town's business council, and stay alive when the bad guys come after her. This book is a joy to read."—Jackie Layton, author of the Low Country Dog Walker Mysteries

"Packed with action and filled with "Oh, man, I didn't see THAT coming" moments, this first installment in the Jules Keene Glamping Mysteries series will not disappoint. And Weidner made glamping sound so glamorous that I think I'll take my husband up on his suggestion to go camping…but only if it's Fern Valley Camping Resort style!"—Jayne Ormerod, author of *Goin' Coastal*

"Smart and persistent businesswoman Jules Keene puts on her amateur sleuth hat to track down murderers at the upscale Fern Valley Camping Resort, set in the beautiful Blue Ridge mountains. The bad guys have met their match in this fast-paced mystery."—Frances Aylor, author of *Money Grab*

"Heather Weidner's *Vintage Trailers and Blackmailers* is an exciting addition to this year's cozy mystery line-up. Fern Valley Camping Resort, with its refurbished vintage trailers and tiny houses, is as enjoyable as can be, but don't be fooled, this book is all excitement. I don't know how she combines charm with a fast-paced story but I'm so glad she did."—Lane Stone, author of the Pet Palace Mysteries and the Tiara Investigations Mysteries

"Heather Weidner writes a fun and intriguing mystery that's full of twists and turns. Jules Keene, the owner of the posh Fern Valley Camping Resort in the Blue Ridge Mountains, brings sass and adventure as she works to figure out what's happening in her glamping get-away. The other characters are also well defined and add romance, humor, and hair-raising antics! Hard to put down once you start!!"—R. Lambertson, Amazon Reviewer

"I really enjoyed this fun read and would highly recommend it for anyone. I especially liked the idea of the vintage trailers. What a great idea for a campground!"—Sandra Fehr, Amazon Reviewer

"With an appealing cast of characters and a smart amateur sleuth, this series kicks off with a bang. I recommend this to readers who like their mysteries with plenty of red herrings before the satisfying end. Five stars!"—K. M. Rich, Amazon Reviewer

"A mystery with humor, full of secrets, one very handsome security guy, Bijou the dog, blackmail, and some interesting strangers. A fun mystery and look forward to what happens next."—Amy, Goodreads Reviewer

"Heather Weidner wrote a really great storyline with great characters. I think Jules's dog, Bijou, will be everyone's favorite character. The town of Fern Valley seems like the ideal spot for tourists, but it has that warm familiarity to it that could easily make it home for anyone. I'm so excited to see what Heather will come up with next for Jules and Bijou."—Valerie Blankenship Book Reviews

"Vintage Trailers and Blackmailers by Heather Weidner is a fantastic start to a new series for Ms. Weidner. I can't wait to read the next book in this series to find out what else Jules can get into when it comes to solving a mystery. Jules, Roxanne, Jake, and Emily are all great characters, and I can't wait to see what else can happen with them. I am giving Vintage Trailers and Blackmailers by Heather Weidner five stars and recommending it to everyone that likes to read cozy mysteries."—Karen Baron, The Baroness

Book Reviews

"This is my first book by this author, but it definitely won't be my last! I was hooked from the very first page!"—Tonya S., BookBub Reviewer

"The unique setting at a campground pulled me in and gave me a vicarious "glamping" escape. Memorable characters, unique setting and twisty-turny plotting made this a great weekend read. Waiting (not so patiently) for the second installment in the Jules Keene Glamping mysteries."—Mystery Loving Mom, Amazon Reviewer

"Take a break from routine with a visit to a charming mountain resort that features vintage trailers and other whimsical lodging options. While there, get caught up in a puzzling death of a guest. Resort owner Jules investigates murder with the help of an interesting cast of characters. A satisfying and enjoyable read."—S. E Warwick

"Now, this is my idea of camping! Cute, upcycled vintage trailers are so much better than tents! (Not that I have camped in a tent in the last 30 years…) If Fern Valley Camping Resort was real, you can bet I'd be vacationing there. As owner of this resort, Jules Keene has got a great thing going. The campers are full, and people are happy. One reason they might be happy too is the delicious breakfasts that they can get in the lodge. I'd fill up on cinnamon rolls.

Vintage Trailers and Blackmailers is a fantastic start to what I'm sure will be a wonderful series! Heather Weidner paints us a vivid picture, and it's easy to feel as if you're in Fern Valley. She describes not only the camping resort but also the town. You're going to get hungry since Jules visits several trendy restaurants in Fern Valley. So, get some cookies or carrots (or better yet, cinnamon rolls) for your book reading snack. I also love the fact that she doesn't tell us about many of the trailers because that leaves more surprises for the next book. And, speaking of more surprises, I can't wait to see how the tiny house village that they're planning comes along.

The book was a light, fun, quirky read with interesting characters. It sets up for a unique series. I found it very entertaining and enjoyable to read this clean, fun cozy mystery! I highly recommend this book and series!"—Nellie Steele, Nellie's Book Nook

"Heather Weidner has done an outstanding job with this engaging and enjoyable debut novel that features Jules Keene. The story introduces a group of realistic characters. Jules is likable and believable in the central role, and the supporting characters are an interesting mix of personalities. The story is not just about a mystery to be solved. It also encompasses secretive behavior, interpersonal relationships, perseverance, political aspirations, business undertakings, the close connection between a pet and its owner, and a juggling act between amateur sleuthing and fulfilling job-related duties."—Diane Woodman, Amazon Review

"*Vintage Trailers and Blackmailers* is the first book in a new series but doesn't read like one. I mean that in the best possible way. Often, first books tend to spend a lot of time setting the scene and introducing the characters, with the murder almost taking a backseat to the series background. This book launches right in with the mystery element, and does an excellent job of introducing characters, relationships, and the location as part of the narrative.

I very much enjoyed the setting at a glamping-style campground near real-life Charlottesville, Virginia. I liked reading about the different themes of some of the refurbished campers, and the tiny houses. I look forward to seeing more featured in the next book in this series. Five out of five slices of perfect Provolone!"—Chewie the Mouse Amazon Review

Film Crews and Rendezvous

Lights! Camera! Action! Heather Weidner has penned a delightfully entertaining cozy mystery with a strong female lead, a handsome love interest, realistic connection to law enforcement, a snuggle-worthy dog, clever nod to Baum's *Wizard of Oz*, and just the right amount of trials and tribulations to keep readers on their toes. Starting with the perfect karmic choice of victim, the additional murder, questionable accidents, evasive suspects, overheard arguments, revealed secrets, and incriminating photos made this a "couldn't put down" tale of illicit affairs, professional conflicts, and a social media smack down. And the final arrest? I didn't see that coming … loved it!

Heather's writing style is very entertaining worthy of reading more of her work. She has created a delightful environment and characters that work, play, and love in endearing ways to make this a book you'd like to enter. Jules is a determined woman with tight family and friend relationships including the Sheriff, a connection which offers a more natural involvement in the murder investigation … sure she goes off on her own snooping and finds herself in jeopardy, but it meets the realism I expect."—Kathleen Costa, *Kings River Life Magazine*

"With the inviting setting of a luxury camping resort in the Blue Ridge Mountains, a plucky protagonist, and a twisty murder to solve, *Film Crews and Rendezvous* has all the ingredients that appeal to cozy mystery readers."—Kim Davis, Reviewer

"Weidner hits it out of the park with this Jules Keene Glamping Mystery. I loved *Film Crews and Rendezvous*. Jules is a fun character in this great mystery. Weidner keeps you guessing throughout this delightful story. Of all her books I've read, this is definitely one of my favorites."—Cat Brennan

"This series is something truly original."—hsim3691, BookBub Reviewer

"This is a fun addition to the Jules Keene glamping mystery series. As always, it presents a cast of quirky characters and a surprise twist at the end. Highly recommended."—Mary Miley, Mystery Author

"I had never heard of glamping until I started reading the Jules Keene mysteries. Jules is a savvy business owner who always seems to be in the middle of a new adventure which includes murder. Fun to read to figure out who done it. Keep these mysteries coming!"—Vince A., Reviewer

"This is a great book!! I really enjoyed it! When I started reading and discovered that it is set pretty close to where I live, I wasn't sure if I would be able to enjoy it or if I was going to constantly be noticing things about the area that are wrong, but the location didn't end up bothering me at all. It held my interest the whole time, too. I'll be keeping an eye out for the next book in this series."—Sarah Manspile, NetGalley Reviewer

"I thoroughly enjoyed this mystery story set in a Hollywood setting. This had me guessing and guessing who the murder was and in the end I was wrong. Heather has created characters who are colorful, and she develops them in a way that you will learn about them as you read."—Katie Edgard, Net Galley Reviewer

"This latest book by Heather Weidner is great fun. The descriptions of the resort setting are visual, the film crew characters come alive, and there are enough plot twists to keep you guessing. In addition, all the references to food make you want a snack. (Spoiler alert: there are recipes at the end.) A good holiday read and stocking stuffer!"—Charlotte Stuart, Mystery Author

"The second of the Jules Keene Glamping mysteries and the apparent arrival of Hollywood in Fern Valley is raising more than a few eyebrows. The glamping resort has, in fact, never seen anything like it —as the divas and the drama arrive in droves. Amidst the menagerie, however, a killer lurks and it's not too long before chaos ensues and bodies pile. Jules needs to act fast before her previously booming business goes bust. With a cast of eccentric characters, a pacy plot and a frothy narrative this is an entertaining entry in the series."—Ruth Giles, NetGalley Reviewer

"Although I haven't yet read Vintage Trailers and Blackmailers, the first book in the Jules Keene Glamping Mystery series, I was soon hooked after beginning Film Crews and Rendezvous! It didn't take long for me to become acquainted with Jules and her dog, Bijou, from Fern Valley in the Blue Ridge Mountains. With an obligatory murder, the characters are beguiling, and the mystery held my attention and kept me guessing. A great tale."—Bridget East, NetGalley Reviewer

"An entertaining story and I like the idea of the tiny houses. They intrigued me and off I went researching them. I do like stories that pique my interest in something new."—Kate Merson, NetGalley Reviewer

"A very fun read!!"—Liz Boeger, Mystery Author

"Film Crews and Rendezvous gets five stars from me! The entertaining characters, cozy small town setting, humor, and twisty mystery make Film Crews and Rendezvous a cozy I highly recommend."—Kristy's Cozy Corners

"Hollywood, glamping, and murder… oh my! *Film Crews and Rendezvous* by Heather Weidner had me at the Blue Ridge Mountains setting (aka, one of my happy places) and then kept me engaged by the various layers to this murder mystery. As the title suggests, Jules' glamping resort is overrun by a film crew – and the crowds it attracts – and trying to keep up with who is rendezvousing with who (all off-scene) becomes an almost full-time job for poor Jules. All in the name of investigating the double murder, of course. The author does a great job of setting the scene and moving the mystery along at a steady pace. Sorting the clues from the misdirections will take some skill for readers-slash-armchair-detectives and keeps us invested in the outcome – a cleverly-crafted outcome, at that. Also, I want the tiny homes at Jules' resort to be real because I want to stay in the Rowling one. Such a fun idea!"—Carrie Schmidt, Reading is my Super Power Blogger

"What a fantastic addition to the series! This has to be my new favorite in the series! I love the setting—Blue Ridge Mountains, the characters (Jules, aunt Roxanne, Jack, Pixel and of course, Jules' dog Bijou), and this time we have a film crew on set. So, more drama, more saucy gossip and rumors, and more action… with a dash or two of murder."—The Book Decoder, Book Blogger and Reviewer

"What do you get when you mix Hollywood people and a small town in the Blue Ridge Mountains: you get this amazing book. I need to read the first book in the series."—Riley Wiederhold, Book Reviewer

"With lots of twists and turns, a little romance, a murder and a strong, take-charge protagonist in Jules Keene and you have a winning cozy murder mystery!"—NorthStarVance, BookBub Reviewer

"All the characters are well written and interesting. The dialogue is smart with a bit of sass. Heather Weidner has done a great job writing *Film Crews and Rendezvous*. I'm looking forward to reading more books in this series."—rmkrejsa42, BookBub Reviewer

"A new to me author and series. It was the first I read and won't surely be the last as the author did a good job in developing a solid plot that kept hooked and guessing.

The fleshed out characters are likeable and I had a lot of fun. Recommended."—Anna Maria Giacomasso, NetGalley Reviewer

"Such a cute, fun read! I really enjoyed the mystery in the book, and I thought the story flowed really nice. Such a good book!"—Noelle S., NetGalley Reviewer

"I really liked this book! The setting was great and very well written. I am now very interested in glamping myself. The author really involved every part of the setting in a well thought out way and it really made the book better. I liked the steady pace which never made the book boring nor to intense. It was a good mix between the author telling us what we needed to know and stuff the reader had to figure out by themselves. I was very invested in the book and liked all aspects of it!"—Molly Bossel, NetGalley Reviewer

"I absolutely loved this book! The story is so well developed, and the characters are so relatable. I love the tiny homes that are in the book. If you are looking for a fun fast paced reed, I highly recommend!!"—Katie Burleson, NetGalley Reviewer

Christmas Lights and Cat Fights

"A resort owner starts solving the murder of the ex-wife of one of her guests. This book literally made me so jealous that I wasn't in a cabin near the mountains with fresh snow and a murder to investigate. The plot is very refreshing and enticing. The writing is sensational, I could envision everything so perfectly."—Shannon Coe, NetGalley Reviewer

"This book reminded of the mysteries I read when I was younger, good clean and fun! I like the author's writing style and she seemed to have a good knowledge of police procedurals without over doing it for this fun styled book. There's some good clean, budding romance, sleuthing and mystery that you won't want to miss!"—Angela Hodge, NetGalley Reviewer

"This was a delightful and suspenseful holiday mystery that will keep you hooked from the very first page. This book combines the festive spirit of Christmas with a thrilling murder mystery, creating a unique and captivating story."—E. A. Andrews, NetGalley Reviewer

"I really am looking forward to the next book! I highly recommend *Christmas Lights and Cat Fights* (and the other Jules Keene books!) for its amazing characters, delightful setting, and puzzling mystery! I think cozy mystery lovers will enjoy it as much as I did."—Christy's Cozy Corners, Book Blogger

"Such a cozy, festive mystery! I binged this in one sitting! Definitely need to pick up a trophy copy. I can't wait to read more by Heather in the future!"—Megan Moore, NetGalley Reviewer

"I thoroughly enjoyed this story, and if you enjoy cozies, I think you will too. Plus, there are cats, and it's Christmas. What's not to like? It's a nice addition to this series by Heather Weidner!"—Jackie Layton, Mystery Author

"Absolutely loved this book! The author's writing style is amazing! I look forward to reading more from them!"—Rebecca May, NetGalley Reviewer

"Christmas Lights and Cat Fights by Heather Weidner is a delightful and cozy mystery that combines the joy of the holiday season with an entertaining feline twist. With engaging characters, a charming small-town setting, and a purr-fectly mysterious plot, this book is sure to keep fans of cozy mysteries entertained."—A Moment with Mystee, NetGalley Reviewer

"Christmas Lights and Cat Fights is a fun cozy with a nice winter-holiday theme."—Rebecca M. Douglass, Author and Book Blogger

   "This is a charming cozy mystery for the Christmas holiday. Heather adds many festive details to the descriptions of Fern Valley, making me wish I could visit Jules' resort and stay in a tiny house. I particularly loved the descriptions of snow in the valley."—Sarah Erwin, *Kings River Life*

"This was a suspenseful holiday mystery that kept me hooked from the first page to the end of the story. It's the 3rd book in the series and is full of surprises. The characters are engaging and entertaining. Many are suspects with secrets that kept me guessing. I also enjoyed reading all the recipes following the end of the story. I look forward to reading another book by Heather Weidner. If you like cozy mysteries, then I am sure you will love this one."—Eadie Burke, NetGalley Reviewer

"A fun cozy. Throw together a wife, ex-wife and Christmas time along with a huge blow up between them and you get mayhem. And some cats are missing! Not your everyday house cats either! Yikes! Jules is trying to keep everyone happy while finding out who did the ex in. Great setting. Good characters."—Renee Winter, NetGalley Reviewer

"Christmas mystery meets the Tiger King! I was excited to read this book. Weidner's book had me guessing until the end. It's a perfect read for a cozy night!"—A Book to Mark, Book Blogger

"I was looking for a fun mystery set during the Christmas season to get me in the holiday spirit. Christmas Lights and Cat Fights by Heather Baker Weidner was just the book! I was delighted to find that it was set in Virginia, and I recognized many of the towns. I want to continue to follow the adventures of Jules Keene."—Theresa Werner, Journalist

"This is a fast-paced mystery with an interesting setting and an engaging amateur sleuth. A fun read around the holiday, or anytime."—Anna St. John, Mystery Author

"This was such an amazing holiday cozy mystery. I couldn't stop reading this book!! I hope more comes out with Jules as the main sleuth. I think that they would be awesome. I loved the writing style of Heather Weidner, and I will definitely be reading more from her."—Lori Clenderin, NetGalley Reviewer

"Christmas, Oh I do love Christmas at any time of year. This is a book that is a bit of fun, a bit of murder and of course an amateur sleuth. A cozy mystery and an entertaining read. A good story and it is very easy to read, I enjoyed the characters and the setting. And to top it off. Recipes! I wasn't expecting that."—Donna Robinson, NetGalley Reviewer

"Heather Weidner's *Christmas Lights and Cat Fights* is a delightful cozy mystery that perfectly captures the holiday spirit while delivering a dose of intrigue and humor."—Tami Boyd, NetGalley Reviewer

Deadlines and Valentines

"I devoured each and every page."—Mariam Mulla, Book Reviewer

"I just finished reading this book. I loved it. I'm looking forward to the next one!"—The Book Decoder, Book Reviewer

"I thought the interactions of the diva authors was hilarious, and really added to the story, we don't normally get funny moments in the true crime genre so it was really a treat."—Terah MacInnes, NetGalley Reviewer

"I liked this book a lot and the animosity among all the authors made this book fun to read. Everyone had a motive, but who is the real killer?"—Lisa Currier, NetGalley Reviewer

"The mystery was really good. I loved the Scooby Doo vibes. I would definitely check out more books by this author!"—Shaina Burris, NetGalley Reviewer

"Weidner's writing is crisp and keeps the story moving at a good pace."—Jennie Bishop, NetGalley Reviewer

"This was a really cute cozy read. Gave me Scooby Doo and the Mystery Machine vibes! I'll definitely have to pick up and read the other books to this series!"—Grace Lee, NetGalley Reviewer

"Loved this book, very interesting and keeps you hooked until the very end."—Rachel Phillips, NetGalley Reviewer

"This was a fun one! It's a cute mystery and a quick read. I liked the Valentine's setting with the spooky vibes of the mystery/death. I like the lighthearted chaos and liked the writer's voice—it was well written."—Rachel Seal, NetGalley Reviewer

"This was such a cozy thriller! I really enjoyed the small town glamping resort in the mountains of Virginia. It was so easy to imagine in my head since I am familiar with the areas that the book mentions. I had no idea what to expect with a thriller/mystery themed novel based on a valentine's book festival. With several quirky, attitude-filled characters, this book did not disappoint. I picked this book up not realizing that it was the fourth book in the series. I will definitely be adding the first three to my "to be read" list."—Kayla Barton, NetGalley Reviewer

"As a fan of this series, I enjoy it for two main reasons: 1) the unique glamping resort theme, which is expanded with fresh ideas in every book, and 2) it's written by Heather Weidner, one of my favorite authors. Heather's writing is like aged wine -rich, full-bodied, and immersive, drawing readers in as if watching a movie unfold.

Heather Weidner masterfully weaves together recurring character developments, the glamorous yet cutthroat world of authors, and lovable furry friends to create the perfect Valentine's-themed cozy mystery. I was hooked from start to finish, unable to put the book down. While the killer's identity wasn't shocking, their motive added a chilling layer, revealing the sinister depths of human psychology."—Rekha Rao, NetGalley Reviewer

"This was an easy cute read. Just read a really heavy difficult book and this was a nice palate cleanser."—Lauren Kilroy, NetGalley Reviewer

"I enjoyed this clever and charming murder mystery. Having writers as characters was a great idea, they are intriguing and quirky. You can also expect suspense and humor. The setting is charming, with the glamping resort adding a unique twist to the typical cozy mystery backdrop.

Cozy murder mysteries are my favorites, and this one did not disappoint."—Julie Botez, NetGalley Reviewer

"This was an enjoyable light read. All the jealousy and underhandedness amongst the authors makes them all suspects, but what I really want to know is if any of the authors are based on real people?!"—Theresa Werner, NetGalley Reviewer

"This series does not disappoint! The author does a fabulous job of developing dimensional characters, a solid mystery filled with twist, turns and red herrings, and brings it all to life and away that makes it hard to put the book down. If you have not read a book in this series yet, I can tell you there is nothing wrong with reading this one first and going back to the others."—Cindi Austin, NetGalley Reviewer

"I absolutely loved this book! It was a Nancy Drew meets book festival mystery. The book was a short, fun, easy read. I loved the characters and the Valentines theme of the book. This was the first book in the series that I have read, but I felt it was easy to understand who the characters were, and I did not feel like I was missing anything."—Megan Slough, NetGalley Reviewer

"This was such a fun read, hooked me right from the beginning."—Corie Sylvester, NetGalley, Reviewer

"A true who-done-it with a lot of suspects especially the divas. I had a few guesses on who the killer was, but the author did a nice jump of showing Jules puzzle out the answer."—Katie Barr, Educator

"*Deadlines and Valentines* by Heather Weidner is a delightful cozy mystery that combines romance with suspense in a charming glamping setting."—Clarissa Cambusano, NetGalley Reviewer

"*Deadlines and Valentines* is a delightful cozy-romance mystery that takes readers to a charming glamping resort in the Blue Ridge Mountains, where a book festival provides the perfect setting for romance and suspense. This was such a fun read!"—Lori Bauswell, NetGalley Reviewer

"I read this as a standalone. However, I will definitely be reading all of them! This was a fun, easy read that kept you guessing the whole time. I enjoy books like this that are relatable to small-town living. I'm excited to read the next one in the series!"—Annie Kirth, Net Galley Reviewer

"If I can't go in person and visit the town of Fern Valley from Heather Weidner's Jules Keene Glamping Mystery Series, reading another entry into this charming cozy mystery series is the next best thing."—Sarah Ervin, *Kings River Life*

Chapter One

Thursday Afternoon

Taking a swig of her iced mocha, Jules Keene threaded her way around piles of boxes and half-assembled, canopied tents as she and Kim Lacy, owner of Knit Wits, scanned Fern Valley's main street. Both sides of the street looked like Santa's workshop with the long line of colorful vendor tents and all their paraphernalia for the town's first Teddy Bear and Toy Extravaganza. A large brown banner covered with cartoon bears stretched across the street and flapped in the warm spring breeze.

"It looks like everyone's checked in. I'm sure Elaine is relieved and ready to get the festivities going. I know she's double and triple-checked everything. All the i's are crossed or dotted or whatever Elaine does," Kim said, brushing a stray brown curl off of her forehead.

Jules smiled at the thought of Elaine James, owner of the Birds and Bees garden shop and chairperson of the town's business council's events committee, fluttering from booth to booth, ensuring that every detail met her standards. "Most of all the vendors have checked into their accommodations at the resort. Tomorrow, we expect a large number of visitors to arrive. Sounds like we are about ready for a festival."

Jules's Fern Valley Luxury Camping Resort had been in her family since the 1970s. After her divorce from the Idiot, she moved back to the Blue Ridge Mountains and helped her father restore vintage trailers to transform the business from traditional campsites to a glamorous camping experience in time for the glamping craze. Jules blinked back the tears when she thought of her dad. The divorce was traumatic, but she was glad to have had those last few years with her father.

"Stop right there! What in tarnation do you think you're doing?" echoed from a large blue tent in front of them. Jules and Kim froze in their tracks. *So much for a peaceful afternoon.*

They hurried over as a woman dressed from head to toe in a red outfit with a large brown bear that stretched from her shoulder to her knee waggled her finger inches from an older man with a trolley full of boxes. The woman's red plastic visor struggled to hold back her graying ringlets. Her head bobbled as she stomped even closer to the man. The man paused and pulled the metal trolley in front of him like a shield to ward off an impending attack. He continued to back up as she encroached on his space.

"You wait a doggone minute," the woman yelled. "Barb and I tried to be polite and neighborly when your brood showed up. But you all have done nothing but harass and infringe on our rights and our patience. We paid a lot of money for this oversized booth, and now your crew is invading our territory. And that. That." The woman pointed a red fingernail at the tent next to hers. "That display is blocking the majority of the entrance to our booth. You've got to do something about it before I take matters into my own hands."

"Not sure what you're flapping your gums about. We're in the process of setting up Vern's Collectibles. It takes a lot of hands and work to maintain our enterprise. We're professionals. And don't get your panties in a bunch, we're not done yet. Just hold your horses." The meatball of a man took off his red ballcap and wiped his brow with his arm.

The woman made a harrumphing sound and stepped toward his tent. Before she could make her case, Kim pulled out her clipboard and scanned several pages. "Uh, Ms. Johnson?"

"No. Barb's my sister," the woman replied, still inspecting the dividing line between the two booths. "I'm Sil. Silvia Gregorio, her business partner."

"It's nice to meet you. I'm Kim Lacy, and this is Jules Keene. We're volunteers for the business council." Turning to face the man, she continued, "Mr. Hogge." She stretched his surname out to two syllables with her southern accent.

"It's Hogge, like the pig. Don't need any fancy pronunciations. I'm Vernon Hogge, and I'm here with my son Vee Jay, his girlfriend, and my nephew. We have a full-scale operation here, and we need space to move around and to showcase our inventory. We do over two hundred and fifty shows a year. This one," he said, pointing a beefy finger at Sil, "Has done nothing but yammer and whine since we've been here. I don't have time for chitchat. I've got work to do. So please move yourself out of my way, or you might get run over."

"It's nice to meet you both," Jules said. "Mr. Hogge, you all seem well on your way to setting up your space. Before you leave tonight, you'll make sure that all the boxes and displays are under your canopy, right? Our fire officials insist that we don't block any exits."

"Of course. Safety first. And all our inventory will be locked in our trailer. We have a security system and cameras, so don't get any ideas about any funny business," he said, turning his head toward Sil.

"I wouldn't dream of it. I want to have a great weekend of sales in the booth I paid for. All of it with no impediments or junk blocking my customers from our merchandise. It's not fair of you to trap our customers in your tent."

"Junk?" His voice echoed through the tent loudly enough for those nearby to stop and stare. "I'll have you know our brick and mortar store, Vern's Toy Emporium, has the finest teddy bears and dolls this side of the Mississippi. We sell collectibles. And for your information, we have quite a few famous clients. You should check out our website. I have scads of pictures with politicians, world leaders, and Hollywood types." He turned and dragged the trolley full of boxes back to the other side of his tent and started moving tables and displays.

"Let us know, Ms. Gregorio, if you have any other issues. We'll check back later," Jules said, waving as she and Kim ducked under the tent's canopy.

"Well, that was interesting," Kim whispered. Before she could finish, a shrill scream rang out across the street. The pair hurried toward a rainbow-colored food truck and a white tent on the opposite side of Main Street. Ten blocks, most of the town's downtown, had been cordoned off for pedestrian traffic, the vendors, and a variety of food trucks. A large stage dominated the small park nestled between a row of businesses and restaurants. A second squeal ripped through the peaceful setting.

"You cheated me, and I don't appreciate that comment you made," a young woman screeched at a guy inside the food truck. "I ordered the taco combo, and I didn't get the side. And the stupid soda is all ice. And do you call this meat? It looks like you waved the meat over the taco. It's full of lettuce and tomatoes. Where's the beef?"

Jules stifled a laugh when she thought of the old TV commercial. Before she could interject into the discussion, the petite woman threw the taco on the street and hoisted herself up on the food truck's counter and leaned into the open window. With one swoop of her arm, she knocked condiments in all directions and swung one leg up on the counter like a gymnast on a high bar.

"Hey, you can't come in here. Get down. What are you doing?" the guy inside said, trying to prevent the woman from climbing into his food truck. "That's a health code violation. You can't be back here while we're cooking. Get out. Get down before you hurt yourself and destroy our stuff. Are you nuts?"

Kim keyed her walkie-talkie. "This is Kim and Jules. We have a disagreement at the food truck near booth thirty-four. Need some assistance. Do we have anyone from the sheriff's office?"

The radio squawked. "Elaine here. I'm on my way. I'll alert the deputy. Code red. Code red."

Ignoring Kim, Jules, and the squawking radio, the woman continued to try to crawl inside the truck's small window. "Don't push me. If I fall, I'll sue you. See. He's trying to push me. Did you see that?" The woman balanced on the counter, squatting on one knee. With her free hand, she knocked more condiments to the ground. "You need to respect me. I'm a customer. Wait until my boyfriend hears what you said to me. You treated me terribly.

Wait until I let all my followers know what happened. You are going to be sorry."

"Lady, I'm not sure what your gripe is, but get down now. I'm sure we can work this out," the food truck guy shouted as Elaine James rushed over, waving both arms as a small crowd gathered nearby on the sidewalk.

"Stop this right now. Young lady, get down immediately, or I'll have you banned from the festival," Elaine yelled.

"Well, lah-di-dah and I'll get down when I feel like it." She hopped down and dusted her hands on her Daisy Duke denim shorts.

"What is going on here?" Elaine demanded, tapping her foot on the asphalt.

"He messed up my order. Then he disrespected me. I will not be treated like this. My boyfriend's dad paid good money for us to come here and work. I shouldn't be treated this way. I am a VIP guest in this town."

"And you are?" Kim asked.

"Simone. Simone Carlson. And you should know," she said, pointing a hot pink talon at the food truck guy. "I'm a social media influencer. You're going to be sorry you crossed paths with me."

As the small crowd continued to grow on the sidewalk, Jules stepped forward. "Ms. Carlson. What if he replaces your order?"

"I only want an apology. I'm done here. I lost my appetite when I saw this rabbit food," Simone said, sweeping her bottle-blond bangs off her forehead with a dramatic wave. She pulled out her phone and pointed it at the vendor.

"I'm sorry," the guy said. "I didn't mean to offend you."

Simone shrugged a shoulder and pocketed her phone.

"Thank you," Elaine said. "And I think you need to apologize to him before he asks the deputy to arrest you for destroying his property and invading his space and probably ruining whatever he was cooking."

Simone stared daggers at Elaine. "What? I'm very passionate about my causes, one of them being the way that women are treated by men." She turned on her heeled sandals and marched off toward Vern's tent.

Kim and Jules picked up the sauce packets and wrapped plasticware as the man came around to survey the damage.

The taco vendor picked up the napkins and dumped several handfuls into the nearby trash can. "Some people," he muttered under his breath. "Thanks for your help." He returned the utensils and the sauce packets to the caddy on the counter.

Elaine looked around and scanned the crowd that had started to disperse.

Deputy Dempsey shuffled next to the taco truck and adjusted his thick, leather belt. "You called for assistance?"

"Too late." Elaine scowled. "We diffused the situation and restored order."

"Glad to help," the deputy said, stepping up to the window and looking at the menu.

Elaine made a harrumphing sound and checked her clipboard before she toddled across the street.

"Not quite the fun start to the Teddy Bear Festival that Elaine was expecting. I hope Simone has no other causes that she's passionate about," Kim said with a wink. "And we may need to keep an eye on those folks. They seem to be a tad abrasive." She pointed toward the overstuffed tent where the pudgy Vern stood in the street, hands planted on his hips. He stared intently at Sil in the next booth.

Chapter Two

Friday Morning

Roxanne Mallory, Jules's fashion plate of an aunt, breezed in and plunked several bags and her pink Coach purse on the other desk in the resort's back room of the store. "Whew. It's getting hot out there already. How are things?" She swept a loose stand of her platinum bob off her forehead.

Jules closed the Dutch dividing door between the two rooms to keep her spunky Jack Russell, Bijou, from being overly enthusiastic when guests arrived. "Good. All of the vendors have checked into their accommodations. I'm expecting fifteen more check-ins from festival goers for the vintage trailers and tiny houses, and another twenty-five for the campsites in the meadow. Jake and Lester are keeping order over there and sending new folks here to register and get their campsite number. So far, everything is running smoothly."

"I heard through the grapevine that there were some feisty vendors and dustups in town. My source said Elaine turned three shades of red and purple." A wry smile crept across Roxanne's face. "At least this time, Elaine didn't end up in a melee."

Jules suppressed a snicker. "Hopefully, that's the worst that will happen this weekend. It was the gal staying in the Baum tiny house. She made a bit of a scene in front of a taco truck. Oh, and two of the vendors were arguing about their display space." Jules let out a sigh. "Maybe, they'll settle down and enjoy the festival. But I did tell Jake to keep an eye out when he does his rounds, just in case."

"Is she one of the vendors, too?"

Jules nodded. "She's with Vernon Hogge and his family, one of the teddy bear guys."

Roxanne wrinkled her nose. "She's no match for Jake and Lester. And I can't forget you, Miss Bijou. You really run security around here." Roxanne reached down and slipped the wiggly brown and white dog a treat from her stash in the desk drawer.

The bells on the front door of the store jingled and halted their conversation. Jules and her aunt made their way to the camp store's large wooden counter, filled with anything needed for a true glamping experience.

Jules and Roxanne spent the next few hours answering questions and welcoming the new check-ins. A few guests popped in for excursion ideas or to check out equipment for croquet and cornhole, or badminton.

"Whew. That was a little intense," Roxanne said, sinking onto the stool behind the store's counter. "Somebody opened the floodgates. You haven't offered campsites in the meadow to traditional camping in a while."

Jules straightened the fliers on the counter and did a quick mental inventory of what needed to be replenished. "It made sense. We had a lot of interest in the festival, the trailers, including my newest fairy forest one, and tiny houses filled up fast. I wanted to help bring as many toy fans to town as I could. And a lot of folks were interested in bringing their own campers. Plus, we also have some paranormal investigators staying in two of the tiny houses. They made their reservations before we had the date for the festival. I'm curious to see what they find in Fern Valley. They should be here tomorrow."

"I love those ghost hunter shows. Though they're not too much fun to watch with Sheriff Matt. He's the consummate skeptic, never suspending belief for even one second that something otherworldly could have happened. He has a scientific explanation for everything." Roxanne rolled her eyes and blushed slightly when she mentioned her beau, Sheriff Matthew Hobbs. "I'm going to get some tea. Want some?"

"No, thanks. Since things are under control here, I'm going to head into town to see if the business council volunteers need any help, and I hope it's quieter than yesterday," Jules said.

"No problem. Bijou and I will have a staff meeting while you're gone."

"Staff meeting? Did I miss it?" Jake Evans said, poking his head through the doorway and laughing. He picked up Bijou, who turned to jelly in his arms.

"Nah," Jules said. "Roxanne's busy planning their afternoon. I'm going to head into town to see how things are there. How's life in the meadow?" A tingle of excitement shot through her when he smiled at her.

She had known Jake and endured all of his teasing during her teen years when he worked for her parents. The guy with the boyish grin and deep green eyes returned to Fern Valley all grown-up and focused after several tours in the mid-east. They started dating about the time they formed a partnership with the tiny house business. They made a good team. Jake created them, Jules themed them, and they shared the proceeds from the rentals. He also used the tiny village as models for his side business.

"Lester and I met some nice people and answered a ton of questions about the area and things to see in the valley. By last count, there are only four spaces that aren't filled," he said.

"You want to go to town with me?" Jules asked Jake.

"If you plan a stop for lunch." Jake winked and kissed Bijou.

"Let me wrap up a few things here, and I'll meet you out front," Jules said. Jake nodded. "I'll go get the 'Stang."

"Do you want me to bring you anything?" Jules asked as her aunt popped a tea pod in the coffee maker.

"I'm good. Sheriff Matt and I have dinner plans. I'm saving room for part of his dessert. Y'all have fun. We'll be here when you get back."

"Be good for Aunt Roxanne," Jules said to Bijou, who circled her puffy pink bed twice and found the perfect spot for a pre-lunch nap.

Before Jules had time to fasten her seat belt in Jake's red Mustang, he floored it out of the parking lot toward the resort's entrance. The trees that lined the main road looked like a blur from the passenger window. They made it to town in record time and without getting caught at Fern Valley's one stoplight. Not finding any open parking places, Jake snagged a spot on a side street. After parallel parking, he jogged around and held the door for her.

"Let's go see what's shaking. I'm hoping that it's quieter than yesterday." Jules grabbed his outstretched hand.

A sly smile crossed Jake's face. "Lester told me that you all had to quell a screaming banshee who was attacking a taco guy for apparently no good reason."

"Yep, and we have the privilege of hosting her for the next week or so. She's staying in the Wizard of Oz house. Let me know if you encounter any problems."

"I heard Elaine threatened to ban her." Jake grinned.

Jules nodded and cracked a smile. "Not sure if it was a ban on this week's events or for the entire town forever."

"With Elaine, you never know."

The pair strolled up and down both sides of the street, checking out booths and food trucks. Most of the vendors had their wares already set up to sell. The signs and displays showcased every kind of bear and stuffed animal imaginable. Jules's favorite was a double tent full of classic toys. She and Jake reminisced as they perused the cases full of dolls, teddy bears, and toys from their childhood.

Jake stopped in front of a huge exhibit. "I wish my mom had saved some of my Hot Wheels and comic books. I'm going to have to check the attic next time I'm home to see if she saved anything. I didn't realize how valuable some of these are."

"I had the Dawn Dolls and the Fisher Price ones," Jules said, pointing to a display of the Little People toys. "And an Easy Bake Oven."

"A Big Wheel," Jake and Jules said in unison.

"If you find your old toys and want to get rid of them, give me a call," a tall woman in a neon yellow "Carla's Classic Collections" shirt said. "Hi, I'm Carla. My son and I travel all over for the best collectibles. Aren't toys wonderful? They bring back so many good memories for people."

"It's been fun browsing through your displays," Jules said. "I think most of mine were given away years ago."

"We'll be here throughout the festival if you see something you like. Grownups like the nostalgia or to buy things they always wanted. And my son Carl will have a big demo at the Miniature Car Show. If you like Mattel and Hot Wheels, you'll see some classics."

"We'll be there," Jake said, pocketing the business card she offered.

When Carla turned to greet a pair of women who wandered into the tent, Jake and Jules stepped out into the street. Jake shaded his eyes with his hand to block the bright sunlight.

Pulling her sunglasses out of her red curls, Jules glanced up and down the street. "Let's go see Vern and his neighbor." She pointed catty-corner across the street. "That's where all the fun was yesterday."

Jake raised an eyebrow and followed her to Vern's oversized tent, bursting at the edges with bears in every size and shape. Ducking under the canopy, Jules and Jake browsed the thousands of stuffed animals that covered every inch of the tent.

Jake approached the table with the cash register. "Hi. I'll take the hot pink one behind you."

"Good choice," Vern said, pulling it down from the hook. "That's ten dollars."

"And I'll take that purple one," Jules added, handing Vern the cash. Jake looked at her. "It's for Pixel," she said. "She has a thing for purple." She took the bag Vern offered her.

Simone sat on a stool behind the table with her arms crossed. Her pursed lips looked like she had licked a pickle.

"Hi, Simone," Jules said.

The younger woman nodded slightly and glanced back at her phone without any response.

"She's Miss Sourpuss this morning. She better perk up, or she'll be looking for a new job soon," Vern said, zeroing in on three new customers who were leaning on a glass display behind Jules and Jake. "Hi. If you're interested in seeing that, it's a classic teddy bear made by the Steiff company, one of the premier manufacturers. And it is perfect for any true collector who knows quality."

Jules tuned out Vern, who rambled on about the value of his classic bears. She paused and stared at Simone. It was odd she didn't react when it was clear people were talking to her. When the young woman finally looked up, Jules waved. "See you around the resort."

Simone nodded and averted her eyes to her phone's screen.

"That was odd," Jake said outside the tent.

"Hopefully, it was nothing. There seems to be a lot of drama with Vern's team."

"Here. This is for you." Jake handed her the bag with the pink bear.

"Awww. Thanks. I don't have a pink bear. It's perfect for my collection. What do you feel like for lunch?" Grilled meat and French fry scents wafted from the line of food trucks across the street and caught the attention of both of them.

"The hot dogs and brats smell out of this world. You up for that?" he asked, leading her toward a bright blue truck with images of cartoon dachshunds on unicycles.

Jules nodded, and the pair found a spot in the fast-moving line that snaked around the Dogs on Wheels truck. When it was their turn, Jules ordered a Coney dog with mustard and chips, and Jake asked for a fully loaded brat and two lemonades.

The pair took their lunches and found an open spot on the curb near the travel agency. The windows behind them featured posters of real bears and adventure vacations. The crowds wandered up and down the sidewalks.

Jules popped the last bite of hot dog in her mouth as Simone rushed out of the tent across the street. She glanced at her phone and scanned the activity on the street. After a couple of seconds, Simone dashed down the pavement in a pair of red stilettos.

"That is odd," Jules said. "I'll be right back."

"Give me your trash. I'll meet you back here." Jake reached for her empty wrapper.

She took one last sip of her lemonade and handed him the cup, too.

"Thanks. Be back in a flash."

Keeping Simone in sight, Jules power-walked down the street. The woman checked her phone again and darted through a throng of people on the sidewalk on the other side of the street.

Jules zigzagged her way around the bystanders and followed Simone to a red tent in front of an alley near J. P. Gross's landscaping company. Jules pushed thoughts of the cranky business owner, J. P., who gave her grief every chance he got, out of her head as she tiptoed around, trying to keep an eye out for Simone. Deciding to duck behind the next tent and loop around it like she's walking toward the alley, Jules spotted Simone in a lip lock with a stocky blond that wasn't Vern's son.

Jules's eyes widened. Deciding not to interrupt the kanoodling, she quickly retraced her steps and caught up with Jake.

"Where'd you go? Simone okay?" Jake asked when she stopped next to him. He had found shade under a tree near the Good Thyme Bistro's outdoor seating.

"She seems fine now," Jules said, catching her breath. "She's over behind the tent making out with her boyfriend's cousin."

Jake raised one eyebrow. "Interesting family dynamics. The holidays are going to be fun at their house."

"It might explain some of the tension. Wanna see anything else while we're here?" she asked.

"We didn't see what's at the other end." Jake pointed to the banner fluttering over the other end of Main Street. "Hopefully, there's less drama down there."

Chapter Three

Saturday

Jules stared at her laptop and rubbed her eyes with the heels of her hands. She had been working on the resort's newsletter and website for several hours. "Bijou, it's time for another round of java juice. I need the caffeine to keep it going this morning."

The plucky dog opened one eye. When she didn't see any chance of scoring a snack, she rolled over in her bed.

As the coffee maker spewed out the last stream of dark roast, the bells on the store's front door tinkled and activated the Jack Russell alarm. Jules managed to grab her coffee and nudge the little dog behind the Dutch door as she headed off to meet her guests before they were greeted by the little, four-legged tornado of energy.

"Good morning." Jules set her mug on the front counter and logged into the reservation computer. "How may I help you?"

A burly man with shaggy curly hair lumbered to the counter and dropped a heavy backpack on the floor. The thud echoed through the store. "Hi, I'm Eliot, and this is Noah. I talked to Jules about a block of reservations for the East Coast Paranormal group." He pointed to the shorter guy behind him.

"I'm Jules. Welcome to Fern Valley." She tapped on the keyboard. "I have the A. A. Milne treehouse reserved for four, and then someone else in your party reserved the J. K. Rowling tiny house for two more. Here are the keys for the treehouse. You all are the first group to stay in this one. It's themed for Milne's works, including the Winnie the Pooh classics and *The Red House Mystery*. The treehouse is a split-level dwelling with a wrap-around deck and a three-sixty view of the beautiful Blue Ridge Mountains. We hope you enjoy your stay."

"Cool," Eliot said. "Noah, Cliffy, Norm, and I will be staying there. We'll be able to get some footage from up there of the mountains. Two others in our group, Suz and Drew, are going to check in later today. They're driving in from Norfolk, so it'll take them longer. Our part of the crew came from Richmond."

"If you have any questions or need anything, please let me or my staff know." Jules pushed the keys across the counter.

Uh, we've got a lot of equipment in our trailer and truck. Is it okay to leave them parked in your lot?" Eliot asked.

"Sure. Or I could have Jake, our security guy, meet you at the house and show you where you could park in the field if you don't mind the grass. Then your equipment would be closer to your accommodations if you need to access it."

"That'd be great," Eliot said, bouncing on his heels. "We've got a lot of electronic gear and cameras. The stuff's expensive and specific to the work we do. I'd like to be able to keep an eye on it. We're filming a documentary of haunted places in the Blue Ridge."

"That sounds interesting. I've heard stories over the years of ghostly encounters and spooky tales in the valley," Jules said.

"Do tell," Noah, the thinner guy with the longish blond hair, said, whipping out a notebook and a pen after handing Eliot one of the keys for the Milne treehouse. Noah pocketed the other keys and pushed a thick lock of hair out of his eyes.

"Let's see. The old Whitaker place that's up the road, about three miles, has always been front and center in a bunch of stories kids told on Halloween. It looks like it belongs in an episode of Scooby-Doo. Lots of people around town have claimed to see spooky lights in the windows, even when the place had no electricity. Rumor has it that it's from old Mrs. Whitaker, who's searching the property for the gold her husband hid. There's also a railroad trestle about ten miles from here, near the ridge that's supposed to be the site where some kids were killed by the train in the 1950s. Legend has it that you can see them or hear them laughing and whistling during a full moon. You may want to check out Between the Covers, our local bookstore. The owner, Elizabeth Rhoney, has a whole section on books about the area. I know there's a haunted places series that she keeps in stock. You may want to talk to my aunt Roxanne, too. She's lived here all her life, and she's our resident expert on all things Fern Valley. She's off today, but she'll be back in the office tomorrow."

"Thanks," Noah said, as he continued to jot in his notebook. "Lots of good stuff to check out."

"We're going to get settled in and work on our plan for this week. We're headed up to the abandoned motel on Afton Mountain starting tomorrow night. We hope to capture a lot of paranormal activity up there. Suz and Drew have done massive research on that place, and there were several deaths that occurred there over the years, so it's probably rife with paranormal activity. Plus, it just looks spooky in all the pictures."

Jules's thoughts flashed to the abandoned roadside attraction that had been several motels and a gas station before I-64 diverted traffic and eventually led to its decline. The restaurant and motor court morphed into different names and chains over the years, only to be abandoned and left to rot. The blighted site looked like a war zone today. Jules hadn't been up there since high school, but she heard that there had been several fires and lots of trespassers.

"Be careful. It's kinda run down and a magnet for squatters," she said, handing Eliot several brochures about area attractions. "Breakfast is served every morning in the lodge, and there are plenty of places in town for lunch, dinner, and takeout. This week, we have a teddy bear and classic toy festival going on, so there are lots of vendors and food trucks downtown. Here's the schedule. Tonight's the concert and fireworks show."

"Cool. Thanks. Come on, Noah. We've got a lot to check out. Oh, did you say someone was going to meet us about the trailer?" Eliot said.

"Sure." She held up a finger and grabbed her phone. When the call connected, she said, "Hey, Jake. Some of the East Coast Paranormal guys are here, and they have a bunch of gear in their trailer. Could you meet them over by the treehouse and show them where they can park in the field?"

"Sure thing, boss. Headed there now," he said before disconnecting.

"Jake will meet you near the tiny houses. He's really tall with wavy brown hair and green eyes. He'll be near the treehouse, which is right past the tiny house village on the other side of the parking lot. You can't miss it. It's the only treehouse on the property."

"He can't miss our trailer with the new phantasmic green wrap of our logo on it," Noah said with a smile.

The two men trudged out on the porch as Jules Googled their organization's website. They had quite the resume of ghostly documentaries, video clips, and a podcast. The theme from "Ghostbusters" bounced around in her head as she skimmed through the black and day-glo green site full of all kinds of hauntings and ghostly tales from all over the East Coast.

Jules's phone alerted. Wanna grab dinner before the fireworks tonight? How about Pop's?

She smiled and tapped a reply of a heart, smiley face, and a hamburger emoji to Jake. Will 6 work for you? Meet me at my cabin.

Jake responded with a thumbs-up emoji, and the ECP guys all settled in. Trailer close to the treehouse. All's well.

A little after six, Jules scooted into the vinyl booth under the Elvis on black velvet, and Jake slid in beside her, taking the two menus that Marsha Stokes, the fifty-something waitress in the pink and white outfit, offered.

"What can I get you two lovebirds?" Marsha asked, pulling a pencil out of her pale pink bouffant. "Save some room for dessert. Pop has lemon chess pie and chocolate tarts on the menu tonight."

"Sounds good," Jules said. "I think I'll have the cobb salad with ranch and a side of onion rings. And an unsweetened iced tea."

"I'll have the double-decker burger with mushrooms and onions and the steak fries," Jake said, pushing the menus closer to Marsha.

"And to drink?"

"Let's do a chocolate malt and a glass of water," he replied.

"Sounds delish. I'll be back in a flash." Marsha turned on her saddle oxfords and headed to the kitchen.

Jules scanned the Elvis memorabilia in their dining room. The diner had been owned by several Pops through the years, and each had added on to the original silver building that was a town fixture and the place to go for burgers and pizza after high school football and basketball games.

"See, I told you I'd be quick," Marsha said, setting down their drinks. "Y'all enjoy. It's been hopping in here today with all those teddy bear fans. Pop even made sure to load all the classics that referred to toys and bears on the juke box in honor of the occasion."

Jules smiled. "It looks like we've got a good crowd. I hope all the local businesses and vendors have great sales."

"We appreciate all that you and the business council do to keep folks coming to our little corner of the Blue Ridge. It's nice that we get tourists now year-round."

"Jules is full of creative ways to bring people in. There's even a group of paranormal hunters at the resort. They're doing some filming around the area," Jake said, pulling the wrapper off his straw.

"Ooooooo, how cool is that. I can't wait to see what they find around here. There are so many old battlefields and graveyards that are supposed to be haunted. Let me know when their stuff airs. Oh, don't forget to tell them about the Brickman house out on Route 650. The main house dates back almost to the Revolutionary War. My grandma saw an apparition of the owner's daughter in one of the front windows. My sister and I snuck out one night after midnight when I was ten or eleven to see for ourselves. We sat in the field staring at the old house for hours and never saw a ghost. We ended up getting a whipping for sneaking out after dark." Marsha waved over her shoulder and moved on to another table.

"The ghost hunters are interesting. They are really passionate about their work. Noah and Eliot showed me some of their special microphones and cameras. They even had some device that picked up electromagnetic pulses. I'm kinda curious what they find around here. We've all heard the spooky tales that kids tell around campfires. My grandma used to tell some about a ghost train that ran through the mountains and one about Civil War soldiers from both sides haunting the battlefields. She was convinced that we had a lot of restless souls around here." Jake slurped on his malt. After a pause, he continued, "We can't forget about the Confederate train full of gold from the treasury that's supposed to be hidden in a cave around here. My uncle told us that an army of ghosts guarded it. People have been looking for that gold for years," Jake said.

Their conversation paused when Marsha returned with a large tray. "Here you go. Mustard and ketchup are on the table. Let me know if you need anything else or if you want dessert. Be back to check on you in a bit."

The pair dug into their dinners, and the conversation faded until Jules wiped her mouth and pushed her plate toward the center of the table. "That was good. You can't go wrong with Pop's fries or onion rings. You want dessert?"

Working on the last few bites of his burger, Jake shook his head. "No. I'm good. We'll get something at the fireworks later. I'll be ready for a snack by then."

Jules waved at Marsha, who drifted by their table and dropped off the check. Grabbing it before Jake could, Jules slid her credit card into the plastic holder. "My treat."

After Marsha returned the card and receipt, Jules and Jake wended their way through the diner's rock and roll-themed dining areas to the Art Deco front doors with the little porthole windows.

* * *

Barricades blocked the main thoroughfares downtown. Jules navigated a warren of side streets to get to the overflow parking near the government center. The name sounded bigger than the complex that housed the library, sheriff's office, and the town administration building actually was.

Finding a spot in the grass at the back of the lot, she made her own space. "Here we go. The show doesn't start until seven, and then the fireworks are scheduled for nine. Elaine said that they're shooting them off from the government center roof. Hopefully, there will be good viewing spots all over town. The stage is set up at the end of Main Street. Do you want to walk around town for a bit? Let's go see what we can see," Jules said.

"Sounds good." Jake took her hand, and they strolled across the grass and ducked down a side street. As they rounded the corner onto Main Street, shouting ripped through the quiet fair. Following the loud voices, Jake and Jules ended up in front of Vern's tent.

"Call the cops. I've been robbed. My antique bear is missing, and the case is wide open. We never leave the case unlocked. I thought little towns were supposed to be safe," Vern yelled, waving his arms around. His son and nephew stood by sullenly, staring at their phones. No sign of Simone or the purloined bear.

Before Jules could say anything, Deputy Mario Caswell made his way through the growing crowd. "What's going on here?"

"Officer, someone stole my teddy bear," Vern wailed.

Jules thought she saw a sly smile creep across the deputy's face, but he quickly recovered his take-charge look. "What exactly happened?"

Vern let out an exasperated sigh and glared at the deputy. "I'm Vern Hogge, and I own Vern's Collectibles. We specialize in classic toys, anything teddy bear, and some very expensive collectibles. Travis, give him one of our cards." Vern snapped his fingers, and his nephew fished a business card out of his pocket and handed it to the deputy.

"Over here," Vern continued, pointing frantically at a glass case. "We have our priceless display of valuable toys. It's always watched and kept locked. When I returned from getting a lemonade, our classic bear was missing. And the case was wide open."

"Who was staffing your store while you were gone?" the deputy asked.

Vern turned his head and glared. "My son Vee Jay and my nephew Travis."

"Who else was in the tent?" the deputy asked, pulling out a small notebook and pen.

Travis shrugged, and his cousin shifted from one red high top to the other.

After a long pause, Vee Jay said, "We were swamped with customers. I was on the floor answering questions, and Travis was working the cash register. We didn't see anyone steal the bear." Travis nodded so vigorously that Jules feared he was going to jar something loose.

"When was the last time you remember seeing it?" Deputy Caswell asked.

"I dunno," Travis said. "It was there when Uncle Vern set up the case. He locks up the valuables every night in the truck. I guess it was here when I arrived. I didn't really go looking for it. I was busy."

"Yep. I'm super busy. I don't remember seeing it when I came back from lunch, but I'm pretty sure I would have noticed an open display case," Vee Jay added.

"Do you have a picture of it?" the deputy asked, looking at the empty case. "And was there anything else in here with it? Anything else missing?"

"No, just the bear," Vern said. "It's extremely valuable. Vee Jay, show him the picture on the website. And I put everything in the cases this morning, so I know it was here today."

Jules glanced around the crowded tent. All the displays gave her a claustrophobic feeling. How would they even know if something was missing with all these bears stuffed in all these cases and display shelves?

His son scrolled through his phone and held the screen up for the deputy to see. "This is it. We had it appraised recently. It's worth close to ten thousand dollars."

Deputy Caswell nodded and continued to take notes. "Anything else about the bear I should know? Anybody overly interested in it?"

The cousins shook their heads and stared at Vern. "A lot of people asked about it. I don't think they've seen such an expensive toy before. It was very popular. I want it back. You need to get out there and find who committed this grave crime. Wait. That nosy so-and-so next door kept remarking about it. I would talk to her. I bet she knows something. She's shifty. And there was this scody guy in a blue hoodie. He asked a lot of questions about toys. It was strange that he was wearing a sweatshirt when it's warm out. I'd go look for him before he gets away. I bet he had my bear under that baggy sweatshirt. And you're going to dust for prints, aren't you?"

"Not sure if that would yield anything valuable," Deputy Caswell said. "It's a glass case out in the public view. I can see hundreds of prints without dusting. What about the feeds from them? Have you checked them yet?"

The deputy pointed at the cameras clipped to the top of the shelves.

The two younger men snickered while Vern silenced them with a scowl. "Uh," Vern said, clearing his throat. "They're a deterrent. They don't actually record."

The tanned deputy nodded. "I'm going to my SUV to write this up and call it in. I'll be back in a few minutes with the paperwork for you to sign. Let me know if you think of anything else."

"You'd better put out an ABB or a BBB. You know, one of those alert things on the bear before it's too late. And go find the guy in the blue hoodie." Vern waved his arms around again. "And I'll need you guys as witnesses. Make sure you give the police your statement."

Deputy Caswell stepped out of the tent and into the large blue one next door. Jules motioned for Jake to follow her as she made her way through the crowd of gawkers outside. Jules wiggled her way inside the tent next door and moved to a good spot to overhear the deputy's conversation with the two women behind the counter.

"Good evening. I'm Deputy Caswell. There has been an incident next door. Vern Hogge is reporting the theft of an antique toy. Did you see anything suspicious in the last hour? Anybody in a blue hoodie?"

"Uh, no," the shorter woman said. "I'm Barb, and this is my sister Sil. We were so busy with customers this evening. I haven't noticed anything unusual."

Sil nodded and added, "I walked through Vern's display yesterday. All of the cases were locked, but if anyone even looked like they could afford his so-called antiques, Vern was all over them, unlocking cases and letting them touch the displays. And when he's not around, his staff are lax. In my opinion, that's no way to run a business. And with all that crap in the store, it's a wonder he even knows what he has."

"Thank you, Miss…"

"I'm Barb Johnson, and this is Silvia Gregorio. Here are our cards in case you need to reach us, but that's about all we know. I'm sorry that Mr. Hogge suffered a loss. That's not good for any small dealer."

Sil tsked as the deputy took the cards.

Jules nodded toward the street, and Jake followed her outside, where "Kokomo" blared from speakers surrounding the stage area. The couple made their way down the street and found a quiet spot near a tree and frozen drink truck.

"I hope Deputy Caswell can locate Vern's antique bear," Jules said, scanning the street for bear-nappers.

"It looks like his team wasn't minding the store," Jake said. "Want an icy drink?"

Jules nodded. "Cherry, please. I wonder if Elaine's team knows about the theft?"

"Probably not. She'd be in the thick of it, arranging a search party if she did. Be back in a sec." Jake ran his hand through his longish hair.

Jules continued to glance around the tents. Most of the people sat near the stage and listened to the cover band. A few people milled around the food trucks. Nobody acted suspicious. A flash of blue ducked into a tent on the other side of the street.

She hustled over to the tent full of bears that customers could personalize with names and decorations. Jules pretended to browse, stepping closer to a pudgy guy with a big black backpack. Her heartbeat pounded in her temples. Was this the guy Vern mentioned? He was wearing a bright, shiny light jacket, not a sweatshirt. Could the bear be in his backpack?

Inching closer to the counter where the man talked to a blond woman with a heart-shaped face, Jules leaned in to hear the conversation. He said something she didn't pick up, and the woman waved her arms around and pointed at displays behind her.

The man leaned forward and pointed to something in the display case. By this time, Jules had scooted closer and stood next to him and his backpack.

"How long have you been in business, and where did you get your start?" He asked, tapping something on his phone.

"Oh, I've always loved bears. I saw an ad for a franchise opportunity, and I started Bearly You as a home-based business. Now I have four employees, and I travel to shows all around the country. It's an amazing opportunity, and now I own my own business. We help our customers design their own bears."

"Do you have a card or a flier? And can I take a picture?" the guy asked.

"Sure. Let's do it in front of these custom bears." The woman smiled while he snapped several shots with his phone. "Thanks. I'll be in touch if I have any more questions," he said, taking the card she offered.

He scooped up his backpack and hurried out of the tent.

"Can I help you?" the woman trilled.

"Uh, no," Jules said, rushing to follow the guy in the jacket. Outside the tent, she looked up and down the street and spotted him heading toward a tent diagonally across from her.

Deciding against tackling him, Jules rushed up to him and tapped him on the arm. "Excuse me. Are you interested in our inaugural bear festival? Are you a collector?" She hoped her question didn't sound as lame to him as it did to her.

The man paused and turned to face her. "Not really. I'm Jackson Pruitt." After a long pause, he continued, "I freelance for the *Blue Ridge Mountain Times*. I'm doing a puff piece on the festival."

"Hi, I'm Jules Keene. I'm the Business Council President for Fern Valley. If you need any information, give me a call or Elaine James at Birds and Bees. She's the chairperson who organized all of this." She fished a business card out of her purse and offered it to the reporter.

"Thanks. People seem to be having fun. If I think of any questions later, I'll be in touch." He slid the card into his front pocket and continued toward the next tent.

Jules let out a long sigh. Then someone grabbed her shoulder. Letting out a whimpery squeal. Her heart leapt up into her throat.

"Where'd you go? Here's your slushie," Jake said, handing her a cup.

"Sorry. I saw the guy in the blue jacket."

"And of course you gave chase. What'd ya find, Nancy Drew?" Jake asked with a wink.

"Mmm. This is good, but I think I gave myself a brain freeze. He's not a bear thief. He's a reporter." She pulled out her phone and Googled the paper he worked for. After a few clicks, she found a more polished photo of the guy on their staff page. This is him, Jackson Pruitt." Jules tapped a quick text with the link to Deputy Caswell.

"I think we missed most of the concert, but let's go see if we can find seats for the fireworks," Jake said.

"I have an idea. Come on." Jules led him back to the government center. When they made it to the parking lot, Jules pulled a blanket out of the back of her silver and black Wrangler. "Here, help me spread this out." Jules tossed the blanket on the hood. "The perfect spot for stargazing and fireworks-watching."

Chapter Four

Sunday Morning

Spotting the paranormal crew at a long table near the wall of windows and the fireplace at the lodge, Jules approached with her plate and coffee. "Good morning. How is the hunting around Fern Valley? I hope you found a lot of places to explore."

"Pop a squat," Eliot said, patting the bench next to him. "We've had a great time here so far. We're talking about our plans tonight. And we met Crystal over there. She is such a fan of our work." He pointed at the daughter-half of the mother and daughter duo who cooked and cleaned at the resort. Crystal gave a tiny wave and a slight smile in their direction.

"Any unusual sightings or good stories?" Jules asked, sliding into the spot next to Eliot.

"Hey guys, this is Jules. She owns this cool place. This is Cliffy, Norm, Suz, Drew, and you already know Noah."

Cliffy shoveled in a forkful of omelet. After a couple of chews, he said, "The treehouse is really dope. But I like all the decorations in the Harry Potter house, too."

"My boyfriend Jake designed and built it." And if by magic, Jake appeared with a to-go box and an oversized coffee. "Oh, hey," she said, turning toward Jake. "Everyone, this is Jake. Jake, these are the East Coast Paranormal explorers. They were telling me about their strategy. And they like the treehouse." She scooted over so he had room to sit next to her.

"Cool." Jake slid onto the bench, and Eliot introduced everyone again.

"We haven't done any full-blown investigations yet. We're still in our reconnaissance phase. But we got lots of good film of the mountains and the wilderness during the day and the night. Your treehouse is perfect. We may never leave," Noah said.

"And we got lots of night sounds that will be awesome to use in the documentary. You have some creepy animal noises around here," Norm said. "I'm going for seconds. Anyone want anything?" Suz was the only one to shake her head as he rose and trotted toward Crystal and the buffet table.

"Tonight, we're going to do our first investigation at the Inn at Afton," Eliot said. "If you all aren't busy, why don't you come and see what happens. You never know. Sometimes, we get lucky, and there's a lot of paranormal activity. Norm invited Crystal. She's going to ride up with us."

Jake looked at Jules with the same look that Bijou had when she wanted to play, and she nodded. "Sounds fun. Count us in. When and where?"

"We're going to caravan up the mountain and be in place by sunset. So, we'll need to get there in plenty of time to set up and scout the area," Eliot said. "Be there by seven."

"Anything special we need to bring?" Jules asked.

"If you want to record it, bring your phone and a big flashlight," Noah said.

"I haven't been up there in a while," Jules said. "Probably since high school, and it wasn't in good shape then. There are squatters from time to time, and a lot of trash everywhere. They've also had several fires on the property, and I doubt those buildings were ever repaired or torn down. I would wear long pants and sturdy shoes."

"We got permission from the current owner. He wanted a mention in the production, but at least he didn't charge us," Eliot said. "It seems like a great place for us to do our research."

"Through the years, it's been several hotel chains, a couple of different restaurants, and a gas station. There was even a log cabin up there at one time. It was a big deal in the fifties and sixties. The motor court and the building that was the Holiday Inn fell into disrepair when the interstate diverted traffic to the other side of the mountain. Now, it's a hot mess that attracts druggies and vandals," Jules said.

"It was kind of a rite of passage for teens to go up there to drink or hang out. The view is nice. It's too bad that the resort looks like a war zone now," Jake said.

"You know the best way to get up there?" Eliot asked.

Jake pulled out his phone and tapped on his map app. When the map popped up, he said, "The easiest is to take I-64 west and get off at the Route 250 East exit. It winds up to the ridge and goes right past the old motor court."

"Sounds good. We'll head up about four or four thirty. We need to poke around the structures that are still there and do some readings," Cliffy said.

"When we did our research, we found that several of the guests had died on the property over the years. One was a girl who drowned in the pool in the seventies. The original motel opened in the 1880s. It was the place to visit and get away from the hot cities in the summers before air conditioning," Suz said. "After the big-name hotel franchises pulled out, there were several overdoses and a murder in one of the rooms. Locals claim to hear screams and see lights in the rooms. There hasn't been electricity up there for years. I'm curious to see what we'll experience. It would be cool to make contact."

"We'll see. Hopefully, it'll be a good night to see or hear the deceased who are trapped here for whatever reason. We'll see you all up there before sunset," Eliot said.

I hope they don't start counting folks who have been murdered around here. When Jules realized she had paused, she quickly added, "I'm looking forward to it." *I wonder what one wears to visit ghosts.*

* * *

After a quick dinner at Pie in the Sky, Jake paid the gal at the register. "About ready?" he asked Jules as he pointed to the glass door.

"I'm up for the adventure. Though I have to admit I'm kind of a skeptic. But I am curious. I hope we don't run into any problems from this world. I packed a bag with a medical kit, a jacket, bug spray, a knife, flashlights, and extra batteries. Oh, I've got water and snacks in a cooler if we need them," Jules said, climbing into the Jeep for the short ride to the top of Afton Mountain.

"Sounds like you've got it all under control. I've got my pocketknife and a long-sleeved shirt to avoid bugs, scratches, and the cool night air. Not sure what kind of trash is abandoned up there. It looked bad the last time I was up there, and that was before I enlisted."

Jules backed out of the parking lot and headed for the interstate as Jake found a classic rock station on the radio. "Let's go have a ghost hunt."

About twenty minutes later, Jules pulled into an overgrown parking lot with grass and weeds running rampant in the cracks. The ESC trailer and truck looked surreal next to the backdrop of the abandoned and dilapidated buildings as twilight descended on the mountains. Several parts of the roof of the old motor court looked like they had caved in, and most of the windows had been broken. Fire had destroyed large chunks of the smaller cabins. Jules snapped a few selfies with Jake and the eerie background.

She grabbed her jacket and spent some time tucking her jeans inside her thick socks and steel-toed boots.

"Good thinking," Jake said. "You never know what's up here, and I'm sure there are bugs and critters."

"Oh, wait. I have spray." She pulled out the aerosol can and sprayed both of their jackets, shoes, and pants. "Hopefully, that'll keep the mosquitoes and ticks at bay."

"Let's hope the bedbugs are long gone." Jake picked up the large flashlights that could double as a weapon if needed. "Ready?"

"As ready as I'll ever be." Slipping her keys and her phone in her back pocket, she locked her purse inside the Wrangler and shook off thoughts of critters and bed bugs. "Let's go see where the gang is."

"The view is really great up here," Jake said, turning to take in the almost three-sixty-degree view of the valley below. The sun's afternoon rays left golden streaks across the blueish-looking trees.

"I always get a little melancholic when I drive past this. It's too bad they couldn't make a go of it. Maybe someone will come along and want to develop it. But it's been like this most of my life," Jules said.

The wind rustled through the leaves and the pine trees. Pausing, Jules heard voices. "I think they're over this way."

The pair carefully picked their way over trash, abandoned furniture from the motel, and overgrown weeds and brambles.

"Hey, there's Jules and Jake." Cliffy waved both hands. The knot of paranormal investigators stood in front of a row of small buildings that were once part of the motor lodge.

"Isn't this great?" Noah asked as they approached.

Crystal Carson gave the pair a little finger wave and returned to holding some piece of recording equipment for Noah.

"What do you need us to do?" Jake asked.

"I think we're almost ready to go here. We're going to get some video of the site while the sun's still up. Y'all follow along. Take pictures or record anything that you want. We'll pull up tomorrow at breakfast and do a debrief of what we experienced," Eliot said. "Everybody ready? Noah, Drew, and I will get stock photos and sounds we can use. The rest of you go and explore to see where we want to put the detectors. Suz, you want to do some call-outs when it gets dark? The old HoJo and the cabins are down here. The old hotel is up there. We'll need to drive up there when we're done here."

"I'm on it," Suz said. "You all know why we do most of our investigations after dark?"

Jules and Crystal shook their heads.

"It's spookier," Jake said.

Drew let out a snicker. "It's when we're in our element."

"It's usually quieter, and in the dark, there's not a lot of interference from electricity or other utilities. With no power up here, we don't have to worry about that. And there doesn't seem to be a lot of traffic for the lights or motors to affect our pulse recordings. Old buildings have outdated wiring, and the buzz often shows up on our detectors. That probably won't be an issue here," Suz said. She glanced around the abandoned buildings like she was listening for something.

After a long pause, Suz continued, "I'm going to poke around over there. I heard some folks OD'd on this part of the property. Then I want to explore what's left of the bigger hotel up there."

Jules and Jake held the equipment and followed the team through the ramshackle cabins full of trash, broken windows and doors, and damaged roofs. As the sun set over the ridge, the team flipped on flashlights. The breeze picked up and whistled around the abandoned buildings and through the trees. Jules strained to hear any other noises. The wind was spooky enough.

"Okay, guys," Suz said. "I'm going to do some call-outs in this section, and we'll see what we get." The petite woman cleared her throat and checked the screen on a handheld device. "Hello. Can you hear me? We're trying to tell your story. Let us know if you're here." The group paused and listened while Noah and Cliffy swung a device around to pick up any activity. Suz repeated her calls in several locations near the old restaurant and cabins. The green lights from the equipment cast an eerie glow on the faces of the crew. The only sounds Jules heard were from the traffic on the interstate up the ridge and the wind.

"Did you all get anything?" Eliot asked, wiping sweat from his brow with his sleeve.

"Nope. Nothing," Norm said.

"Me either," Noah said.

"I didn't get any unusual readings either," Suz said. "How about we head up to the other complex? I definitely want to check out the pool area."

"The team dispersed and climbed into a van and the truck. Jules and Jake jogged to her Jeep and followed the caravan to what was a Holiday Inn in a past life.

They parked near the lobby and jumped out with large flashlights. "You all be careful," Eliot said. "When Noah and I were up here earlier, there was a lot of debris and overgrown landscaping. And the railings on the steps and balconies aren't that safe. Don't lean on anything. I don't want anyone to fall. Suz wants to start at the pool."

"I wish we knew what room the people died in. It might help. But we'll have to work with what we have," Suz said.

"Hey, guys," Noah yelled. There's no fencing around the pool. It's over there near all that cement, and it looked like a Super Fund site when we took pictures of it earlier. Don't fall into that either. There's no telling what kind of hazmat situation that is. And without a lot of ambient light around, this place is pitch black." He flipped a switch on his large camera, and the light bathed the immediate area.

The paranormal investigators fanned out with their equipment. Jules and Jake followed Suz, who was inviting the spirits to join them. An icy shiver sped down Jules's spine. *I'm not sure if it's all the spooky talk, the wind off the mountain, or the creepy surroundings. I feel like something is going to jump out at me at any moment.* She stepped closer to Jake and clutched his arm.

He pulled her closer, and they picked their way around the debris and the overgrown bushes that were once part of the landscaping. The broken sidewalk made it difficult to navigate. Jules paused for a moment and looked out at the dark vastness and the mountains. Tiny dots of light twinkled in the distance. Red lights on the towers across the valley twinkled on and off like heartbeats.

Suz broke the silence with her call-outs. Every few minutes, she would pause, and the team would listen for any kind of response.

"Hey, guys," Eliot said, interrupting Suz's singsong chants.

"Shhhh!" Suz ordered. "I felt something brush by me."

"It was probably Norm," Cliffy snickered.

Everyone moved closer to Suz on the broken cement around the pool. Cliffy and Norm swung their lights near the inky water. "If you're here with us. Let us know. We know you had a tragic death in the pool here. I think you're trying to reach out. I can feel your presence. Let us know that you're here. You've been here a long time."

Suz paused.

Jules heard a thud, and a scream echoed across the patio area. Her heart leapt into her throat, and she dug her fingernails into Jake's arm.

Chapter Five

Sunday Evening

The team rushed toward the scream, and a halo of flashlight beams jumped around and encircled Crystal like the lights at some movie premiere. She looked down at a pile of clothing and screamed again.

"Crystal, are you okay?" Jules asked as she and Jake raced to her side.

"Yes," she said quietly. "But he's not." She pointed at what looked like a mound of abandoned clothes.

Noah turned on his video camera's external light and flooded the area with brightness. Jules blinked several times, trying to get her eyes to adjust. The sudden whiteness lit up this side of the patio where every crack, speck of peeling paint, and graffiti seemed front and center. The pool area, a place that brought joy to so many kids in a bygone era, looked like something out of a horror movie. The water, almost to the top of the decking, shimmered in the same bright green and black that was on the ECP trailer. Branches and abandoned furniture floated in the murky goop. The old motel looked even more decrepit when the light accentuated the decay and vandalism.

Drew nudged the Hawaiian print shirt with the toe of his boot. "He's kinda stiff. I wonder if he's been here for some time, but he doesn't look or smell like it's been weeks."

Suz, looking slightly squeamish, glared at Drew.

"What, it's not like this is the first body we've found on a site," Drew said.

"Maybe we should do a podcast on that."

"Not quite what any of us expected tonight," Eliot said.

Jules pulled out her phone and tapped 9-1-1. When the dispatcher answered, she said, "Hi. I'm with a group at the old Inn at Afton up near the old motel on the hill. By the pool. We found a body, and he's unresponsive."

"Where exactly are you on the property?" the dispatcher asked.

"Tell them we're at 38.0293° N, 78.8587° W," Cliffy said.

"Did you catch that?" Jules asked.

"No. Have him repeat it slowly."

Jules held the phone toward Cliffy, and he repeated the GPS coordinates like he was talking to a toddler.

"Thanks. Is he bleeding or breathing? Any sign of trauma?" the dispatcher asked.

Drew grabbed the body by the shoulder and flipped the man over. A dark stain covered the cement and the front of the man's shirt.

"There's blood on the cement," Cliffy shouted. "But I can't tell where it's coming from."

Jules gasped. "Vernon Hogge! What is he doing all the way out here?"

"You know the man?" the dispatcher asked.

"I'm Jules Keene from Fern Valley. We're hosting a festival in town. He's one of the vendors, and he's staying at my resort. There's a lot of blood on the front of him. It looks like he's been shot or stabbed. It's hard to tell."

"Y'all step back and don't touch anything else. Police and rescue are on their way. I'm going to stay on the line in case they have trouble finding you."

"We're at the top of the hill. I think this building used to be the old Holiday Inn. We're out on the patio near the pool."

"I'll let the responding officer know," the dispatcher said.

"This is definitely not what I thought we would encounter," Eliot said, shaking his shaggy head.

"It ruined our hunt. Now we'll have to come back another evening to make contact. There's too much light and noise around here now," Suz muttered. "Too much bad energy." The petite woman shuddered and zipped up her jacket.

About fifteen minutes later, headlights pierced the darkness and moved up the road. They danced as a car crept up the winding road.

"Drew, let's go wave him this way," Norm said.

The pair picked their way around the old building as the rest of the group huddled closer and stared at the very dead Vernon.

The noise of a large engine approached, and a car door slammed. The darkness seemed to creep up and surround them. The mood and the mountains made Jules feel like she was trapped in the small puddle of light, jittery about what was going to happen next. She scooted closer to Jake, and he hugged her with one arm.

A few minutes later, beams of light bounced around the corner of the three-story wing. A state trooper, followed by Drew and Norm, hiked over to the group.

"Over here," Cliffy said. "The dead guy's over here." He waved his arm at the approaching police officer.

The trooper looked around and scanned the faces encircling the body. He clicked his shoulder mic and said, "This is 215 requesting forensics and ETA of rescue."

"215, forensics has been notified. They're leaving an incident now. The ambulance is inbound. Expect it in about six minutes."

The radio squawked as he replied, "Ten-four."

"I'm Trooper Isaacs. What are you all doing up here?" He scanned the faces of those in a semicircle at the edge of the pool.

"I'm Eliot Kellogg with East Coast Paranormal. We have permission from the owners to film as part of our documentary, *Haunts of the Blue Ridge*. We were conducting our investigation when we stumbled upon him."

"Was he like that? Did you touch anything?" he asked, looking at the faces, illuminated only by the camera's light.

"Drew flipped him over. When we found him, he was lying on his stomach. We didn't see the blood until we saw the front of him," Cliffy said. "Did anyone get any pictures before he was moved?"

After a long pause, Noah raised two fingers. "I did," he said quietly as

Trooper Isaacs handed him a business card.

"Send them to me and any other footage you have," the trooper said.

More engine sounds cut through the night, and then a series of car door slams echoed off the mountains. A few minutes later, a rolling sound approached as a deputy and two EMTs guided a gurney across the cement.

"Just a minute. Everyone, stay put," the trooper said.

"Deputy, could you secure and photograph the area while rescue does its thing? Forensics is on the way. I'm going to take this group around front and get statements."

"Sure, but I've only got my phone. Not sure how well the pictures will come out."

"Just capture as much of the scene as you can. The team will be here soon with their equipment."

"Uh, Noah can send the recordings that we took earlier. Who knows? We might have caught something as we were exploring during the daylight hours. I don't remember seeing anyone else on the property, but you never know," Eliot said.

The state trooper nodded, "Noah, could you stay here with your camera and lights while the deputy takes photos?"

"Sure," Noah said, eager to be in on the action.

"The rest of you follow me around front. I need to talk to you one at a time." The state trooper motioned toward the building.

The tiny band marched around the abandoned motel behind the tall policeman. Once beside his blue and gray SUV, he rummaged in his vehicle and then went down the line collecting names and contact information, jotting furiously on a legal pad.

After what seemed like an eternity, the two EMTs pushed the gurney around the building, and it bumped along over the cracked pavement. Jules paused as they loaded the covered body into the back of an ambulance. A few minutes later, the EMTs drove away with only lights flashing. She tried to shake the gloomy feeling. *What was Vern doing all by himself up here? How did he even know about his place?*

As each member took turns giving Trooper Isaacs his or her update, Jake leaned over and whispered to Jules, "It looks like ole Vern definitely ticked off the wrong person."

Chapter Six

Monday Morning

Jules tossed and turned all night. The whole Afton Mountain experience gave her the heebie jeebies, and she couldn't fall asleep no matter how hard she tried. When the sun started turning the sky pinky purple, she and Bijou hiked over to the office to get a jump start on the day. Hoping that resort work would take her mind off of what had happened to Vern, her plan was to plow through a bunch of reservation and business council emails with the hope of finally getting caught up.

Thwarted by a big message on her screen to upload critical patches, she waited for her laptop to finish the download and popped a dark roast coffee pod into the machine. Not seeing any snacks or breakfast, Bijou settled in her puffy bed next to Jules's desk for an after-breakfast nap.

As the coffee maker spewed out the last few dribbles, the bells on the front door jangled. Jules made a mad dash to close the dividing door before Bijou turned on the charm as the resort's official greeter and yipper.

"Good morning, Sheriff," Jules said, pulling the bottom half of the door shut behind her. "What brings you out so early?"

"Heard you and Jake had a little adventure last night with those ghost hunters. I'm here with Trooper Isaacs." He pointed at the window. The other man stood outside near the porch swing, talking on his cell. "We stopped by to notify the family. We're hoping to catch them before they head into town for today's events."

Jules nodded and woke up the laptop on the front counter. "Vern Hogge, his son Vee Jay, a nephew named Travis, and Vee Jay's girlfriend Simone are staying in the Baum house. It's the one with the Wizard of Oz flag on the porch."

"Got it. Anything else we should know?" Sheriff Hobbs asked, shifting his weight to his other foot. His thick leather utility belt squeaked when he moved.

"Vern is, well, was a bit abrasive. He had a dust up with his vendor neighbor the other day in town, and then he called your department when his antique bear was stolen."

"And it seems the girlfriend caused her own little stir with one of the food vendors. They definitely don't fly under the radar. Nothing like getting yourself noticed," the sheriff said with a wry smile. "When he's done with his call, we're going to head over and talk to the family."

"The lodge is open for breakfast. Stop by afterward if you haven't eaten. Crystal was with us last night. She was the one who stumbled over the body in case you need to talk to her too," Jules added.

Sheriff Hobbs raised one eyebrow and nodded. "We'll stop by and see if she can chat. Thanks. I'll let you know if we have any more questions." Her aunt's beau turned and headed to the front door.

After looking at the upcoming registrations, Jules grabbed her keys and phone. "I'll be back in a bit. I'm going to see what Mel and Crystal have on the breakfast menu this morning." Bijou opened one eye and barked to remind her that she loved anything with egg and cheese.

The short walk to the lodge, the focal point of the resort, brought a sense of calmness to Jules. The crisp mountain air laced with scents of pine and wildflowers reminded Jules of why the valley was her happy place. She paused and closed her eyes for a moment to soak up some of the serenity before she had to return to the business of her resort and the reality of Vern's sudden death.

Chatter and a lilting laugh jolted her out of her daydream. Jules smiled when she spotted four women in colorful teddy bear t-shirts. The friends laughed and teased each other on their way to breakfast. Jules fell in behind them and enjoyed their banter about how much fun they were having on this excursion.

Jules slipped into the buffet line and added biscuits and gravy and a fruit mix to her plate. At the beverage table, she selected pineapple juice and glanced around for an empty table. Most were filled with guests getting ready to start their day. Spotting the sheriff and the state trooper in a corner near the windows with Crystal Carlson, Jules made her way through a maze of tables. The daughter-half of the mother-daughter duo sat next to the sheriff. Her long blond braid bobbed as she nodded her responses.

Sheriff Hobbs gave Jules a thumbs-up. "Good recommendation on breakfast, Jules. Crystal's spread this morning was very good. And we always appreciate coffee. Pull up a chair and join us."

Jules scooted into the empty seat next to the trooper and dug into her breakfast.

"Crystal, you're central to all of this. You found the body last night," Sheriff Hobbs said. "Is there anything else you remember that you didn't tell the officers last night?"

"I don't think so." Crystal paused and stared at her neatly filed nails. "I met Noah and Norm, two of the paranormal investigators, the other morning. They came in for breakfast, and he and some of his guys were telling me about what they do. I'm a fan of those ghost-hunting shows. I was excited to meet them and over the moon when they invited me to see it firsthand. I even got to help with some of the equipment. I rode over to Afton Mountain with them. You know that old inn site, the one that looks like Baghdad or Kabul or something. Pretty nasty stuff there. There was trash and graffiti everywhere. I tried to be careful not to trip or step on anything. Anyway, we trekked around for quite a while. It was definitely spooky, and finding a real body was the last thing I expected. I was walking around the patio while Suz was conducting her investigation. I almost stepped on him." Crystal shuddered. "The body was partially lying on the cement near some overgrown bushes. At first, I thought it was a pile of clothes. I almost kicked it out of the way. I'm glad now that I didn't." Her voice faded as she paused again and looked at the police officers.

"Anything else?" the trooper asked.

"Nope. I was hoping to get to see some paranormal action in person, and instead, we found a body from this world." Crystal shivered again. "Any idea how he died?" She looked down at her hands again. "I went straight home and took the longest shower. I still feel like I walked through a giant spider web."

Sheriff Hobbs pursed his lips. Before he could respond, the trooper said, "He was stabbed several times in the chest. We didn't recover the weapon."

Crystal's hand flew to her mouth, and her eyes widened. "Oh, how awful. I was kinda hoping that it was natural causes. But there is a lot of blood." When no one else added anything, she continued, "That was about it. I hung out with the guys while the police did their work and asked us questions. I got back here sometime close to midnight."

"And you?" the trooper asked, looking at Jules.

Finishing the bite of biscuit, she replied, "That's about the same for us. Jake and I rode up to the abandoned site after dinner. We explored with the team a little bit before the sun went down, and they started their ghost hunt in earnest. I heard Crystal scream, and that's when they found the body. We rushed over to where she was."

"You saw the victim prior to last evening, right?" the trooper asked.

"Just coming through the food lines," Crystal said.

Jules nodded. I saw him at check-in and at his booth in town. Vern Hogge and his crew had a couple of incidents in the short time he was here, so he was kinda memorable."

"What kind of incidents?" The trooper's stare felt like it bored into her.

"He and the vendor in the next tent had a loud discussion about his displays that blocked the entrance to her area. And then later, he had a valuable toy stolen. Deputy Caswell took his statement on that one."

"Uh, huh. Anything else?" the trooper asked as he continued to jot notes on a yellow legal pad.

"That's about it," Jules said. "We came back to the resort after we talked with you."

"Nobody saw any kinds of weapons on the Afton property?" Trooper

Isaacs asked.

Jules and Crystal shook their heads.

"Just a lot of trash," Crystal said in a soft voice. "Did you need me anymore? Can I get you anything else? Refills on coffee?"

Both men shook their heads.

"I'd rather experience ghostly connections. Tonight, I'm going with the ECP guys tonight to UVA to investigate some haunted places like Poe's room and the old cemetery that had grave robbers. I hope they are able to make contact this time. But right now, I need to go check on mom and the kitchen." Crystal's voice trailed off as she rose and headed toward the door near the coffee station.

"You attending any more ghost adventures?" Sheriff Hobbs asked Jules.

"I hadn't planned on it. That one was enough to last me for a while." She hoped her smile didn't look fake. "I've had enough adventures this week. Last night was proof that humans are more scary and deadlier than ghosts. I'm hoping the rest of the of the week is quiet."

The sheriff raised an eyebrow and took a bite of his biscuit.

"Thanks for the hospitality," the trooper said. "You have a beautiful place here. I need to tell my family about it. They've been wanting to come and visit me and see the Blue Ridge. I'm going to send them your way. My efficiency apartment is too small for a lot of visitors, but this place is great. They'd love to stay here," the trooper said.

"We'd be glad to have them." She slid a business card out of her phone case across the table. Jules rose and picked up the discarded plates and glasses. "Let me know if I can help with anything."

She disappeared into the large, industrial kitchen where Mel and Crystal buzzed around cleaning and refilling food trays.

"I would have gotten that," Crystal said, taking the dirty plates from Jules.

"No problem. I was standing there. Everyone enjoyed breakfast. You ladies outdid yourselves again. I didn't know you were a ghost hunter fan."

Mel wrinkled her nose and shook her head hard enough to make her brown curls bob around in all directions.

"I am. I love every paranormal show I can find. I was so excited to find that

Discovery Plus has its own section with a ton of different shows. I watch something on it every night," Crystal gushed. "And I'm going out with Noah and his friends to Charlottesville this evening. I hope we get to see or hear something. Wouldn't it be so cool to make contact with Poe in his dorm room?" Her cheeks flushed, and she scurried back into the dining room to replace a tray of biscuits and another of bacon on the buffet table.

Her mother rolled her eyes and continued loading the industrial dishwasher. "If it makes her happy. She has always been a fan of horror stories since she was a little girl. Not my cup of tea."

Jules patted her on the shoulder. "Jake likes Halloween and haunted houses, and corn mazes. Not really my thing either. I'll take a British mystery or a thriller any day. Steven King or Dean Koontz keep me awake at night."

Mel waved over her shoulder as Jules headed out the back door. Breathing in the mountain air, laced with the loamy scents of the woods, Jules soaked in the majesty of the three-sixty view of the mountains. *Time to get back to work. You need to make sure all the spaces are filled through the rest of the year.*

She took two steps, and a loud shriek came from near the other side of the lodge. More screaming and muffled voices. She hurried to the barn where Lester, the groundskeeper, kept his mowing equipment, and Jake constructed his tiny houses. Before she made it to the large doors, a flash of pink ducked around the building.

Jules followed the person and skidded to a stop in the grassy area between the barn and the woods. She caught her breath and glanced at Simone, Travis, and Vee Jay. Not noticing Jules's approach, Simone waggled her index finger with its hot pink dagger of a nail in Vee Jay's face. "Stop the yammering and give us the keys to the truck. We need to get set up in town. They're expecting big crowds, and we can't afford to miss any sales. You should be all over this now since you're the new owner of Vern's bears."

Vee Jay's eyes filled, and he wiped his nose on his T-shirt. "I can't believe he's gone. And sometimes you can be such a…" He paused and looked up at Jules. Travis stood sullenly with his arms crossed across his chest behind Simone.

Vee Jay continued, "It's all that crazy witch's fault. All she did was pick,

pick, pick about our booth. I know her and her hateful sister had something to do with this. I've got to figure out what to do. I'm going to call Phil."

"What can his poker buddy do?" Simone rolled her eyes and looked at Travis.

"He's his lawyer," Travis said.

"You two go into town and take care of the business. I've got to make some calls." Vee Jay tossed his keys at Travis and trekked toward the tiny houses.

"Find out definitely who inherits the business while you're at it," Simone screamed at this back. "I'm not working my tail off for nothing. When he was out of sight, she turned and stared bullets at Jules. "And what do you want? We're busy here with some personal stuff. Were you listening to our conversation?"

"I wanted to offer my condolences and see if you all needed anything." Jules hoped her smile looked sincere. "Let me know if my team can help." She walked slowly toward the office, watching to see what Simone and Travis did next.

Chapter Seven

Jules stood near the tree line as Simone and Travis trekked from the barn to the parking lot. Simone wobbled on her stilettos on the uneven grass. She only picked up a few of the shrill words, but Simone's wild hand motions in Travis's direction gave her a pretty good idea of the mood. She followed them to the edge of the parking lot, where the pair hopped in the black truck and gunned it down the maintenance road. *Hopefully, she'll calm down before she gets to town and has to deal with customers.*

Jules adjusted the pillows on the swing and rocking chairs on the store's porch and opened the front door.

"Good morning and welcome to the Fern Valley Camping Resort," floated from the back as her aunt Roxanne, in white capri pants and a red striped shirt, made her way to the front. "Hey, Jules. Where have you been this fine morning? Bijou and I have been having a dance off back there."

"I popped over to the lodge and spoke to the sheriff and his trooper friend."

"I heard you found another body." Her aunt raised one perfectly manicured eyebrow and then winked at her niece. "You have a knack for that, don't you?"

"Actually, Crystal found this one, and it was up at the old, abandoned motel site at Afton. So, nowhere near Fern Valley."

"Tell me all about the ghost hunt." Her aunt's eyes sparkled as she pulled the stool around to the edge of the counter and sat.

"There wasn't much action after they found the body, who was one of our guests. The ghost hunters claimed that all the noise ruined their chance to make contact with the spirits. We talked to the police and headed home. Crystal said that she's going with the paranormal guys to the University of Virginia tonight."

"How exciting. I can't wait to see what these guys find in our little neck of the woods." A somber expression crossed her face. "Sorry to hear about our guest. Who was it?"

"Vern Hogge. He was staying with his team in the Baum house."

"Are they checking out early?" Roxanne asked.

"It doesn't look like it. The girlfriend and nephew headed into town to staff their booth. They didn't act like they needed anything. I'll check on the son Vee Jay later."

"I'm going to walk over to the lodge to get the scoop on the paranormal team. Need me to bring you anything?" Jules shook her head as Roxanne disappeared out the door.

Settling at her desk, Jules took a deep breath when she saw the number of unread emails. "Bijou, you could have taken care of some of these while I was busy."

The brown and white Jack Russell Terrier opened one eye and closed it again quickly, not interested in any type of communication at the moment.

Twenty minutes later, Jules stared quizzically at the corner of her desk and hopped out of her chair. Circling the desk and peeking under it, Jules straightened up and said, "Hmmm."

"What's up?" Roxanne asked, closing the back door behind her. Bijou scampered to greet her. "Hey, puppy. Are you happy to see me or my sausage biscuits?"

"She loves you, but I think your breakfast caught her attention." Bijou followed Roxanne to the table near the kitchenette.

"This is strange," Jules muttered. "Jake bought me a pink bear the other day, and I set it right here next to the inbox. And now it's gone." She opened the desk drawer and looked under a folder. "The purple one I bought for Pixel is still here."

"That is odd," her aunt said. "I don't think anyone besides Lester, Jake, and us have been back here. Though we've had a steady stream of folks in the store for supplies and information over the past few days. Anything else missing? Bijou, did you take it?"

The brown and white terrier gave her best "who me" look.

Jules checked the other drawers as her aunt verified that the other desk was locked.

"Nope. It is bizarre." Jules ducked down and checked under the furniture. "No pink bear. Let me know if you find it. It's going to drive me nuts. Things don't disappear." Her aunt made a woo-woo noise and fluttered her hands. "Maybe those investigators came to the right place." Jules shrugged and pulled out her phone. She texted a note to Jake.

Good morning. Have you seen the pink bear you bought me in town?

A few minutes later, her phone alerted. It's on your desk.

Can't find it. BOLO for it.

Sounds like a mystery, he replied with a smiley emoji.

"That is very strange. I know I left it here." Jules checked the cabinets and supply closet.

The front doorbells jangled, and Bijou dashed to the dividing door and barked at whoever entered on the other side.

"Well, good morning, y'all," Roxanne said. "What can I do for you?"

"Hi, we're staying in the Winnie the Pooh house. Love that treehouse. We got some awesome shots from that great wrap-around deck. Anyway, wanted to see if you had any local attraction brochures."

"Help yourself. These are for Fern Valley and the surrounding areas. I heard from Jules and Crystal that you all were heading to UVA tonight."

"Hi, I'm Noah, and this is Cliffy. Yep. We hope to catch some righteous activity there. Plus, we're all huge Poe fans."

"Me too. He's a Virginia favorite," Roxanne said. "Where can I see your work?"

Cliffy pulled out something from one of the pockets of his utility vest. "Here's a postcard. This has our website with the stories that we stream, the documentaries, and the podcast episodes."

Roxanne took the postcard he offered and cooed, "Thank you. I am a fan. I'll definitely watch your videos. Can I get a picture with y'all?"

"I'll take it for you." Jules stepped into the store and reached for her aunt's phone. The trio mugged for the camera, and Jules snapped several photos.

"Thanks, y'all. I can't wait to see what you find in and around Fern Valley." Roxanne took the phone Jules handed her and scrolled through the pictures.

"Any suggestions for area haunts that we should add to our list? We heard about the train trestle and a haunted farm up the road. Anything else you can think of?" Noah asked, picking up one of each of the brochures.

"The Exchange Hotel over in Gordonsville is purported to be haunted," Roxanne mused. "Staunton has a lot of stuff. There's an old state mental hospital up there. I went on a ghost tour there once. You all need to see it. The experience creeped me out."

"Ooooh. An abandoned mental facility," Cliffy said, tapping something into his phone. "That'll definitely have some energy. I'm adding it to the list."

"Thanks for the info. I'll drop off some posters and swag for you all later. Suz did our cool new logo, and we rebranded everything ahead of our new season. The documentaries will be available on Hulu," Noah said.

"That's exciting. I want autographs from you all," Roxanne winked.

"Cool. Cliffy, why don't you come back later this week and interview Miss Roxanne for the podcast?" Noah suggested.

"Sounds like fun." Roxanne beamed as the pair bounded out the front and down the porch steps.

"You'll be famous," Jules said.

"Hardly, but it will be fun. I'm looking forward to it. Can't wait to hear what Matt will say about it," her aunt said.

"Do you mind keeping an eye on things and Bijou for a bit. I'm going to swing by town."

"What's going on today?" Roxanne asked, reaching for an event schedule.

"More food trucks, a puppet show, and the street vendors. The toy car show is this afternoon, and the train show is on Thursday at the high school." Jules waved over her shoulder. "Jake wants to go to the car thing. I'll be back way before you head out."

"No problem. Bijou and I have everything covered."

A few minutes later, Jules opened all the Wrangler's windows and blasted the air conditioning. For a spring day, the sun's rays heated up the interior to almost roasting. When the temperature was bearable, she found a classic rock station and headed to town.

Encountering no traffic, she zipped down an alley and found parking on a side street. Perusing the vendor stalls as she walked across Main Street, Jules made a beeline toward Barb and Sil's tent.

Sil held court in the corner, pointing out outfits for their teddy bears as a woman and her two daughters oohed and ahhed over the clothes for the bears they had selected.

"Can I help you?" Barb asked as Jules turned toward a row of shelves.

"Oh, hi. How are things going today?" Jules asked, looking at shelf after shelf of stuffed bears, cats, dogs, and lambs. "These are cute."

"We get them from a small company in New Hampshire. They're top-notch. Plus, you can have about any outfit or costume you're interested in." Barb straightened a lamb that was leaning off the shelf. "It's been really quiet around here. Hopefully, the crowds will pick up after lunch. At least that bunch over there is behaving. Maybe they'll focus on selling instead of minding everybody else's business."

Not sure if the sisters had heard about Vern, Jules decided not to break the news. They'd hear about it soon enough. "Glad things are going well. I'm looking forward to the events later in the week."

"I'm doing a workshop at the Teddy Bear Extravaganza on Friday. Make sure to stop by and see me. I'm also on a panel about toy trends."

"Sounds like fun." Jules waved and wandered to Vern's tent. She approached the back where Simone sat on the counter, her phone propped against her knee.

Jules gasped when she saw the display behind Simone.

"Can I help you with something?" Simone asked, looking like she had been interrupted.

"Hi. My boyfriend and I were here the other day and saw your rainbow bears. Are you sold out?"

"Uh, I guess." Simone pushed her long hair over her shoulder and glanced at the empty racks behind her. "Must have been a good week." She glanced around the tent. "Travis, hey Travis. Do we have anything that can go on these empty racks?"

He mumbled something and left the tent.

"Do you have any more of those colorful bears?" Jules asked.

"I don't think so. I guess they were popular. You interested in anything else?" Simone paused a couple of beats and then glanced at her phone.

Jules shook her head and scanned the displays as she left. The empty glass case that had held the stolen bear stood out amongst all the other shelves packed with toys.

They must be doing well if they sold out that quickly. There had to have been a hundred bears on that rack.

Smells of grilled meat and onions tickled Jules's nose as she exited Vern's tent, and her stomach rumbled, reminding her that it was near lunchtime. After narrowing down her choices, Jules made a pit stop at the fusion BBQ for a new take on a southern classic. *Maybe the food and lemonade will help me make some sense of the events lately. Could the rainbow bears be that popular?* Thoughts of the missing bears, including hers, kept rumbling around in the back of her head.

Chapter Eight

Tuesday

Jules grabbed a yogurt and a granola bar and headed to the office for an early start. Time to plow through the email inbox and update her social media sites with some teddy bear festival pictures. She made a mental note to get some of the ECP guys and their gear.

After her second mug of coffee and a completed list of her administrative tasks, Jules opened a blank spreadsheet and typed in everything she knew about Vern and his crew. Why was he at the abandoned motel site? It seemed odd and unrelated to the festival.

Jules paused to look at the sparse content and the few facts that she had. She rubbed her eyes with her hands. Glancing at the time on her laptop, she picked up her phone and dialed her friend, Gwen "Pixel" Pierce. If anyone could dig up information, it was her former college roommate and white hat hacker who recently started working for the FBI. *I hope she still has time to research some things for me.* She was Jules's best source for uncovering hidden secrets.

After the third ring, she heard, "Hey there. I was thinking about you yesterday. How are things going?"

"Good. We're gearing up for our busy season. How are things with your new job at the FBI?" Jules asked.

"Great. I'm still doing a lot of training, but I've been assigned to a fusion team. The good part is that I get to work from home some days. My focus is on doing research and support for the teams."

"Sounds perfect for you. Do you have time to talk?" Jules asked.

"Sure, I've got a few minutes before I need to log in. What's up?" Pixel asked.

"Jake and I went out with some of our guests who are paranormal investigators…"

"Whaaatttt? How cool is that? Details. I want details. I've probably had too much caffeine already this morning. Sorry to interrupt. Please go on," Pixel said.

"It was kind of fun. We went up to that old, abandoned motel on Afton Mountain."

"Did you see or hear anything from the other dimension?"

"No. But we found a dead guy and spent the rest of the evening talking to the police. Oh, and he was one of my guests. I have no idea why he was up there because he had nothing to do with the paranormal folks. He was one of our vendors at the town's teddy bear festival."

"Wow. You have the most interesting stories. What do you know about the dead guy?" Pixel asked.

"Next to nothing. He was grouchy and complained a lot. He also had an antique bear stolen from him. His son, the son's girlfriend, and a nephew are here with him, and I get a weird vibe every time I talk with them. Something's not right. You'd think toy vendors would be friendly and all about the fun. This crew is on the grinchy side."

"Hey, your intuition never fails you. You've got a great track record of hunting down killers and solving murders. I have faith that you'll figure this one out," Pixel said.

"Not without your amazing computer skills," Jules replied. "If I send you a list of names, can you see what you can find? Something's hinky with this one."

"Hey, at least it didn't happen on your property this time. And tell me more about these ghost hunters. They sound so cool. Are you going out with them again? And do they have all that fancy Ghostbuster gear?"

Jules laughed. "No decked-out ambulances or proton packs. But they did have a trailer full of gear. They're from East Coast Paranormal, and they make films and podcasts. I hadn't planned on going out on another adventure, but I'm definitely going to watch for their documentary. They've been doing some recording around the resort. It would be neat to see the property in an episode or two. The guys are staying in the treehouse that Jake built."

"Treehouse. Awesome. Have you got paranormal activity at the campground? Their website is pretty cool. I'm going to check them out."

Jules picked at a hangnail. "No, not here at the resort. I would have heard stories. All our local ghosts are from nearby places."

"Too bad. That would give you something else to highlight in your marketing. Send the list over on the dead guy, and I'll see what I can uncover when I get some free time. Maybe the teddy bears are a cover for something nefarious. I'll see what's buried deep on the dark web."

Jules laughed. "Thanks. Just sent you an email. We always seem to attract interesting folks to the area. So maybe the paranormal research will send us some new guests."

"Keep doing what you're doing. You're crazy successful at your business, and you're a good amateur sleuth. I'll let you know what I find. Ciao."

"Bye," Jules said to a dead line. Pixel was definitely wired today. *Hopefully, she can find something about Vern and his crew that would help me figure out why he was targeted.*

Before Jules could start another project, the front door opened, and Bijou jumped into attack mode at the dividing door. Gently moving her out of the way, Jules stepped into the office. "Good morning, Eliot. What can I do for you?" she asked.

"It's a great day. Just got a call from the police. Their teams have finished with the old motel site. We are free to go back and film. Suz thinks we should strike while the iron is hot. She thinks all the turmoil and recent death will stir up the energy at the site, so we're going back tonight. Crystal said she's in. Do you and Jake want to go back up there with us?"

"Thanks for thinking of us. Let me see if he's available." Jules pulled out her phone and texted, What are you up to? The ECP guys want us to go back to Afton tonight. Interested? She added a couple of ghost emojis for good measure.

A few seconds later, her phone binged. Sounds fun. We can head over after dinner. Having a blast right now at the Matchbox car show.

Have fun. Meet me at my cabin around 5:30?

That works, he responded. Now I have to find my old track set. It's probably in my mom's attic.

Jules smiled as she pocketed her phone. "We'd love to. We'll head over there after dinner. Do we need to bring anything?"

Eliot bobbed on his toes. "Nope. Nothing special. Dress like you did last time and bring flashlights. See you then." He clomped toward the door and headed for the porch.

Jules straightened the brochures on the front counter. *I hope ghosts are the only things we encounter up there tonight.*

Not finding anything exciting on Vern's brood on the internet. Jules locked her laptop screen and said, "Come on, puppy. Let's take a quick walk and see what we have for lunch at home."

After a longer-than-expected trek to the cabin because Bijou had to sniff every flower and chase a bee, Jules rummaged through the fridge for leftovers. Finally settling on spaghetti, she warmed it in the microwave and poured herself a raspberry tea. Bijou took up residence on the couch and peeked over the arm occasionally to see if there was any food for her.

Jules ate her lunch at the counter, flipping through a week's worth of junk mail. "Not much exciting going on the home front." Jules did a quick clean-up and gave Bijou a treat. "Okay, let's go back to work. We need to purge our photo file and work on this month's newsletter." Bijou tore through the living room and stood on her hind legs at the cabin's front door, waiting not so patiently for her leash and for Jules to get a move on. The little dog was ready at the word "go."

Outside, Jules nudged Bijou toward the office as the little dog tried a repeat of her flowerbed exploration. A shriek echoed across the property. Then a long scream followed and sent goosebumps down Jules's arms.

Bijou growled and darted toward the village of tiny houses, and Jules jogged to catch up.

Simone, weighed down with two large duffel bags and an oversized purse, stomped after Travis. She hefted her things into a truck's backseat and glared at the tall guy. "What am I supposed to do? This is your family's thing. I shouldn't have to do everything! Where the heck is he?"

Travis shrugged and ambled to the driver's side. "I dunno. He's your boyfriend."

"Grrrrrrrrr. But he's your family. You are no help. I swear he does things to set me off. I should leave. I'm tired of always having to be the adult." Simone stamped her foot and stared at Travis through the open passenger door. "We need to do something about him."

"Can I help you with anything?" Jules asked, picking up Bijou to keep her from darting toward the guests.

Simone spun around on her high heels. "I don't think anything can help right now. First Vern goes and gets himself killed, and now Vee Jay has disappeared. I can't take much more of this. I didn't sign up to do all the work. And if that's the case, he's going to have to pay me a whole lot more. He thinks family and friends work for cheap. Sheesh."

"Do you have any idea where he went?" Jules asked.

"No. Who knows? I got this stupid text from him this morning. It said that he had been kidnapped and to wait for further instructions. I don't even know if it's real. Kidnapped and instructions were misspelled. I think it's one of Vee Jay's stupid pranks."

"Did you call the sheriff?" Jules asked.

"Why? It's probably him trying to get out of work. He never really wanted this business. He likes strutting around pretending he's the boss. Travis and I do all the work. Vee Jay has been complaining for days about a stalker and weird voicemail messages. I think he was setting us up for his stupid antics. He's off doing something fun and laughing at us. He fancies himself some kind of practical joker. I bet he's recording it for TikTok."

Travis nodded and started the truck. Simone huffed and pulled herself up to the passenger's seat.

Before she closed the door completely, Travis threw the giant truck in gear and zoomed toward the resort's entrance.

Jules kissed Bijou on the head and set her down on the pavement. *Well, that was odd. Was there really a kidnapping?* Simone was more worried about how Vern's death and Vee Jay's disappearance imposed on her and affected her day. *My spidey senses are tingling. I hope he's not in danger.* She pulled out her phone and tapped an email to Sheriff Hobbs.

Chapter Nine

Tuesday Evening

After a quick dinner with Jake at the Good Thyme Bistro, Jules put the Jeep in gear and headed back to the abandoned property near Charlottesville.

"Let's see what happens this time. Ready for an adventure?" he asked, scanning the presets for a radio station.

"I don't want to jinx it. Hopefully not a repeat of last time." Jules raised one eyebrow.

Jake's grin showed his dimples. "Hey, you never know what could happen. Maybe we'll meet a ghost. Oh, I picked this up for you at the car show." He handed her a plastic bag.

"A pink Wrangler! I love it," Jules exclaimed, setting the tiny vehicle on the dashboard.

"They didn't have a silver one. I found a whole bunch of Mustang stuff, too. Now, I'm probably going to have to go build a shelf for all of it," he said.

Jules pointed the car toward the interstate, and Jake turned up the radio. They listened to Queen, Black Sabbath, Kiss, and Aerosmith on their ride up the mountain.

The Wrangler chugged up the mountain, and Jules changed lanes ahead of the exit. She followed the signs for the scenic Skyline Drive on the Rockfish Gap Turnpike and hugged the back roads for several miles. Putting the Jeep into a lower gear, she applied the gas for the trek up to the abandoned site.

Jake's Mustang, great for interstate driving, would have balked at the uphill climb.

As they rounded the bend, she spotted the ECP trailer and truck. The last few rays of the sun glinted off the chrome work.

"We made it," Jake said. "Let's see what kind of encounters we have." He winked as she rolled her eyes. "Hey, maybe Eliot's team will be able to convince even you, Miss Skeptic."

"I'm open-minded. It's that I always come up with some rational explanation. And it's probably because I've encountered too many real-live monsters and hobgoblins."

Jake patted her arm as she swung the Jeep in between two trucks. He hopped out and grabbed flashlights. Jules fished out a hoodie from the back and slid her keys, phone, and pepper spray in the front pocket.

"That stuff doesn't work on spirits," he said with a snicker.

"I know. But it's not the ghosts that I'm worried about." He shut the door, and she looped her arm in his. The pair picked their way over the garbage-strewn lot with weeds popping through every crack and pothole. Nature was slowly reclaiming the site. They followed the voices around to what was left of the smaller drive-up motel with the former gas station and its missing roof.

No one around. They heard voices in the distance and followed them up the old road to the larger motel.

"This must have been something in its heyday. They built the old Holiday Inn into the side of the mountain. One wing has three stories to take advantage of the scenery, and that part has two levels, so it doesn't block the view." Jules hoped she didn't sound winded as they trudged up the ascending asphalt. "The view of the mountain range goes on for miles. Too bad they couldn't sustain it."

"I remember coming to the steak house when I was little. I can't remember if it was still the Aberdeen Barn then or some other name. It was fancy according to my five-year-old standards," Jake said.

Jules laughed. "My dad and Roxanne talked about going to the HoJo restaurant for ice cream when they were kids."

Around the corner, there was a beehive of activity. Crystal and Noah set up tripods near the pool area, and Cliffy toddled behind Suz with something that looked like a light meter.

Suz stopped her pacing, and Cliffy almost ran into the back of her. "What about here? Do a reading at this spot," she said.

"The EMF reader is higher in this region," Cliffy said, stretching his arms in two directions."

"Magnetic or electric?" she asked.

"Both."

"What about radioactivity?"

Cliffy shook his head. "Nothing yet."

"You don't have your cell phone on again?" she asked, glaring at Cliffy.

Cliffy rolled his eyes and pulled out his phone. "No, smarty pants. I turned it off."

"This time," Suz said under her breath. She nodded at Jake and Jules and headed over to talk to Noah and Crystal. "Are you all picking up anything on the mics?"

"Nope. Just chatter from the humans," Noah replied.

"Hi, Cliffy. What's that?" Jules asked, staring at the handheld device with the flashing green and red lights.

"Oh, hey. Glad y'all came back. We're hopeful to have more success this time. It's an EMF device. An Electromagnetic detector. See here," he pointed to a small screen. "It tells me the temperature and the amount of electricity nearby, and it also measures radioactivity. I can check the settings of the area and compare them to the audio and video recordings later."

"She means, what does it tell you about the ghosts?" Suz yelled over her shoulder.

"Oh, yeah. It measures fluctuations in electric or magnetic energies, and that lets us know when unseen forces are moving around us. Sometimes it's man made, like from electrical outlets, generators, or cell phones, but many times it's otherworldly. We do a lot of investigations after dark with the lights out to reduce the influence of man made energy and noise." Cliffy paused and scanned the patio area. "Noah has some really sensitive microphones and recording devices over there. Sometimes, he's able to pick up sounds that human ears can't hear. There are spectrums of sound that are inaudible. We don't want to miss any type of communication."

Suz gave him a side-eye from across the pool. "Uh, I gotta go. We still got stuff to do before the sun sets completely." Cliffy followed along behind her like a puppy.

Jules walked to the edge of the hill on the other side, near what remained of the fencing. She snapped a few pictures with her camera while the investigators continued their research.

"Don't let Suz catch you," Jake whispered. "You're creating your own energy field over there."

Jules smiled. "This view, highlighted by the last few of the sun's rays, is too good not to capture."

"It's a nice property," Jake said. "Too bad most everyone drives by it these days on the interstate. You thinking about investing? They used to call this area Afton Baghdad."

"Nice view, but it would take some serious cash to clean it up and remove all the hazards. That rusted tank over there looks like it's ready to collapse at any minute."

Jake and Jules found spots on the cracked cement decking behind Noah, Crystal, and Norm.

Suz clapped her hands to get everyone's attention. "Okay, people, it's almost dark. Find a place and get ready. We're going to start in a minute. Jake and Jules moved closer to the pool deck and stood behind Noah, Crystal, Eliot, and Norm.

As darkness descended and the sun's last rays dropped behind the mountains, Suz cleared her throat. "Good evening. Thank you for letting us share this space with you. We are ECP, and we want to make sure the world knows your story. Hello. We know your energy is with us. Are you the little girl who tragically drowned in this pool? Hello." Suz walked around the edge of the decking where the diving board used to be. "What about here?" she whispered to Cliffy.

He waved one arm. "Yessss. The energy levels are much higher there. Stay there and keep talking," he said with a strained whisper.

"Hello. Little girl, are you with us? Reach out. Let us know if you're there. Hello. Can you hear me? Please make contact," she said.

A knock echoed from inside the motel. "Did you hear that?" Norm yelled. "We got it."

Suz shone her flashlight in Norm's direction and waved both arms at him to tone it down. "Hello. Little girl, was that you? Are you with us? Let us know that you're in our presence. What do you want us to do? We'd like to know that you're here with us."

The group strained to hear any non-human noise. Only crickets and tree frogs serenaded the group for what seemed like an eternity.

As Jules fidgeted to keep her leg from falling asleep, something nearby made several scraping noises. To Jules, it sounded like it came from one of the lower deck rooms behind them. More scraping and then some banging. The hair on her neck stood up, and a cool breeze caused her to shiver.

"We got it. We got it. I knew his place was going to be a gold mine," Norm yelled. "Whooo hoo. This is going to be a great one."

"Shhhhhh!" Eliot and Suz ordered in stereo.

"Little girl," Suz said, moving toward the building with all its shattered windows and broken slider doors. "Little girl. We know you were left here after that tragic summer day. Are you Stacey, who drowned in the pool? Are you trying to find your family?"

Several loud bangs and a scream, "I'm free!" echoed across the pool deck. "I've been trapped in here forever!"

Cliffy screamed and ran away from the motel. Everyone else froze where they were. Blood coursed through Jules's veins, and she felt the urge to run too. Her heartbeat pounded in her head, pushing out all rational thoughts.

Jake squeezed her arm and whispered, "That wasn't a little girl's voice unless you count Cliffy's shrieking."

Jules tried to stifle a laugh. Before she could offer a retort, something burst out of one of the downstairs rooms. It pushed the drapes outward and stumbled to the patio. "Help me. Help me. I've been trapped here! I'm finally freeeeeeeeee!"

Noah swung his large camera light and illuminated the area. Whoever it was looked like they were battling with what was left of the curtains. For a few seconds, it looked like a jumble of arms and legs, and it was hard to tell if the person had freed himself from the drapes. Jules hoped whoever it was wouldn't stumble into the pool.

A red-faced Vee Jay with a bandana hanging from his neck waved his arms and kicked what was left of the curtains across the broken cement. "So glad to be out of that pig sty. Can y'all take me back to Fern Valley? I don't know how long I've been here. The smell in there was terrible."

A collective sigh seemed to emanate from the entire group. "Keep rolling," Eliot said to Noah.

"Are you okay?" Suz asked.

"I think so." Vee Jay rested his hands on both knees and breathed heavily. "Some guy stopped me at my truck at the festival and asked me for a light. Then something hit me on the back of my head. I woke up in a dump of a motel. What is this place? I saw rats the size of small dogs. Hey, I recognize you guys from the campground."

"This is an abandoned motel," Norm said. "We're here doing some paranormal investigations."

"I think you need to sit down. We need to call the police in case there are any clues about who grabbed you," Norm said.

"This is the second time that something has happened while we were here," Eliot said.

"And it ruined our recordings. I'm not sure we'll be able to return to trying to connect with the little girl who drowned," Suz said with a long sigh that sounded like air escaping from a punctured balloon.

"And the last time we were here, we found a dead guy," Norm said.

"That was my dad. You guys are the ones who found him? I still have no idea what he was doing up here, and now I don't know why I'm here. This whole thing is creepy, especially you all trying to talk to ghosts," Vee Jay said.

Jules whipped out her phone and dialed 9-1-1. She explained to the dispatcher where they were. After she disconnected, she told the group, "The police and rescue are on the way. You might want to sit down in case you're concussed or something."

"I feel fine. Sore and hungry. And thirsty, but I'm okay," Vee Jay said, scanning the faces surrounding him, illuminated only by flashlight beams and Noah's camera.

"Crystal, get him a water," Noah said, pointing to the cooler.

"Thanks. Anybody got any snacks or a cigarette? I don't know how long it's been since I've eaten," Vee Jay said, shifting his weight from one foot to the other.

"Look in Cliffy's bag," Suz said. "He's always good for having a stash of food. Speaking of him, where is he?"

Eliot tossed Vee Jay a granola bar. "I don't know. I'm going to check on him. Sometimes, these events get too intense for people." He disappeared into the darkness near the hotel.

Everyone stood quietly as Vee Jay crunched on the bar and guzzled his drink.

A few minutes later, engine noises grew louder, and headlights bounced around the dark side of the motel. Car doors slammed, and they watched flashlight beams sweep the landscape. Trooper Isaacs, Eliot, and Cliffy approached.

"Evening, folks. It didn't take long for you all to come back here. What's going on tonight?" The trooper asked. "Who's injured?"

"Me," Vee Jay yelled, waving one arm like he was the kid in the front row who wanted to answer the teacher's question. "I was kidnapped and left to die here. But I managed to free myself and alert these folks. I wonder if it was the same people who killed my dad. I have no idea why they brought me here. Or why they were even holding me. I barely escaped with my life. What if my captors were the murderers?"

"What's your name, and what happened? An ambulance is on the way. We'll get you checked out," the trooper said.

"I was in Fern Valley for the festival. We were selling toys when I stepped out for a smoke break. This guy asked me for a light, and the next thing I know, I woke up with a giant goose egg on the back of my head. I'm not sure how long I've been in this disaster area. I think there might have been another guy with him, but I don't remember. Now that I think about it, I remember two captors. And they had guns. And I have no idea how long I've been here."

"Just stay still. I'll get your full statement after the EMTs finish," the trooper said. "And you all are back for more exploring, I see."

"We had some great energy, but we keep getting interrupted," Suz said. "Cliffy, want to get some more readings while we're waiting?"

Cliffy, who looked like he had recovered from the fright, nodded and hustled next to her. The pair huddled around the device's tiny screen while the ambulance crew surrounded Vee Jay.

The trooper moved from cluster to cluster, asking each group questions and jotting notes. When he got to Jules and Jake, he asked, "When you all got here, did you see anyone else?"

Jake shook his head. "Just the paranormal people."

"No, we didn't even know Vee Jay was here. I saw his girlfriend and cousin earlier at the resort. They were headed to town." Jules looked over her shoulder and lowered her voice. "She was annoyed that Vee Jay had left her to do all the work. She mentioned a weird text message from Vee Jay and complaints about someone stalking him. I let Sheriff Hobbs know in case he was really kidnapped. His girlfriend and cousin acted like it was one of Vee Jay's pranks."

"Did she report him missing?" the trooper asked.

"I don't know. She and Vee Jay's cousin, Travis, were headed to town to open their shop. They talked like he did stunts like this all the time."

"Thanks. I'll reach out to him. Anything else you can think of?" he asked.

Jake shook his head again as Vee Jay yelled, "I don't need to go to the hospital. I don't need any more of your tests. I'm fine. I need to get back to my girlfriend and see about my business. I have a lot of responsibilities now that my dad is gone. And I still have to deal with funeral arrangements and my dad's estate. I don't have time for this."

One of the EMTs said something that Jules didn't catch. Vee Jay, illuminated by Noah's camera light, waved his arms as his face reddened. Then he seemed to deflate like an empty Christmas lawn blow-up. He climbed up on the gurney and let the EMTs finish their evaluation.

Before the trooper could move on to the next group of witnesses, one of the EMTs tightened the strap around Vee Jay's legs, and the EMTs guided the gurney over the cracked cement. As they passed, the trooper, the taller one said, "We're taking him to Sentra Martha Jefferson Hospital."

"Thanks. I'll be right behind you all." Turning to the ECP team, Trooper Isaacs said, "If you all think of anything else or have any more human encounters, let me know."

The team nodded and slowly moved closer to Suz and Cliffy.

"Wanna see what else happens?" Jake whispered in her ear.

"Not really. I think I've had enough of this place. You about ready to head out?" she asked.

He nodded, and she said to the others, "Thanks for inviting us. We have an early morning tomorrow, so we're going to drive back to the resort."

After a chorus of goodbyes, Jules and Jake hiked back toward her Jeep. When they were out of earshot of the group, she said, "That was a little weird. Vee Jay's hollering about being kidnapped, and his girlfriend and cousin acted like nothing happened and that he planned the whole thing. She said that he liked to pull pranks. And Vee Jay acted like he had no idea why he was there. No ransom demands or threats. Just one weird text that his girlfriend didn't take seriously. And he ends up in the same abandoned motel where his father was found dead. It can't be a coincidence."

"There's way more excitement in the physical world than anything the ECP guys found," Jake said, swinging his flashlight in wide arcs to get the best view of the broken pavement ahead of them.

"It all sounds fishy. I asked Pixel to do some digging for me in the dark corners of the wild web. Would someone really be murdered over something related to his toy business?"

"Everybody's got secrets," Jake said. "It basically boils down to money and power. Maybe it all stems from his personal life."

"But why here?" She paused and pulled out her phone. "Vee Jay seems to be the only one profited from this father's death. And now he might be a victim too?"

"The paranormal guys weren't shy about talking about their plans. I heard them several times at the lodge discussing the abandoned motel, so it's possible others heard about this site. Their schedule is posted on their website, too," Jake said.

"That's what I was checking. Their pictures of this place are all over their stuff. So, it's probably not a stretch to assume that if the killer wasn't connected to Vern personally, then he or she may have seized on an opportunity to use this place, too. Hey, it says here that tomorrow, they're going to Staunton. Roxanne told them about some sites there. She'll be thrilled they took her advice."

"Makes sense," Jake said as they neared the Jeep. "There are lots of ghost stories in these here hills."

Inside the Jeep, their conversation paused as she drove down the mountain. Popping on her high beams, Jules made sure she had a good view of the narrow and curvy back roads.

Her thoughts ping ponged around in her head. *I wonder if Vern came up here to meet someone, possibly about his stolen antique bear. Then, days later, his son, who complained of a stalker, said he was kidnapped by some guy who wanted a light. What are these guests into that would cause this much danger and chaos?*

Chapter Ten

Late Tuesday Night/Very Early Wednesday Morning

After dropping Jake off and a long, good night kiss, Jules parked in her driveway and hurried in to give Bijou her bedtime walk. The enthusiastic dog greeted her like she hadn't seen her in days. "Come on, puppy. Let's go sniff something."

Bijou moseyed around the perimeter of the cabin while Jules tried to piece together what was going on with the Hogges. Vee Jay was outspoken like his dad. Simone had her own impulse-control issues, and nephew Travis never said much. And Vern ended up murdered. "Come on, Bijou. There's got to be more to this than what's on the surface," Jules whispered as they walked the tree line behind the cabin. Something was niggling at the back of her thoughts, but she couldn't quite get it to surface.

Once inside her cabin, Jules put the TV on a classical music station and grabbed her laptop and notebook. She spent the next several hours searching for anything that referenced Vern while Bijou snuggled up next to her on the lap blanket. There had to be something related to his family or his business. Vern, a native of Camden, New Jersey, had a warehouse address. No storefront, and they only did internet sales in bulk. The website hadn't been updated in months. *I thought he told me they had a store. I can't find any record of one.* No sign of his antique wares or classic toy business either. According to the About Us section, Vern had always been a collector, and he started the bear business because of his late wife's love for the toys. Vee

Jay, short for Vernon Junior, was his only child and supposedly a marketing guru. There was no mention of Simone or Travis on any of Vernon's "I love me" pages, full of glowing accomplishments and photos of him at hundreds of events.

Not learning much that was new, Jules searched for each of the family members. Vee Jay and Simone had active social media sites with tons of party pictures. No surprise there. Vee Jay's showed him often with Simone or other bikini-clad women. Simone's portfolio was mostly selfies. Though she did post occasionally about Marcus, her cat. Travis, like in life, flew under the radar with no presence on social media.

Shifting gears a bit, she searched for the three younger members of the family on an online school yearbook site. Bingo. All three were in the same class at Camden High School. In the four online high school books, Simone appeared on the most pages in the drama club, the future fashion designers club, and on multiple student government committees. Vee Jay played baseball, and Travis played lacrosse and was in the Dungeons and Dragons club. All, proud graduates of the class of 2022. Simone attended a community college after that. Vee Jay attended college for one year, but Jules couldn't find anything that indicated he had ever graduated. After their school years, she found several candids of Vee Jay and Simone through the years. She'd been with Vee Jay since high school. But where does Travis fit into this? Maybe she likes the strong, silent type, too? Something is not right with this family.

* * *

Jules rolled over and shoved her laptop that was stabbing her in the ribs. The sun streamed in around the living room curtains. She rubbed her eyes and tried to remember why she was in last night's clothes on the couch. "Looks like we finally drifted off, Bijou. We need to get a move on. I didn't mean to sleep this late."

Jules zoomed around her cabin, picking up a mug and a pair of boots from last night. After a shower, she grabbed a banana and a cinnamon muffin.

"We need to check on the office." She leashed up Bijou, and it was off to work.

Juggling her bag, laptop, purse, and leash, Jules managed to lock the cabin door without tripping over Bijou. On her way down the steps, she froze, and a squeak escaped.

An ugly hunting knife pinned a note to her porch column. The note, in black marker on a sheet of copy paper, read, "Mind your own business, or you're next." The bottom of the note fluttered in the warm breeze.

Jules's heartbeat pounded in her temples. She dropped her things on the porch steps and managed to hold onto Bijou's leash as she fished her phone out of her purse.

After a couple of rings, Sheriff Hobbs said, "Good morning, Jules. What's going on? I heard from Trooper Isaacs about your adventure last night. I'm glad Vee Jay turned up relatively unscathed."

"That was definitely unexpected. I haven't had the chance to go check on Vee Jay this morning. But that's not why I'm calling. Bijou and I found something on my cabin porch. It's a note that someone left with a knife stuck in the wood."

"Let me guess. Not a love note?"

"Nope. The knife looks old and dirty." Jules let out a long sigh.

"Stay put and don't touch it. I'll be there in a few. You're at your cabin?"

"Yep," she said.

"Anything on the cameras?"

"I haven't looked yet. I don't have any pointing at the residences, but maybe one of the other ones caught something," Jules said in almost a whisper.

"Okay. Stay there. Be there as soon as I can."

Jules disconnected and snapped several photos of the note and the gnarly knife. Dueling desires of wanting to rip it down in a rage and self-warnings not to touch anything before the sheriff got here battled it out in her head. *Why me?*

Before she could check the cameras, her phone alerted from Roxanne. You okay? Did I miss something? It's not like you to be late.

Sorry, she typed. We got a late start, and I found something on my porch this morning. Sheriff's on his way over.

Please tell me it's not a snake or a possum.

Nope. A note stuck to my porch with a knife. She added a couple of crying emojis for effect.

Oh, my stars. It's never a dull moment. You okay? Roxanne texted.

Jules sent her a crazy smiley emoji. Be there as soon as I can.

Spending the next twenty minutes combing through surveillance camera footage didn't provide any clues. No one carrying a knife prowled around. She also didn't notice anyone except Jake and Lester walking toward the cabins last night. There were hours and hours of guests walking to and from the lodge and the parking lot, but nothing suspicious.

Bijou yipped and tried to dart toward the sheriff when he hiked up the small hill. "Good morning, ladies. Lovely day. What have you found?" He pulled out his phone and a pair of gloves from his utility belt.

"Somebody left me a present," Jules said, standing and pointing like Vanna White at her porch. "And nothing showed up on any of the camera feeds."

He sighed and snapped several pictures. "Anybody acting weird or threatening? Have any run-ins lately?"

"Nope. It's been fairly quiet here. We did encounter a very dead Vern Hogge and his kidnapped son on two occasions with the paranormal investigators, but the only connection is that they are resort guests. None of the outbursts or bad stuff happened here."

"Except for this ominous warning," he said, pursing his lips.

"I'm baffled," she said. "I'll ask the team, but I can't think of anyone who might have done this. It really has been quiet around here. We haven't had any cranky guests in a while."

"If you think of anything, let me know." Sheriff Hobbs carefully removed the knife and the note and placed them in an evidence bag. He sealed it and filled in the information about the find with a black Sharpie.

When he dropped the bag on the ground, Bijou darted after it. She got in several good sniffs before the sheriff scooped it up. "No, no girl. I need that."

"Thanks for coming out. Can I get you anything?"

"Nope. Tell Rox I'll call her later. I've got to go meet Trooper Isaacs about his investigation." He saluted with two fingers and headed toward the parking lot.

"Come on, Bijou. We've got work to do, too." Jules and the Jack Russell trotted to the office's back door.

They were barely inside before Roxanne swooped in. "Where's Matt?"

"He said he'd call you later. He's got a meeting with a state trooper."

"Okay." Her lips formed a thin line. "I was making tea. You want anything?"

"I was going to get some strong coffee. Very strong coffee." Sliding her mug under the spout, she pressed the blue button. While Jules waited, she retold her adventures, starting with finding Vee Jay and ending with the scary warning on her porch. When she finished her recap of the last twelve hours, Jules picked up her mug and settled in at her desk. Rifling through the bottom drawer, she pulled out the purple bear. Bijou barked and jumped into her lap. Instead of cuddles, she wanted the bear. She kept sniffing and lunging for it. She tried to chew on its ears.

"Hey, girl. This is for Pixel. What has gotten you all riled up?" Jules dropped the bear back in the drawer and closed it.

Bijou hopped down and focused on the drawer. She pawed at it and whined until Roxanne picked her up for a hug. "You are in a mood this morning."

"That's odd. She's obsessed with tennis balls and flying discs. She usually doesn't mess with stuffed animals."

"Well, she is a ratter," Roxanne said, slipping Bijou a peanut butter treat from her stash. "Maybe she doesn't like the way it stares at her. I'm that way about creepy dolls and clowns."

"Maybe she's picking up on the craziness vibe around here lately. The ECP guys have gadgets for detecting energy and sounds. Maybe she's uncovered something. She's usually a good judge of character," Jules mused.

"Or she doesn't like Vernon Hogge's bears," Roxanne said.

Chapter Eleven

Later Wednesday

Jules spent the time in between guest questions and emails to search for anything more she could find on Vernon's business. There had to be something out there that might explain his death. Anyone that brusque was bound to have baggage and a string of haters.

Her phone vibrated, distracting her from her online search. "Hey, Pixel. What's up?"

"I found some bits of information I wanted to share with you before I got too engaged with my latest work project. Do you have a few minutes to talk now?"

"Sure. Thanks so much for digging around for me. Whatcha got?"

"Vern has had his business for over twenty years. Vee Jay was a kid when he and his late wife started it. They work out of a warehouse in Camden, New Jersey. He does a lot of business with Chinese manufacturers and distributors. He's been involved in a couple of lawsuits with his vendors, but I couldn't find anything too serious or hinky. His sales seem to be cyclical. They make a lot of money at trade shows and during the Christmas holidays. Nothing in his background stands out. Simone Carson has been dating Vee Jay since middle school. She dropped out of community college to try modeling. Then she tried acting. Now, she works full-time for Vern and considers herself a social media influencer."

"Is she?"

"Not by her social numbers and posts. But she tells everyone online that she is. There are tons of pictures of her in different outfits mugging for the camera," Pixel said, pausing. "Let's see what else. The boys in this family are a bit more interesting. Vee Jay got into some scrapes after high school. Let's see. There was a DUI, street racing, and a couple of bar fights. Cousin Travis was involved in a lot of the same incidents, but his resume includes some drug charges that were pleaded down. It seems ole Vern and his lawyer came to the boys' rescue a lot."

"So not really angels. But Vern is the one who ends up dead at a spooky old motel. No one knows why he was really there. And then his son is kidnapped, but his girlfriend doesn't seem all that concerned. A lot of weird stuff."

"I'll let you know if I find anything else," Pixel said. "Gotta run."

"Thanks," Jules said before her friend clicked off. Lots of bits to think about. *I wish I had something more concrete. What is the connection between Vernon's group and the old motel? Maybe if I could discover that, the other stuff would fall into place.*

Before Jules could formulate her next steps, the screen door slammed so hard the hinges rattled for several seconds. Bijou ran toward the Dutch door and started a barking jag. Jules scooped up the tiny tornado and pointed her toward the fuzzy bed. She had a few seconds to escape to the office and pull the door behind her before Bijou realized what had happened.

Jules approached the counter where Roxanne leaned toward a flushed Simone. "How can we help you?"

The younger woman screwed up her face and shouted, "I need you to call the police. Someone is trying to sabotage us. I knew they were out to ruin our business! This is so unfair!"

"Who, Ms. Carson?" Jules asked.

"Those two, a two…" she sputtered. After gulping in air, she continued, "We were repacking the trailer to go over to the high school to set up for the teddy bear day tomorrow, and those two witches were nosing around. I caught one of them trying to get into our trailer. I want to press charges. They'll do anything to ruin us."

Roxanne picked up her phone. "Hey, Matt. We've got a guest at the resort who wants to report someone trying to break into her trailer. Her name is Simone."

"It's Simone Carson, and I want to report theft, sabotage, vandalism, assault…And I could go on…" the younger woman yelled.

Roxanne paused. "Yes. Yes, you're exactly right. Okay." When she disconnected, she looked up at the beet-red Simone. "He's sending a deputy over. He'll be here in a couple of minutes."

"I should hope so. I'm going to wait out on the porch. And tell them not to waste my precious time. I am a victim here. I don't know what it is about this place, but I want you all to fix it." She huffed and slammed the door again on her way out.

"Someone is a bit melodramatic," Roxanne said, staring at the door.

Jules shrugged. "That family seems to thrive on it."

"Makes the quiet afternoon pass faster," her aunt said, pulling out a nail file from her pale-yellow Michael Kors bag. "Let's see how many times she comes back in here before the deputy gets here. I have 'too hot' and 'it's taking too long' on my Simone bingo card."

Before Jules could brew a mug of coffee and settle in her desk chair, Roxanne called out, "Deputy's here." She hurried to the front to peek out the window, and her aunt continued, "Wish I could hear them. I'm sure it's as good as any of the daytime soaps. Look at her waving her arms around. Her wild hair and eyes made her look cartoon crazy. I'm sure that's not the look she's going for, even though it is entertaining."

"Be right back," Jules whispered.

"I want deets," her aunt called after her.

Jules looked out the front window again, and when Deputy Caswell and Simone walked toward the parking lot, Jules opened the door. On the porch, she pulled out her phone and pretended to talk. She moseyed along the porch and then down the path the pair took a few moments before. Jules continued along, pretending to be oblivious to the deputy's visit.

Getting close enough to eavesdrop, she made sure to add a few yesses and uh-huhs every few seconds to keep up the ruse.

"I want her arrested!" Simone bellowed. "I caught that old woman trying to get into our trailer. I saw it with my own two little eyes. And she and her sister are probably the ones who stole Vern's precious bear. And maybe even did him in. And my boyfriend claims he's being harassed and stalked. Maybe they did that too. This is too much. Why do they keep bothering us? I demand you do something about it!" Simone crossed her arms over her ample chest and tapped her toe.

Deputy Caswell said something Jules couldn't hear, so she tentatively stepped closer.

Simone waved her arms. "I know it's her. She yelled at me when I confronted her. Then she and her sister hightailed it out of here in her SUV. I'm sure they're over there at the high school right now, laughing about how clever they are. I want you to go over there and arrest her."

Jules's phone let out a trill, and a wave of panic shot through her. "Uh, I've got another call. I'll call you back." She punched the button.

"What's going on? I can't see from the front," Roxanne said.

"I'm outside near the parking lot. Nothing new out here. I'll be in in a sec." Jules disconnected and scrolled through her email.

"Ms. Carson, I will question the two ladies and find out why they were near your property. I need to get some contact information from you," the deputy said.

"My number is 856-231-8873," she snapped. "And I'll be at the high school by the time you get around to calling me back. You can give me an update then in person." She turned on her high heels and stomped toward the tiny houses.

When Deputy Caswell looked at Jules, she gave him a finger wave and power-walked toward the office.

Before Jules closed the front door, Roxanne said, "Well, anything new?"

"Nah, it was a repeat of her earlier claims. She wants the deputy to arrest Barb and Sil and throw them under the jail."

A wry smile crossed her aunt's face. "Bijou and I can keep things humming here. Why don't you go check out things at the high school? And come back with some good intel. I'm curious how all this will play out."

"Sounds like a plan." Jules headed to the back for her keys and purse. "Be back soon."

"With details. Lots of them," her aunt yelled.

Jules rolled down the Wrangler's windows to let in some cooler air and sped toward the outskirts of town. A road trip, even if it was a short one with the wind in her hair and great tunes, was what she needed to block out the morning's drama.

At the school, she found an empty spot in the teachers' lot and trotted over to a side door where Darlene Denunzio stood with a clipboard.

"Good morning," Jules said as she approached. "How's life in teddy bear world?"

Darlene laughed. "Just peachy. All but two of the vendors have arrived. They're getting set up in the gym and the hallways. We should have a good inaugural event. Elizabeth and Elaine are around here somewhere. They're waiting for the TV crew to do some interviews with folks."

"I'm sure it's going to be a fun event. I'm going to pop in to see if anyone needs anything. What about you? Doing okay?"

"It's all teddy bears and sunshine here. I've had my iced mocha this morning, so I'm rip roaring to go."

Jules smiled and gave Darlene a little wave as an elderly couple, dragging a wooden wagon up the sidewalk, approached. A small Maltese poked its head out from the middle of a pile of teddy bears. It looked like E.T. in the closet.

Jules smiled and followed the noise inside the school past the information tables in front of the cafeteria and down a series of halls toward the gym. Vendors buzzed around, setting up displays and unpacking bears in all shapes and sizes. At a corner display, Sil stood on a stepladder. She dropped the end of her shop's banner and swore under her breath.

"Here, let me get that," Jules said, picking up the end on the floor.

"Thanks," Sil said when she handed it to her. "Is it straight?"

"Down a little. There's that's good."

"Finally," Sil said, climbing down and collapsing the stepladder. "Barb will be back in a minute. She had to get some more stuff from the trailer. We're a tad behind schedule this morning."

"Everything okay?" Jules asked, looking at the bear jewelry on the racks on the table.

"Don't get me wrong. It's been fun, and sales have been great. I'll be glad when we don't have to deal with those people anymore." She made a prune face and dusted her hands off on her jeans. "I mean, every time I turn around, one of those Hogges is there mouthing off at us for no reason. How do I get so lucky to keep running into them?"

"Is it something Elaine or the volunteers can help you with?" Jules asked.

"No. Keep us away from that banshee and her boy toys. That will make things better. If I never have to talk to them again, I'll be happy. She keeps accusing us of sabotaging her stuff and breathing her air. And a whole list of other crimes. The woman is daft." Sil twirled a finger beside her temple. "Like I told that deputy this morning, it's the other way around. We're not doing stuff to them. We're too busy. I caught the stupid boyfriend rifling through our stuff the other day. I almost smacked him. I was spitting tacks mad. He keeps saying that we are stealing his valuables. We've never stolen anything in our lives. Barb's too nice. She keeps telling me to ignore them. I want them arrested, and I want to smack that smug look off of Vee Jay's face." Sil's lips curled into an evil sneer.

Before Jules could reply, Sil slammed one fist on her hip and continued, "I mean that Simone needs to get off her high horse and make up her mind. She's either kissing the boyfriend or his cousin. Too much hanky panky if you ask me. And his whole stupid story about him being kidnapped. He blamed us for masterminding that, too. He must think we have a lot of free time. Sheesh."

"More ancient history?" Barb set a large box on a side table. "I found three more cartons in the back of the trailer. Gimme that cart, and I'll be right back with the rest of them."

When her sister, in the long green teddy bear tunic, was out of earshot, Sil continued, "The other day downtown, I had to hear him recount his tale of pain and how he managed to scare off some stalker with his karate prowess. He claimed some guys were following him. I mean, he man-splained that story too many times to count, like he does everything he talks about. He told anybody who would listen. If you ask me, his story has as many holes as a sieve and way too many contradictions. I'm flummoxed that the police would even entertain his tale of woe. I think he made the whole stupid thing up."

"Still more ancient history," Barb said, parking the cart next to the booth.

Ignoring her sister, she continued, "That hussy of a girlfriend told the cops today that I messed with their trailer. I mean, really."

"Well, didn't you?" Barb asked, looking over the top of her bifocals.

Sil turned her head and started moving the boxes off the cart. "That's beside the point."

As the sisters continued their squabble, Jules tried to extricate herself. "It was nice talking to you both. Let me know if I can help with anything."

"Just keep the whackadoos away from us," Sil yelled in a singsong voice.

Jules wandered around the corner and spotted Vee Jay and Simone at a table midway down the hallway.

"Hi, y'all," Jules said, turning on the charm. "Your booth looks great. Oh, hi, Vee Jay. I haven't seen you since your, uh, incident. How are you feeling?"

He hopped off a stool and puffed out his chest. "I'm a fighter. I preserved and escaped my captors. All three of them were no match for me. I have a black belt and all kinds of other tactical training. I showed them a thing or two. I scared them off, and then I escaped."

"You are so brave. It's so good that you weren't hurt," Jules cooed, trying not to choke on her sarcasm.

"If there hadn't been so many of them, they wouldn't have taken me. Now that I think about it, there could have been four of them."

"Well, I'm glad you used your resolve and wits to free yourself. You outsmarted the criminals," she said.

Simone rolled her eyes and made a harrumphing sound.

"I'm still bruised, and I may have a cracked rib or two, but I told that deputy to keep a lookout at all the hospitals for a gang of guys with bruises and broken arms. I put up one heck of a fight. They had foreign accents, and I'm sure they're all hurting. Make sure to call the cops if you see them around or if they try to check in at your place. The cops need to find out who hired them to attack me."

"I'll definitely be on the lookout," Jules said, hoping that she didn't roll her eyes. *I guess that was a better story than middle-aged women Barb and Sil kidnapping him and dragging him to an abandoned motel room.*

While Jules was trying to suppress any more sarcastic thoughts, Simone didn't even try to make an attempt. Her eye roll was epic. "Haven't you told that story enough? And it gets bigger and bolder each time you tell it. It's worse than your stalking tales. Not many are buying what you're trying to sell." She waved her hand dismissively at Vee Jay.

Changing the subject, Jules interjected, "Hey, do you have any more of those brightly colored bears? I'd like to get some of the pink and blue ones for my friend's baby shower."

Vee Jay opened his mouth and then closed it again.

"We don't carry those anymore," Simone said. "It wasn't the best investment that Bruce Lee over here made."

A dark look crossed Vee Jay's face, but he remained silent.

"Well, thanks so much for your time. I'm so glad that you're on the mend." Jules turned and ran into Travis, who was lurking behind her. "Oh, excuse me. I didn't see you there."

Travis stared at her and then stepped closer to Simone.

Making her own escape, Jules hurried back down the hallway, trying to shake off the hair-raising feeling. There was definitely bad energy with that group. Something was going on with the mouthy Simone, the puffed-up bantam Vee Jay, and the strong, silent Travis. It's time for more poking around, but first, a call to Sheriff Hobbs.

Chapter Twelve

Still Wednesday

Jules hopped in the Jeep and locked the door, glad to be away from Simone, Travis, and Vee Jay. Something yellow on her Jeep's hood caught her eye. Hopping out, she picked up a rubber ducky with sunglasses and turned it over in her hands. There was a card next to it that read, "Duck, Duck, Jeep." She smiled. At least this wasn't another note with a creepy knife.

She jumped back inside the Wrangler and put the duck on the dashboard next to the tiny pink Jeep. It was nice to be included in the Jeep owners' game, where other drivers played tag by leaving a duckie on your car. She made a mental note to order some rubber ducks, so she could play too. Thoughts of the ominous warning left at her cabin crept back into her brain, and she reached over and locked the door before she dialed Sheriff Hobbs.

After several rings, a "What's up, Jules?" made her jump.

"Hi, Sheriff. Just checking to see if you had a few minutes to talk this fine morning."

"About that. I've got a meeting in about ten minutes. What's on your mind?"

"Simone stormed in the office this morning, complaining about some of the other vendors."

"I know. I got an earful from Marco, Elaine, and Rox. Miss Simone has a reputation that precedes her."

"Yep. The Hogges have had a lot of bad luck since they've been here."

"If you see a deputy at your place, don't panic. We're watching Vee Jay and his bunch. After they took him to the hospital the other night, the deputy found a couple hanging out at a lover's lane near the old motel. Earlier that night, they had spotted what turned out to be Travis dropping Vee Jay off near the back of the property. They thought it was odd that the truck drove off and left the guy trekking through the underbrush in the dark."

"How did they know it was them?" she asked.

"The two Einsteins got out and talked in front of the truck's headlights, giving the couple a well-lit, clear view of their faces. The lovebirds were so puzzled by it, they jotted down the plates, which are registered to one Travis Bates. We're going to give Vee Jay some rope and see what he does. Mario wants to haul him in to look at a lineup and nail him for lying. We'll see. We hope it provides a lead in the case. So, let's keep all this on the down low."

"Of course. I got the same feeling about Vee Jay. I heard his story multiple times, and the details kept changing. Any ideas about who left me the note and knife?"

"We sent the knife to the lab. There was blood on it. They'll be able to tell whether it's human or animal. Speaking of your warning, I don't want you asking a lot of questions. Just call us if you see or hear anything. This is bigger than a couple of dust-ups. Got it?"

"Yes, sir," she said. "And come by the resort any time. Crystal and Mel have a whole new summer brunch menu. Roxanne likes it when you stop by."

"Thanks. Gotta run," he said, disconnecting. *We both know it's not in my nature to stand around and watch. I am minding my business and making sure these clowns don't cause trouble for my resort.*

Before she could back out of her space, someone ran out of a side exit of the school and caught Jules's attention. Then Simone toddled out, screaming as she tried to give chase in stilettos. The pair headed for the grassy soccer field near the stadium.

Jules shut off the engine and slammed the Wrangler's door. She pushed her conversation with the sheriff out of her head as she ran toward the field. She came within a few feet of the wobbling Simone.

Jules paused to catch her breath when someone let out a scream. Before Jules could determine the origin, Simone swore loudly and kicked off her shoes. She picked up speed on the uneven ground. Simone launched herself onto Sil's back. The older woman teetered forward and landed in the grass with an oompf. They looked like a tumbleweed of arms and legs.

Jules paused long enough to text the sheriff and Elaine for help with the tussle.

Distracted by the string of quick responses, Jules glanced at her phone. We're on our way. Keep them from killing each other, Elaine responded.

The sheriff replied, Sending over a deputy. So much for staying out of it.

Jules pocketed her phone and waded into the scrabble.

"You pulled my hair," Simone screamed. "You better not have yanked any out. It took me years to get it all to be the same length."

"You tried to bite me," Sil said. "Get off me, harpy."

"I don't even know what that is. You're trying to ruin my business and my life. I want you to leave us alone. You're creeping me out. Stay away from me and my boyfriend."

"Which one?" Sil sneered.

Simone jerked back her arm, and Jules grabbed it with both hands, pulling her off of Sil. The older woman jumped to her feet and dove toward Simone, knocking Jules over in the process.

Before she could recover, Deputy Caswell yelled, "Stop it now! What is going on here?"

"I want her charged with assault," Sil hollered, wiping blood off of her split lip with the back of her hand. "See, I'm injured. I came outside to make a phone call, and she started screaming and chasing me. Then the next thing I know, she jumped on my back."

"Oh, sister. That's not what happened, and you know it. You were taunting me and my boyfriend…."

"Again, which one?" Sil asked.

"Youuuuuuuuu creeeeep!" Simone lunged toward Sil, but Deputy Caswell was faster. He grabbed her around the waist and moved her a few feet away.

"Knock it off, ladies. I'm taking you both in for disturbing the peace. We'll sort it out at the station."

"You can't do that. I have a business to run. It's all her fault," Simone whined. "I'm a victim in all of this. Everyone is always picking on me."

"Tell it to the magistrate. You two have caused enough ruckus." Deputy Caswell stood between the two women. Both were covered in dirt and grass. Simone's hair stuck out in all directions, giving her a manic look.

Elaine and Deputy Charles Dempsey huffed and puffed toward the group. "What in tarnation is going on here? Ladies, you both agreed to a code of conduct when you signed your contract to be vendors. This behavior is appalling and so unprofessional. I doubt if either of you will be asked back for future events. This is disgraceful," Elaine said.

"She started it," Sil and Simone said in unison.

"What's the plan?" Deputy Dempsey asked, hiking up his pants and adjusting his gun belt.

"We're taking them both in. We'll sort it out in the interrogation room. You transport her." He grabbed Sil by the elbow.

Charles, who would always be Bubba from middle school to Jules, tried the same move on Simone, and she jerked away, swatting at him. "Knock it off. Turn around and put your hands behind your back. This is for both our safety," he muttered.

She started crying and gyrating, and it took Charles several minutes to cuff her. "Now calm down," he said, wiping his brow with one hand.

"This is so unfair," she shrieked. "This isn't my fault. I'm being falsely accused and falsely imprisoned. And where are my shoes?"

Deputy Dempsey guided her across the field, and he picked up her shoes on their way to his cruiser.

"Well," Elaine said. "I'm done with those two. They are going to go on the no list for any future events. Thanks, Jules, for the heads up. Such despicable behavior." She turned on her sensible shoes and marched toward the school.

Jules dusted the grass and dirt off her jeans and made her way back to the Wrangler. *I'm no closer to uncovering who murdered Vern, but at least I have a good story to tell Roxanne.*

Jules pulled out her phone and texted Jake and Roxanne, I'm bringing boxed lunches. Meet me in the office in a bit.

Both responded with hearts or thumbs-up emojis.

Jules drove a few blocks and found a spot in front of Fern Valley's favorite lunch counter, Lula Belle's. The scent of baking brownies wafted from the kitchen and made her stomach rumble.

"Hey, Jules. Long time no see," Mitch Hill said from behind the long white and glass counter filled with deli and dessert specialties.

"It's good to see you. It smells wonderful in here."

"Donna's on a baking kick this morning. She's trying out some new desserts for the festival. What can I get you?"

"Let's do a turkey, ham, and pimento cheese box lunches with your famous strawberry lemonade."

"Sounds good," Mitch rang up her order as she handed him her card. He handed her an oatmeal teddy bear cookie. "While you're waiting."

"Aww. These are cute. Thanks. It's been a crazy morning."

"I was going to ask you if you've been gardening," he said, pointing to the grass stains on her shoulder.

"Nah, I had to break up a fight between two vendors at the high school."

"And that's why you're in charge," Mitch said with a smile. "Always going above and beyond the call of duty."

Before Jules could finish her snack, he handed her a shopping bag with her order and a drink caddy. "Here you go. You're all set. And I put some coupons in the bag for your guests. Keep 'em coming to town."

"Thanks. I appreciate you keeping us well-fed. Send my love to Donna," Jules said, hip-checking the front door.

Pulling into her driveway, she took several deep breaths to help her get back in the right frame of mind. "Enough bad behavior today," she said, shutting the door behind her and heading for the office.

Juggling lunches, the drinks, and her purse, she managed to open the back door to the office a few minutes later. Jake, Roxanne, and Bijou waited for whatever was in the bags.

"Here, let me help you," Roxanne said. "Thanks for bringing Lula Belle's."

"I figured we all needed a treat. I did after my day so far."

The trio chose boxes, and Jake handed out napkins as the three settled in at the worktable. Bijou found a spot where she was equidistant from everyone in case any food hit the floor.

Mitch and Donna Hill did not disappoint. Their sandwiches, made on thick, crusty bread, came with pasta salad, seasonal fruit, kettle chips, and a gooey teddy bear-shaped brownie.

After a few moments of silence except for chomping and swigging, Roxanne said, "So what did happen? You've got mud all over you."

"And grass in your hair," Jake said, pulling out a sprig from her red curls.

"Souvenirs, I guess. Simone and Sil were sniping at each other, and it ended up as a footrace across the soccer field and then a wrestling match."

"More like a smackdown." Roxanne cocked one of her well-manicured eyebrows. "Sounds like some of those chick fights you had to break up at the Christmas parade a while back."

"Something like that. Mario ended up hauling both of them in. Maybe while they wait in the sheriff's lock-up, they'll have time to cool off," Jules said.

"I'll see what I can find out," Roxanne said, whipping out her phone.

"I think I'm going to change. Call me if you all need anything, and let me know if the sheriff has any news." Jules picked up the empty containers.

"Thanks for lunch. I'm going over to Mike Cooley's place to talk to him about a tiny house order. He and his dad have some property by the river, and they're looking for some kind of fishing cabin," Jake said. "I'm not sure when I'll be back."

"Have fun," Jules said. "I haven't seen him since he fingerprinted me last summer after I touched some evidence in the Ira Perkins's murder case. Tell him I said hello."

Roxanne ended her phone call. "No luck. I left Sheriff Matt a voicemail."

"Y'all go ahead. I'll clean up here and keep everything under control." Roxanne wiped crumbs off the worktable.

Jules picked up her things and leashed Bijou. "Bye. Just lock it up when you leave, and I'll be back early tomorrow." *I really need some aspirin and a hot shower.*

Chapter Thirteen

Wednesday

Jules ran her fingers through her long curls as she blasted the hair dryer one last time. A long, hot shower had eased the tension in her muscles, but the greenish blue bruises on her arms and legs would be a reminder of the tussle for a while. Maybe it was time to steer clear of Simone and clan. "A guest was murdered, but it's not really endangering your business. Just let the police handle it. These folks will be packed up and gone in a few days," she said to her reflection. Jules took a deep breath and wiped the condensation off the mirror. "But I can't let it go," she whispered to her foggy image.

She put her hair dryer and brushes away and flipped off the bathroom light. "But a lot of this weirdness is going on here at the resort. And you have a knack for finding clues. Maybe a little more research wouldn't hurt."

Jules poured herself a glass of iced coffee and settled in at her dining room table. She perused her spreadsheet of random facts. "Okay, Bijou. We have lots of little pieces of information. It's time to tie some of this together. There has to be some order to this."

The brown and white dog yawned and waddled toward the couch.

Remembering the sisters, Jules dashed off a quick text to Pixel with their names. Maybe she could dig up something that would make this mystery clearer.

"Okay, Barb and Sil, let's see what's out on the big wide web about you."

Jules yawned after what felt like endless searching. She stretched and did some quick yoga moves. Not much on the sisters. What she did find was on their website and from a handful of interviews. Barb and Sil had owned their business for about ten years. Barb, the eldest, had loved bears since Pooh and Paddington. Her blog detailed her collections and the dollhouses and miniatures she had created. Sil had bounced around a variety of gigs that included makeup, kitchen supplies, and vitamins after she retired from a twenty-five-year career as a drama teacher. The pair seemed to travel quite a lot up and down the East Coast with their business, Teddy Bear Dreams. Both women were in their sixties. Barb was a widow with grown twin sons. It didn't look like Sil had ever been married.

Spotting an article buried deep in the pages, Jules clicked on the link. "What's this? Interesting. Both ladies have been arrested more than six times." Jules found a blog post where the women answered questions about protesting at hundreds of human rights rallies.

"Hey, Bijou, for all that time researching, this isn't a lot of helpful information. I thought I was onto something when I saw the sisters' arrests. Rats. Another dead end." Jules picked up her laptop and notes and moved to the couch. She turned the TV to a murder documentary and continued her online surfing.

Jules's phone alerted with a string of texts. She rolled over and reached for her phone. Blinking several times, she tried to figure out how long she had been asleep. Two-fifteen. *I was more tired than I realized.*

Hope you're still up. Found some interesting stuff.

Sent you an email in case you're sleeping.

You sure have interesting folks at your place, Pixel texted.

Thanks. You're the best, Jules responded.

Pixel sent a string of smiley emojis.

Jules opened the email and let out a little squeal. Pixel had documented several long paragraphs of life facts for Barb and Sil. Nothing stood out as odd except that an Over the Hill Sil was a regular contributor on several protest sites on regular social media sites and the dark web. Nothing looked threatening, but her opinions cut to the bone. *That seemed to match her feistiness and desire to rumble with Simone.*

At the bottom of the third page, Pixel had added a note that Travis Eugene Bates, also known as Travis Baker and Travis Bateman, had several arrests after high school for public intoxication, breaking and entering, and assault. Several of them had been dismissed. *It's always the quiet ones.*

Ms. Simone Carson had a string of unpaid parking tickets and several arrests for public intoxication. She had been to court four times in the past three years for speeding violations and had one assault charge, where she counter-sued a Suzi Beamon for a fight in a mall's food court.

Too wired to fall back to sleep, Jules rummaged through her hall closet and found a roll of craft paper with her wrapping paper stash. She unfurled a four-foot length on the dining room table and drew a timeline. There had to be a link to the murder and the fake kidnapping. Maybe looking at it from a different angle would help.

Jules groaned and stretched. The next thing she remembered was waking up with her crossed arms on top of the timeline. She had to get up and move around to get some feeling back in her arms and legs, and her back ached from sleeping slumped over on the table. "Oh, Bijou. I'm too old for this." She stumbled to the kitchen to make a mug of dark-roasted coffee.

The caffeine and sugar kicked in after her steamy shower. "Come on, doggie. Let's take a long walk. Sometimes, thoughts make more sense if I take a break and let my mind wander."

Jules slipped on her tennis shoes and stuffed her notes and laptop in her messenger bag. "Adventure time," she announced as the Jack Russell raced to the door.

Jules opened the office and checked the messages. After answering a handful of business council emails, mostly about the big fight at the high school, Jules stretched. "I'm going to go see what Mel and Crystal have on the menu this morning. Be back in a sec."

Jules wandered into the empty lodge. Eight forty-five. Still the breakfast hour. She pulled out her phone and checked the festival's schedule on the business council's website. Today was the Great Train Roundup and Miniature Show at the high school. *That's where everybody is.*

She hurried through the buffet line. Jules smiled when she spotted the teddy bear pancakes. She added several to her to-go box along with some fruit salad. She topped her breakfast off with a vanilla latte.

Setting her breakfast on her desk, she stepped through the open door to find Roxanne checking in a family. Bijou lay on the floor with all four legs skyward. A curly-headed kid sat beside her, petting the dog's tummy.

"Hey, Jules. This is Pete, Amy, and Hannah, the Jack Russell Whisperer. The Hathaways are going to be our guests for a week in the 1959 Sunliner Caravan, decked out in honor of Barbie, who also debuted that year. Hannah, I hope you like pink," Roxanne said.

Hannah squealed and kissed Bijou on the head. "I have forty-eight Barbies. But I could only bring two on our trip."

Roxanne handed a welcome bag, the keys, and his credit card to Hannah's father. "From the porch, the vintage trailers are on your right."

Hannah kissed Bijou again and followed her parents. "Bye, Bijou. I'll be back to see you soon."

"What's on the menu this morning?" Roxanne asked, straightening the brochures on the counter.

"Teddy bear pancakes and baby quiche. There's lots of fresh fruit and lattes."

"You had me at latte. Be back in a bit."

Jules settled in at her desk to check the resort's social media sites and enjoy her breakfast, but thoughts of Vee Jay, Simone, and Travis kept bouncing around in her head. Long after Roxanne's return, she kept staring at Vern's website.

What am I missing? Why does this family seem to dominate my every waking moment lately? Probably because of the dead body. But then there's the lying, sneaking around, the dalliances, and altercations galore. But nothing points to a reason for Vern's murder.

Jules checked the time on her fitness band. "Hey, Roxanne. I've got to check on something. I'll be right back."

"Okay," drifted from the front desk.

Slipping out the back door while Bijou snored loudly in her fluffy bed,

Jules breathed in the warm morning air and felt an immediate calmness envelop her. She wandered around the parking lot to the tiny houses where Vern's trailer sat next to the ECP ghost mobile.

Jules spotted Vee Jay on the bottom steps of the Baum porch, smoking and looking at his phone. When he glanced up and saw her, he flicked the butt in the grass and covered it with his boot. "Morning," he said, his glance darted around rapidly, not seeming to settle on anything.

"Good morning. I thought I'd stop by and check on things. How are you and your family doing?" she asked.

"We're fine. The medical examiner's office said I could send ole Vern to New Jersey, so I guess I'll be planning a funeral when I get back. He'd have wanted a big to-do with a buffet table at his viewing. You know, with lots of people and classy refreshments. He always focused on the optics."

"I'm so sorry for your family's loss. Do you need help with any of the arrangements here?"

"Nah, I'm waiting for Travis to get back from bailing out Simone. I swear, that girl has a mouth. And she's been hinting that she wants a change in our relationship. I hope I'm not planning a wedding too. That's all I need right now."

Thoughts of Travis and Simone's make-out session flashed across Jules's brain, but ignoring them, Jules asked, "Have the police had any leads on your father's murder or your kidnapping? Do you think they're related?"

"Uh, maybe. Who knows? The night he left after dinner, the last night I saw him, my dad said he got a call about that stupid antique bear. He was convinced it was one of the other vendors. He was excited that he had a chance to get it back. He was meeting someone at some secret location, and he was all pumped about it."

"It must have been valuable," she said.

"I guess. He has every dime he ever earned. He couldn't stand to lose money or inventory. I kept telling him that he had to expand, and he wouldn't hear of it. He said when I inherited it, I could do what I want, but I better not ruin what he had built. He had to control everything."

Jules paused, and when he stared at her, she said, "He had been in the business a while. He must know his bears. Are you planning to keep the store? I mean, since you're the heir."

Vee Jay nodded, and his shaggy blond bangs covered his eyes. "Yep. I have some ideas to expand into new markets. We need to stay ahead of the competition. Simone's going to help me revamp our logo and web presence. I want to do more IG and TikTok. Vern wouldn't hear of it. It's time for a change. We need to take the teddy bear into the twenty-first century. He only liked to do things the way he had always done them. The industry is passing us by. We've got to modernize. Kids today are more sophisticated."

"I wish you all well with your business. I know how much time and energy go into keeping it viable. Any news on your kidnappers?"

"Uh, nah," he said, glancing at his phone again. "Like I told you before. I went out for a Coke and a break from Simone and Travis. Her whining was getting on my nerves, and my stupid cousin always takes her side. I had had enough, so I took a walk to cool off. A dark car pulled up. This guy asked me for directions, and the next thing I remember, I was tied up in the trunk."

"That must have been frightening," she said in her throatiest whisper. *His story keeps changing.*

"I don't remember all that much. I woke up in that dump. Despite getting whacked on the head, I managed to free myself when I heard voices outside. I was glad that the big-time film crew called the police for me and documented my ordeal. I hope they do an interview with me."

I wonder if he knows they're paranormal investigators.

Before Jules could comment, Vee Jay continued, "I'm sure I was kidnapped because the crime syndicate thought they could get a big ransom for my return." He paused and glanced at his phone. "Simone and Travis are on their way back, and he said she's wound up tight. It may take both of us to calm her down. I gotta go." He rose and opened the door to the tiny house. "Hey, he said over his shoulder. "Do you know any reporters who'd want to interview me?"

"You could try Jane Jenkins. She's the star reporter for our local paper. I'm sure she'd love to talk with you."

"Cool. Thanks. I'll look her up. I need to get my side of the story out there.

Who knows, maybe one of the big networks will pick it up. It could go viral." He slammed the front door behind him.

Jules felt a slight smile creep across her face as she thought of Jane the Pain and Vee Jay. They'd make quite a pair.

After checking her phone, Jules headed to the office to see if Roxanne had heard any news. Vee Jay's story morphed with each telling. She made a mental note to try to bump into Simone later. Maybe she'd be in a talkative mood, especially after a night in the slammer.

"Find out anything interesting?" Roxanne asked her as the back door closed behind her, and Bijou rushed over with a greeting.

"Simone's on her way back from jail. I talked to Vee Jay. His story about his kidnapping sounded a bit far-fetched and wilder than last time. I'm not sure which version is true."

"Wait, if the dad is dead, and he was here chatting with you. Who picked her up from jail?" her aunt asked.

"Travis, his cousin."

Roxanne's eyebrows shot up about two inches. "Well, that's interesting."

"Oh, it is. I caught them out behind the barn the other day, and they weren't discussing teddy bear business."

"Hmmm. Keeping it in the family." Roxanne wrinkled her nose. "I finished the sales tax reports and payroll, and I left folders on your desk. Not as exciting as the teddy bear love triangle."

"Thanks for getting all that done." While Jules was reviewing Roxanne's forms, Bijou zipped over and started pawing her desk drawer. "What's gotten into you? I don't have any snacks in there." Jules leaned over and pulled the drawer out. Bijou lunged and grabbed the purple bear. Before Jules could catch her, she zoomed around the desks and worktable and out into the store with her prize.

Jules managed to wrestle the bear away from the dog after she moved several metal display stands to get to Bijou's hiding place. "What is up with you? You know you can't have this. It was supposed to be for Aunt Pixel. I think you tore a hole in it." She squeezed the purple bear and felt something other than stuffing. "That's weird." Feeling around the seam, she mashed on something hard, something that felt like beads among the fluffy stuffing.

"What is that?" Jules asked as Bijou let out a long, plaintive whine. She mashed the seam and made the hole that Bijou started wider. Jules squeezed the bear, and white fluff poked out. Jules mashed the bear again.

"What the heck?" Roxanne said, leaning over her niece's shoulder as something slick flew out and flopped on the floor.

Chapter Fourteen

Wednesday

Both women dove for whatever popped out of the stuff bear before Bijou grabbed it.

"Well, look at that," her aunt said, dangling a small baggie full of pills. "That's not what I expected to see inside a cute little bear. I thought Bijou didn't like the look of the toy. Hey, puppy. You've got a good sniffer on you."

Jules's eyes widened as she pulled out her phone and punched in the sheriff's number.

"Hey, Jules, what's up?" Sheriff Hobbs asked.

"Good morning," she said quietly.

"You don't sound very convincing."

"I've got you on speaker phone. Roxanne and I had a wrestling match with Bijou. She got hold of a stuffed bear that I bought in town. When I retrieved it, we found a stash of pills inside of it. I think you need to see this."

"Is Bijou okay?"

"She didn't get any of the pills. She's annoyed that I took the bear from her."

"Glad she's okay. Y'all wash your hands. There's no telling what it is. I'll be there as soon as I can."

Roxanne returned to the front counter and handed Jules a bottle of hand sanitizer. The pair stared at the gutted bear and the bag of white pills.

"Who would do such a thing?" Roxanne shook her head.

Jules poked the bag with a pen. "They're about the size of aspirin." She snapped a picture and asked Google what it was. Six pages of possible results popped on her screen. "It could be anything from diet pills to opioids." Jules let out a long puff of air.

"Wait until Elaine gets a hold of this. She'll fret and rant for days. I can almost hear her now. Our teddy bear event was a front for drug smuggling in Fern Valley." Roxanne shook her head with a flip, "Tsk, tsk."

The women fell silent and stared at their phones until they heard shuffling on the front porch. Bijou did her best Rottweiler growl and barreled toward the door. Her security shtick melted when she saw Sheriff Hobbs step inside. Patting her on the head, he said, "I may have to hire you as a drug-sniffing dog. Good job, kiddo. What did y'all find?"

Jules pushed the baggie with a pen toward his end of the counter. He photographed all sides of the bear and baggie and pulled out a device and a pair of disposable gloves. Jules and Roxanne watched him test one of the pills. When the test alerted, a dark look crossed the sheriff's face.

He dropped the pills, bear, Jules's pen, and his gloves in a paper evidence bag and sealed it.

"What is it?" Roxanne asked.

"We'll have it tested further, but it's showing up on the field test as fentanyl. Where'd you get the bear?"

"At Vern's booth," she whispered. "Jake bought me a pink one. You know the one that was stolen."

Sheriff Hobbs shook his head slowly. "I wonder how many of these were sold to kids?" He grabbed the bag and stormed out the front door. "I'm going to walk over to the tiny houses."

"Oh, my stars," Roxanne said, twisting her pearls and sinking onto the stool.

"I'll be right back." Jules dashed out after the sheriff. *Those were the bears that disappeared off of Vern's display.* Blood raced through her veins, and she could hear the swooshing along with her heartbeat. They had oodles of those bears on display, and then they were suddenly gone. Drug smuggling with toys. Jules's stomach did a flip-flop.

As she approached the tiny houses, she spotted Sheriff Hobbs on the porch of the Baum house. He pounded on the door. The sheriff scowled slightly as she approached, and he banged on the door again. "Sheriff's Department!"

After what seemed like an eternity with no answer, he walked around the house and then headed toward Jules. "I'll be back later. Do you see their vehicles in the lot?" he asked.

The pair looked across the field at the almost empty parking lot. "No. They have two big black trucks and a giant black trailer with a teddy bear wrap on it. It's got 'Vern's Collectibles' in red letters. I can check the cameras to see when they left."

"Just send it to me if you find anything. Tell Rox I'll call her when I can." Sheriff Hobbs trekked toward his cruiser with his head down and shoulders hunched. He looked ten years older than we he arrived.

As Jules turned toward the office, a flash of yellow darted between two vintage trailers. She spotted it again, a few seconds later, a few rows over. She jogged in that direction to see who was running around her trailers.

When she ducked around the "Rebel without a Cause" trailer, she heard a loud voice. "Shut up. I said Listen to me. The cop was nosing around the house. I snuck out the back window. He's coming your way. Make yourselves scarce." Vee Jay, in a neon yellow muscle shirt with his back toward her, cradled the phone under his chin and waved both arms around like he was swatting bees.

"Just be cautious and don't say anything. Who knows what they're after? But whatever it is, we know nothing. Shut up, Simone. You don't know everything. Less is better. This can't have anything to do with us. We've been set up. It's probably those old broads again. Let Travis take care of things. When the cops show up, be quiet. I know it's hard for you. Why don't you hurry up and come and get me?" Vee Jay asked.

After a pause, he continued, "I don't care if the King of England is there. If you know what's good for you, do it now. Travis can take care of things. I need to get out of here."

He disconnected by jamming his sausage-like finger on the screen. "You better be smart about this. Don't talk to the cops," he said loudly.

"Hey, Vee Jay. You doing okay out here?" Jules asked as she approached.

"Whoa, what?" he said, spinning around. "Oh, hey. I'm fine. Had to take a call."

"Simone said that you all were getting some more of those cute, rainbow bears. Do you think you'll have them before you leave, or should I order some from your website?"

"She said that? Rainbow bears…Do you mean the neon ones? She doesn't know anything about inventory. Simone needs to keep her mouth shut and stop promising stuff she can't deliver. Our distributor is having a hard time restocking my order. Not sure when we'll get them. You know, supply chain issues." Vee Jay jammed the phone in his pocket.

Jules made her best pouty face and said, "Oh, phooey. I wanted to place a big order for the holidays. I guess I'll have to go somewhere else. I was hoping you and I could make a deal. They would have been perfect for a display in the camp store. I know my guests would love them."

"Here's my card. Call me in a couple of weeks. I'll see what I can do." He turned and stalked off toward the parking lot.

Jules jogged back to the office to check the camera feeds. On the way back, she called the sheriff and left an abbreviated version of her conversation with Vee Jay on his voicemail. Who was doing the smuggling? Either Vern's team was part of the crime, or they had no idea the stuff was hidden in the bears. Vee Jay's half of the conversation sounded suspicious. *I need to see if there have been any strangers lurking around.*

"Find anything else interesting?" Roxanne asked when Jules closed the screen door.

"Not as good as what we found in the bear. The sheriff was looking for Simone and the cousins. I spotted Vee Jay near the trailers after the sheriff left. He was acting a little odd."

Roxanne laughed. "They're all a little odd. So, which one do you think is smuggling pills?"

"It's hard to tell. Vee Jay's whole kidnapping story was made up. He acts like he's guilty of something. My guess is that one or more of them are in on it. Why else would I be getting notes with knives? I find it hard to believe that none of them know something's going on with their bears that suddenly disappeared."

"If I do talk to Matt, I'll see if I can wheedle out any tidbits of info."

Jules settled in at her desk and scrolled through the camera footage from the parking lot. "A ha. That didn't take long. Travis left at eight thirty-seven this morning with the truck and trailer, and Simone left in the other truck twenty minutes later after sitting in the parking lot for a while. Hmm, that's interesting."

"What?" Roxanne peered over her shoulder as Jules stared at her screen. Travis and Simone entered the lot about five minutes apart. They kissed and hugged behind the trailer before they took off.

"Something's definitely going on," Jules said, making a copy for the sheriff.

"They're probably all going to claim that they had no idea how the pills ended up in the bears. Poor Matt has his hands full with this one," Roxanne said.

Jules spent the next hour scrolling through footage from the past few days. She almost giggled when she sped through the images. People moving in and out of the shots looked funny at high speed. Not seeing anything other than her guests in the shots, Jules pulled out her spreadsheet of facts and updated it with the new material. There were no marauding strangers skulking around the resort. She Googled fentanyl and drug smuggling. "Wow. People come up with some unique ways to smuggle drugs."

"Matt's talked about it a lot, especially since the opioid crisis hit the news a while back. Anything to enhance a high, and the dealers don't care if people get hurt or die. He's always insisting that his guys need to be careful and always vigilant of what's going on. Even little towns are affected by this scourge."

"I still can't believe they'd use toys to transport drugs."

"Matt's worried about how many were sold to unwitting parents or kids," Roxanne said.

"Vern, what were you and your family into?" Jules whispered.

Chapter Fifteen

Thursday

Jules's phone alerted with a series of rapid-fire texts while Bijou busily sniffed flowers on their morning walk. "Somebody's wide awake this morning." Jules glanced down at her phone.

You up? Found some stuff. Can I swing by? Pixel texted.

Sure. We can grab some breakfast, Jules replied.

Cool. I'm on your porch swing.

Jules smiled. "Come on, puppy. Let's go see Pixel." The brown and white ball of energy dashed off toward the office.

Pixel had her feet propped up on one end of the swing as she busied herself with her phone. "Hey, good morning. Sorry to show up unannounced, but I found some stuff after I got your text last night about the hidden pills, and I wanted to share what I found before we both got busy."

"No problem. It's good to see you. I appreciate all the information. Let's go grab some food and a table at the lodge. How have things been?"

"I'm loving the new job. I had to give up teaching classes at UVA. Maybe when I get in a routine, I can teach one or two classes here and there. I still feel I'm fumbling my way through things. I don't like being the newbie, but other than that, things are good. There is so much to learn."

"What an opportunity! I'm excited for you," Jules said as they approached the large doors of the resort's multipurpose facility. "Let's see what Mel and Crystal have for us today."

The pair filled plates and mugs as they made their way down the buffet filled with generous portions of oatmeal, breakfast casseroles, sweet bread, and pancakes. Past the beverage table with coffee, teas, juices, and smoothies, Jules and Pixel found a table in the corner near the windows.

"What a spread. I could get used to this every day," Pixel said, digging into her breakfast casserole. "I'm going to have to go back for one of those smoothies. They look really good."

"Help yourself. Mel and Crystal have really come into their own with the food service. This week, they've even been slipping in bear and toy-themed foods," Jules said.

Pixel took several more bites and reached for her phone. "Let's see. I couldn't find any arrests related to drug smuggling with the Hogge crew, per se. Though way back in the dark corners of the internet, I did find that Travis Bates did have some minor drug charges. He had the intent to distribute charges dropped. It seems Vee Jay Hogge was also arrested as an accessory, but those charges were also dropped. And later, Vee Jay did a stint in rehab."

"Interesting, so it wouldn't be that much of a stretch to link the drug-filled bears to them. It was weird that there was a display with so many of the colorful toys one day, and then they had vanished the next. They were so bright and cute, made to attract kids, but so dangerous. The purple one was supposed to be for you, and someone swiped my pink one."

Pixel's eyes widened. "You need to be careful."

"I'm sure it was an isolated incident," Jules said quietly.

"You still need to be vigilant. This is a big deal."

"It was the bears and, well, the note," Jules said with a sigh.

"What note?" Pixel exclaimed a bit too loudly.

"The note. Someone left a warning on my porch. The sheriff said he sent the knife and paper for forensics analysis. It looked like it had blood on it, but he didn't know if it was human," Jules whispered.

"Knife?" Pixel's eyes widened, and she leaned forward and lowered her voice. "What if it's the murder weapon?"

Jules shook off the icy feeling that crawled down her spine. "We're all paying attention. The note was concerning, but I have a business to run. I think someone was just trying to scare me." Jules took a sip of her drink. "Hey, anything else on the Hogge love triangle or the victim?" she asked, trying to change the subject.

"I did a little poking around in Vern's background. He had a lot of complaints about his business. He liked to rant on social media about politics, and he fancied himself as some armchair economist. He was always dishing out advice, even if people didn't want it. He had a string of lawsuits against him. Most were related to his business dealings or partnerships. From what I could tell, they were all about business deals. In a couple of cases, he felt he was cheated, and then there were some where the vendor was suing him for nonpayment."

"Somehow, his business wasn't as picture-perfect as he claimed. I'm assuming Vee Jay is the heir. Wonder if he'll keep it going? He doesn't seem as focused as his father," Jules said.

"He's an only child. The only other relative I could find was Travis. It was odd that Vern ended up dead at an abandoned motel. I was wondering if it had something to do with the drugs, but I couldn't find anything from his past that would connect him to the pills." Pixel took another bite of her egg casserole.

Before Jules could continue, the ECP gang surrounded the food and claimed a long table beside Pixel. The noise level shot through the roof as the gang laughed and joked while filling their plates.

"Those are the paranormal investigators." Jules pointed to the group surrounding the buffet.

Pixel looked up from her phone like a prairie dog poking its head out of the burrow.

Before she could say anything, Jules said, "Hey, Eliot, I'd like for you to meet someone. This is my friend Pixel from college, and she's interested in what you all do."

"Hey," Eliot said, reaching across the table to shake her hand. "That's Noah, Suz, and Norm. Cliffy and Drew are over there trying to see how much food they can get on one plate, and like she said, I'm Eliot."

"It's so nice to meet you. You have a neat website. When Jules told me about your adventures up at Afton, I checked it out. You have some cool videos. Have y'all been able to find anything here?"

"Noah does all our videos." Eliot pointed to the blond guy with the mouthful of pancakes. Noah made a quick salute and continued to devour his breakfast.

"Our adventures at Afton weren't otherworldly," Cliffy said, sitting down next to Eliot. "But they'll make a good episode with a dead body and a kidnapping victim. We're going to do an episode about strange things we find at sites."

"We had fun at UVA," Norm added. "It was cool to see Poe's room. And that graveyard at night would be the perfect setting for a gothic novel. Cool stuff here in the Blue Ridge."

"I think we got the best readings at the sanitorium in Staunton," Suz said.

"The meters were off the charts there and at that creepy bed and breakfast," Norm said.

"We're going to do some battlefields next." Eliot reached for the salt and pepper. "We usually have good luck in war zones. This place has been great. And we're enjoying your resort. The treehouse is off the chain. Oh, you'll like this. Cliffy moved into the nook under the stairs in the Harry Potter house. I think he's been playing wizard, and he'll probably never want to leave."

"He's thinking about moving in permanently," Noah said.

A grin lit up Cliffy's face. "Hey, I may have to talk to you about having my own Harry Potter house built. It is too cool."

"Thanks for all the hospitality. This is a great place. I want a treehouse of my own, too," Eliot said. "It'd be the perfect place for me to write."

Pixel's phone alerted. "Oh, sorry. I gotta run. Thanks for breakfast. It was nice meeting you all. Good luck with your paranormal hunts. Jules, I'll call you if I find anything else," she said, picking up her plates.

"Thanks for all of your help. I'll get those. See you soon."

Pixel waved over her shoulder and zipped toward the door.

"I need to get to work too," Jules said, picking up discarded plates and utensils. "See you all around." Noah waved, and the rest of the ECP team continued their conversation.

Outside, Jules passed Lester on Old Bessie, the tractor. The groundskeeper, whom Jake had dubbed the Lawn Ranger, waved as he made a turn. She saluted and hustled back to the office.

Bijou rushed her at the door and followed her around the store as she woke up the laptops and unlocked the front door.

A stomping sound on the porch distracted both of them. Eliot shuffled in. His hair and clothes looked disheveled, different from a few minutes ago in the lodge.

"Hi, Eliot. Is everything okay?" She picked up Bijou, who was trying to get the tall guy's attention.

"I think we found something. After you gals left, we pulled up feeds to see what we captured recently. This was from the day that we scouted the motel site. It was the day before we found the body." He pressed play and moved his phone closer to Jules.

The video showed Eliot and Cliffy walking around the burned-out cabins. They chatted with Noah, who was off camera. Then the group hiked up the hill and around the larger motel. Jules recognized the pool deck and the two wings of rooms, and the restaurant. The ECP guys wandered inside the restaurant and through the dilapidated kitchen. The interior hallway was covered in peeling paint, old mattresses, and trash. The guys chattered and picked their way over the debris and stepped through a broken sliding door to the side of the motel, where brambles and grass covered the old sidewalk.

"Here, it's right about here," Eliot said, pointing a finger at his phone.

In the background, Jules watched as Travis and Simone climbed into a red truck and bumped over the grass to the old road. "Well, that's interesting. Can you send that clip to the sheriff?" She jotted his email on a sticky note and handed it to Eliot when he nodded. *Where did the red truck come from? They registered two black ones with trailers when they checked in. And what were they doing at the abandoned site?*

"None of us remember seeing them at the motel site, but I recognized them from here when I saw the clip. They're in one of the tiny houses across from us."

It was Jules's turn to nod. "And they're kin to the man who was murdered and the one who was kidnapped."

"Thought it might be important. I'll send the sheriff an email with it. Maybe they can figure out something. Cliffy wants to interview the sheriff and his team later if our video leads to anything. We like to show our followers where our research has been used. It would be cool if it turns out to be useful evidence." Eliot pocketed his phone and glanced around the store.

"Our sheriff is Aunt Roxanne's boyfriend," Jules said.

"Oh, cool. Maybe she could put in a good word for us for an interview. Gotta run. I wanted to show you what we found. That old site seems to be quite popular with the humans, but not so much with ghosts," Eliot said, plodding out toward the porch.

Jules fired off a quick text to the sheriff. He already knew about Travis and Vee Jay being at that old motel right before the kidnapping claim. Now, there's a clip of Simone and Travis there before Vern's body was found.

Grabbing a peach tea from the refrigerator in the back, she sat in her office chair and looked at all her notes about Simone, Vern, Vee Jay, and Travis. *There has got to be something related to their business or lifestyle that ties all these random incidents together. And the three younger ones were guilty of something. I just have to figure out what.*

"Okay, Bijou. From what the sheriff said, Vee Jay and Travis were involved in the fake kidnapping. Now, we have Simone and Travis at the site on the day before Vern was killed."

The little dog looked up and turned her head. Not having anything to add to the conversation, she rolled over to get comfy in her bed.

Why do these people keep coming back to that abandoned site? They aren't even from around here. *I wonder if the sheriff knows when exactly Vern died.*

Chapter Sixteen

Thursday Morning

The back door opened, and Bijou turned into the director of security until she recognized Jake. "Good morning, princess," he said, patting the terrier on the head.

"Good morning, sunshine," he said, turning to Jules and kissing her. "How's life?"

"Good. Just looking through all my notes on the Hogge family. They seemed to be involved in all kinds of things." Jules ran her fingers through her long red curls.

Jake dropped a coffee pod in the machine and said, "The part-time security guy stopped me on his way out this morning. He saw something on his rounds that he wanted us to know about. I'm going to take a walk over after more coffee to take a look. Wanna go?"

"What did he see?" Jules sat straighter in her chair with enough force that caused her to roll backward.

Jake grinned and pushed her and the chair back to her desk. "It may be nothing, but it struck him as odd. It was a vehicle parked deep in the woods."

"Let me change my shoes. Sandals may not be the best for a hike." Jules found her navy and tan duck boots and slid them on as Jake poured his coffee into his to-go mug. "Bijou, you guard the place until we get back."

After putting a "be right back" sign on the front door, the pair trekked toward the tree line behind the barn. The temperature dropped fifteen degrees as they headed under the thick, dark canopy.

"I don't think I've been back here since Sawyer Kelley's car was jacked and set on fire last summer," she said, picking her way over several large branches.

"The burned-out spot has almost regrown. I walk back through here occasionally," Jake said, taking her hand. "Not as much since you hired Mark O'Rourke's guys to cover the late shift."

"Business has finally reached the point where I can hire more help. If it keeps up, we're probably going to need some part-timers to help Mel and Crystal with the cleaning and food service."

"A good problem to have." Jake led her through the trees toward the clearing at the back. "He said it was over near the road and in the field. It's been a while since we've had squatters back here."

Pausing their conversation, they picked their way over the uneven ground filled with dead leaves and sticks. Every once in a while, a chipmunk or squirrel would scamper by, or a bird would land on a nearby branch. Without the traffic and other human noises, the animals' movements seemed to echo through the woods. Jules jumped a couple of times when something scampered by under the cover of the dead leaves.

When they neared the clearing, Jake said, "Over there." They trudged toward the grassy meadow that buffered the woods from the nearby road.

A red truck and a small tow-behind trailer sat near a copse of trees, not anywhere near the road. An old brown tarp covered most of the trailer.

"Looks too far from the road to be a breakdown or out of gas. Plus, someone took the time to cover the trailer." Jules walked around the older truck. The tinted windows made it difficult to see in. "Not that many leaves and debris on it, so it may not have been out here for a long time."

"I think the guard said he noticed it a couple of days ago. He made it a point to look for it on all his rounds since then," Jake said, checking to see if all the doors were locked.

Jules had a flashback to the last campsite they had found hidden here in the woods. That belonged to a guy who killed one of her guests. Shaking off the bad memory, she said, "Eliot showed me a clip of some video that Noah and his guys captured. It was at Afton, and it showed Travis and Simone climbing into a red truck." She pointed with two index fingers to the vehicle. "That may explain why this is out here and not in the parking lot."

"Interesting," he said, circling the trailer. "There's a rusty padlock on the back of this. Why would they hide it back here?"

"Someone doesn't want to be tied to the red truck, Afton, and the murder scene. It's really hard to see in the windows." She held up her flashlight app toward the driver's window. Trying another tactic, she used the front tire to climb on the hood to peer in the windshield.

"That's one way to do it." Jake laughed.

She snapped a few photos of the interior and slid off of the hood. "The front plate is all dented and curled. I can hardly read it. She scooted closer to the ground for a better shot.

"Let me see if there's one in the back," Jake yelled. "Nope. And nothing on the trailer except a faded sticker for the Handle Bar in Philadelphia," he said.

Jules hurried around and snapped a photo of the sticker. "Let's have the night security guys keep an eye on it. Make sure they do a report each shift. I'm going to send my pictures to Sheriff Hobbs. Maybe he can figure out the partial plate." She pocketed her phone and dusted off her hands on her jeans.

Jake circled the vehicle and did several laps that spread out into concentric circles. When he returned to where Jules was standing, he said, "Just seeing if there was anything else on the ground. I didn't see any footprints, and nothing looked disturbed. Just a few cigarette butts scattered around. Let's see what the sheriff says." He took her hand, and they headed back to the office.

"Philadelphia is really close to Camden, New Jersey," Jules said. "I'm pretty sure it's one of the Hogges' vehicles. It's too much of a coincidence to not be the same red truck in the video. Who knows what they're up to? There's a lot of hinkiness going on with that family."

Jules and Jake retraced their way through the woods to the edge of the property. After stepping out from the thick canopy of leaves, Jules blinked her eyes several times to adjust to the sunlight.

"I'm going to head over to Mike Cooley's place to work on the tiny house.

We're going to tackle the wiring and the drywall today. Hopefully, we can wrap it up soon, so we can move on to finishing and installing his appliances. Call me if you need me."

Jules opened the back door, and Bijou scampered out to greet them. Jake kissed Jules, and Bijou wended her way around Jake's legs to make she he didn't forget her. After a quick cuddle with the dog, he handed Bijou to Jules. "See you two later."

"Let me know if you feel like dinner," Jules yelled as he headed for the barn.

Jules kicked off her rubber boots and plopped down in her chair, and fired off a text to the sheriff with several of her pictures of the truck and trailer.

No sooner than Jules had settled in her chair to stare at her spreadsheet again than a loud rap echoed through the store. Before she could answer it, someone banged again. This time, much harder on the front door.

Jules gently nudged Bijou behind the Dutch door and hustled to the front, chiding herself for forgetting to remove her sign and unlock the office door.

"Good morning," she said, opening the door and pulling down her sign.

Two large, bald men in black T-shirts and jeans barreled through the door. Their black motorcycle boots thumped on the wood floor. "Good morning," the taller one said. "We're looking for one of your guests. A Simone Carlson. We were supposed to meet her here, and she's not around. I don't see the trucks in the lot."

The other man looked around the store and then at the brochures on the counter.

"I can take a message for her if you'd like to leave your name and number. I'm not sure when she'll be back, but I'll make sure that she gets it." Jules looked the men up and down.

"Tell her Vick and Petey stopped by. She knows how to reach us."

He turned to his partner, who looked more like his twin with matching buzz cuts and mirrored aviator glasses. "Petey, you ready to head out?"

Petey nodded and picked up a schedule for the teddy bear festival. The pair made it to the door in two steps, and their thunderous footsteps echoed through the store. When the door closed and rattled behind them, Jules slipped over to the window and took a few photos of them climbing into a large black Suburban.

Scrambling to fire off another text to the sheriff about Simone's visitors, her thoughts jumped from conclusion to conclusion as she tapped out her message about what happened.

The front door opened, and Jules jumped. "Mighty excitable this morning." Roxanne breezed in and dumped her red Coach purse and a shopping bag on the front counter. "Who were they?"

Jules shrugged. "They were looking for Simone." She wiggled the pink sticky note. "I took a message for her."

"Interesting. Anything else I need to know about around here?" Roxanne asked, picking up her bags and heading to the workroom.

"Nope. Other than the twins out there, it's been pretty quiet. The night security reported a truck and trailer in the woods. Jake and I walked over and looked at it this morning. I sent the sheriff a picture. I'm pretty sure it belongs to the Hogges. Though I'm not sure why it's parked in the woods. I'm going to head over to the school this morning to see if I can find Simone and let her know about her visitors."

"Wow! Delivering messages to our guests. Such service." Her aunt winked. "We'll be fine here. Just be sure to let Bijou and me know what you find out. I'm sure there's a good story behind it." Roxanne smiled at her niece. "You have skills. And as much as Matt fusses about you not meddling in his investigations, he does appreciate you as a source. You always seem to find out interesting things."

"Be back as soon as I can. The workshops are at the library, and the teddy bear tea is at the high school. Not quite sure where Simone is, but I'll find her." She patted Bijou and grabbed her purse.

She jogged to her driveway and hopped in the Jeep. She had a fifty-fifty shot, so she made a snap decision to try the library first since it was on the way.

Not seeing any available parking in the lot by the brick building, she found a spot near the sheriff's office and hiked over. She paused in front of the glass doors and smoothed her shirt and patted down her wild curls before venturing inside.

"Whoo hoo, Jules," rang out from the checkout desk. "Hey, how's it going?" Gail Mathews asked, as she fanned herself with a pamphlet. "It's a bit hot in here with all these folks. That poor AC is cranking extra hard. I hope it doesn't give up the ghost. What brings you over this way?"

"I'm looking for one of my guests. She's one of the vendors. I have a message for her."

"You're so nice. Darlene and Kim are running the show. They'll know who's here. The rest of the folks are over at the high school with Elaine and Elizabeth. I can't wait for the tea party this afternoon. It should be fun. I'm going to head over when I get off, but first, I need to stop by the house and get gussied up. I have the perfect hat for the shindig."

"It does sound like fun. I hope it draws a big crowd. Thanks for the info. It's good to see you." Jules waved and threaded her way around tables, chairs, and bookcases to the multipurpose room at the back of the library.

Darlene Denuzio, owner of On Pins and Needles, looked up from her phone. "Hey, Jules. I didn't think you were on the volunteer schedule today."

"I'm not. I'm looking for one of my guests."

"These are the speakers on the doll and toy panels." Darlene pushed a list of names toward her.

"Thanks," Jules said, skimming the list. "I don't see her. Mind if I take a quick peek?"

"Help yourself. It's all humming along here. Kim headed to the high school to help Elizabeth and Elaine. We wrap up here at twelve. It's been pretty ho-hum, but I guess that's better than the alternative."

Jules opened the door a crack and scanned the room. No Simone in sight. Closing the door as quietly as possible, she said to Darlene, "Thanks. I'll try the school." Then pausing after a few steps, she said, "Has anyone else been by looking for Simone Carson or the Hogges?"

"Nope. Like I said, it's been uneventful. I had one question about some missing keys. It's been kinda nice, but it's still early. We could still get a whackadoo or two," she whispered.

Jules snickered. "Fingers crossed for smooth sailing." She ducked out the side exit and hustled to her vehicle.

At the high school, trucks, trailers, and vans covered every inch of the bus loop as vendors hauled boxes and bins inside. Stepping inside to the lobby in front of the cafeteria, it looked and sounded like a beehive. People with arms piled high hustled down each of the corridors.

Spotting Elizabeth Rhoney and her elegant silver bob behind the information table, Jules fell in behind a man and woman who were asking the bookseller for directions to the nearest place with "cawfee."

"Thanks," the man said, taking the town map where Elizabeth had circled Lula Belles and Pop's Diner. "We'll try both before we leave." Jules stepped to the table when the man and woman in matching Hawaiian print shirts headed outside.

"Hey, Jules," Elizabeth said. "How is it going?"

"Good. It looks busy around here." Jules looked up and down the hallway at all the activity.

"Yep. All the vendors are getting set up for the shopping that starts with today's tea and runs through tomorrow. We're billing it as the land of thousands of bears. Welcome to the zoo."

"What fun. I'm on the schedule tomorrow to volunteer, but right now, I'm looking for one of my guests, Simone Carlson. She's with Vern Hogge's team. You know the one they found up at Afton." Jules lowered her voice and looked over her shoulder.

Elizabeth whipped out her clipboard and flipped through several pages. "They're in the science hall. Down there and to your left. It should be the booth on the end near the back door of the gym."

"Thanks so much. Do you need anything? I can cover if you need a break," Jules said.

"Nope. Everything's good here. Lunch for the volunteers will be soon. Have fun," Elizabeth turned toward the two women who approached the table.

Jules dodged boxes, tables, and people with carts. Booths, in all stages of setup, overflowed with teddy bears and stuffed animals. She picked her way around half-assembled displays and headed down the next hallway.

Spotting Vern's large banner, she eased around the crowd of people who scurried in every direction. Travis stacked boxes in the corner as Vee Jay sat on a stool scrolling through something on his phone.

She cleared her throat and said, "Hi, guys. Excuse me. Is Simone here?"

"She's around somewhere," Vee Jay said, without looking up.

"A message came into the resort office while you all were out. I thought I would let her know since I was in town." Jules scanned the throngs of people who were in constant motion. No, Simone is sight.

"What's the message?" Vee Jay said, looking up and glaring at her. "We can tell her. Who knows when she'll be back? She's probably slacking again."

Travis coughed but didn't say anything when Vee Jay and Jules looked at him.

Jules paused, not sure how much she should say to these two. "Uh, I don't mind waiting if she's here. I'm sure she'll be back to help you soon."

"Not likely," Vee Jay said, still scrolling through the feed on his phone. "We're used to doing all the work."

Travis coughed, and when Vee Jay looked up, he said, "She's coming up the hall." He pointed about three booths away.

"Thanks. I see her," Jules said, hurrying in the direction where he indicated. *That's more words than I've ever heard Travis say at one time.*

Jules rushed forward. "Hi. Some guys came by the resort, looking for you."

"Shhhh!" Simone said, digging her red acrylic nails into Jules's arm. "Come with me." She hurried Jules out the side door into the grassy courtyard at the center of the school. Picnic tables and benches dotted the outdoor common area, and flowers and a small tree provided a focal point for a small garden with a plaque.

"That's better." Simone looked around to make sure no one had followed them. "What did you say?"

"Two very big bald guys showed up in the office this morning. They said to tell you that Vick and Petey are looking for you."

"You didn't tell anybody else, did you?" Simone's dark eyebrows formed a "V" between her eyes.

Jules shook her head. "I told your boyfriend and his cousin that a message came in while you were out. I didn't say who it was from."

"Good. Keep it that way if you know what's good for you. They're my friends, and nobody needs to know anything about it. Tell your staff that it's none of their business either." Simone turned on her three-inch heels and stomped back into the building. *So much for learning any details from Miss Congeniality.*

Jules, feeling a little deflated, rubbed her arm and walked across the courtyard to the school's main hall and out the front door. *First, the red truck and trailer in the woods, and then the visit by Simone's two burly friends. And it's not suspicious at all that she doesn't want anyone to know about her visitors.*

Jules rolled down the windows in the Wrangler and cranked up the air conditioning to cool off the black interior. She settled on an eighties station for company and headed to the resort. Cyndi Lauper, the Bangles, and Devo brightened her mood.

Then out of nowhere, a vehicle zoomed up behind her. She mashed the accelerator and glanced up to see a black vehicle barreling toward her. She pressed the gas again, and the Jeep leapt forward. Putting some space between her and the approaching vehicle, she bypassed the route through town, hoping the aggressive driver would turn off and let her enjoy the rest of her ride in peace.

"No such luck," she said to herself as the bulky SUV closed the distance quickly. Before she could react, the other vehicle pulled up on her bumper and squealed its tires.

Jules white-knuckled the steering wheel and slowly edged her vehicle off on the shoulder. The Jeep bumped and banged along the ruts and tall grass. The black vehicle behind her roared to life and zoomed past too quickly for her to see a license plate or who was inside the heavily tinted windows.

She gulped air until the bats in her stomach calmed down. Easing the Jeep back on the pavement, she checked the rear view mirror every few seconds to see if the SUV returned.

No other cars in sight. *What was that idiot's issue? He could have passed me without any tailgating. Simone's friends again?* Jules shivered. It felt like icy fingers playing the piano on her spine.

Chapter Seventeen

Thursday

Jules sat in her Jeep in her driveway until her blood pressure returned to normal. Why would someone road rage on an otherwise empty road? Jules took two more deep breaths and headed toward the office.

Scooping up Bijou at the back door, she hugged the wiggly dog closely.

"What's shaking?" Roxanne asked, poking her head through the doorway. "Did you find Simone?"

"Yep. She was as cordial as ever." Jules rolled her eyes.

Roxanne laughed. "I wouldn't expect anything less. Not." Her aunt turned toward the store's door when footsteps thumped on the porch.

"Hey, Matt. Why so serious?" Roxanne asked.

Jules set Bijou down and slipped behind the counter next to her aunt.

"Morning, ladies. Deputy Caswell and I have a warrant to search the rooms of Vee Jay Hogge. Can I get the spare key?" Sheriff Hobbs handed Jules a piece of paper.

She scanned the document as Roxanne located the key in the lock box.

"Here you go. One key to the Baum house," Roxanne said, giving Jules a side-eye.

Jules handed him the warrant. "The cousins and the girlfriend are at the high school setting up their booth."

The sheriff nodded. "I know. Trooper Isaacs and his team are there to arrest him."

"What for?" Roxanne asked.

"The murder of his father," he said with a stony look.

Roxanne's eyes widened, and she covered her mouth with her hand.

"This morning, the two guys I sent you a picture of stopped in to see Simone Carlson," Jules said.

The sheriff's head bobbed slightly as he followed the deputy toward the door. "I sent the picture and stuff you sent me to the team. Maybe Vee Jay can supply some of the missing pieces when they question him." He pulled the door shut firmly behind them.

No one said anything as the footsteps faded. Bijou yipped from the back, and Roxanne picked her up. "Wow. I guess it's plausible, but I didn't picture Vee Jay as a killer," Roxanne said, stroking the soft fur on the terrier's neck. "Though he did get an inheritance from Vernon's death."

"He definitely had the most to gain as the sole heir," Jules mused. "But he didn't strike me as the killer either." She made her way to the back and pulled up her spreadsheet. After she entered her notes from recent events, she stared at Vee Jay's information for what seemed to be hours.

"I'm not making much progress here. I'm going to walk home for lunch. You want me to bring you anything?" Jules asked.

"Nope," her aunt said. "I packed leftovers. I was planning on dinner with Sheriff Matt tonight, but I guess that's iffy with today's arrest. You go ahead. I'll be here when you get back."

"Come on, Bijou. Let's go take a walk." She leashed up the dog and picked up her phone and keys.

"Make sure to go by the tiny houses," her aunt yelled after her.

"My plan exactly. Miss Bijou, let's head that way." The Jack Russell Terrier trotted around the building and across the almost empty parking lot.

Two police cruisers and a forensic van sat at all angles on the grass near the tiny houses. Jules stared at the *Wizard of Oz* flag that flapped in the breeze. The purple, red, and blue petunias on the porch provided a welcoming look. Too bad the police were inside looking for proof of something sinister. Jules stood outside, trying to catch a glimpse of what was going on through the windows while Bijou sniffed around the flower beds.

A whistle ripped through the quiet, and Jules looked around. She followed the sound of a second whistle to the treehouse's deck, where Cliffy waved both arms and leaned over the railing.

Jules picked up the little dog and hustled to the copse of trees.

"Come on up," Cliffy said, motioning her to climb the steps to the wrap-around deck.

After trudging up the thirty steps with the dog, Jules paused at the top to catch her breath.

"I'm glad you saw me. The view is better up here. You can see through the windows down there," Cliffy said, handing her a pair of binoculars. "I watched them on the other side for a while. I could see them searching the back of the little house. From here, you can see the front room and the kitchen. They seem to be going through everything. What's going on?"

"That's the house where the guy killed at Afton was staying." Jules pulled up one of the Adirondack chairs, and Bijou settled on her lap.

"That makes sense." Cliffy whipped out a small notebook and a pen from his shirt pocket and furiously jotted notes. "I thought it was about the kidnapping. But a murder makes a better story."

The pair watched in silence except for the occasional scratching of Cliffy's pen.

"They seem to be gathering stuff. Too bad we can't tell what it is. I've never had a front row seat for a raid before. We're supposed to talk to the sheriff tomorrow. Hopefully, he'll be able to give us some details. We will interview your aunt tomorrow, too. This is going to be an interesting episode for the podcast," Cliffy said.

Jules nodded and peeked through the binoculars. Mario searched several suitcases and moved on to the front room. She couldn't tell what the sheriff was up to. When he realized Cliffy was staring at her, she said, "That will be neat. I can't wait to hear your podcast."

"Maybe if you have some time later, we could interview you. We heard that you have a pretty good track record with solving true crimes," Cliffy said.

Jules shrugged. "We've had a few incidents that affected the resort, so I wanted to know what happened before it damaged my business."

Cliffy nodded as the Baum house's front door opened and two forensic techs, Mario, and the sheriff made their way outside with equipment and a bin full of evidence bags. The sheriff paused to lock the door.

As the others made their way to the vehicles, the sheriff nodded toward Jules and Cliffy and said, "We're done here. I'll give the key to Roxanne."

Jules waved and rose, which sent Bijou into motion. Jules picked her up before she bolted down the treehouse's steps.

"Well, that was an interesting morning," Cliffy said. "I hope you'll have some time to talk to us. Hey, what about this afternoon? I think it'll be a good addition to the story I'm working on. The gang is off scouting sites, and I stayed back to do some editing. I'm glad I did. I would have missed all of this."

"How about after lunch?" she suggested.

"That works. That amphitheater you guys have is pretty cool. Wanna meet there like around two?"

"Sounds good. See you then." She handed him the binoculars and carried Bijou down the steps. When she set the dog down, Bijou took off like a shot after a bumblebee. Jules jogged behind until the dog lost interest.

Inside the cabin, Jules noticed the scattered dog toys and the basket of towels. She picked up the living room and folded the load of laundry before she whipped up a quick lunch of leftover spaghetti and an apple. When Bijou realized the spaghetti had all but disappeared, she trotted over to her bed in the living room, and Jules wiped down the counter and ordered the kitchen.

"I'm glad you're back. I told Cliffy he could interview me at one," Roxanne said. Jules closed the door as Bijou did zoomies around the workroom table after being unleashed. "Someone's excited. Oh, I got a text from Matt. He thinks he'll be able to do dinner, which was a total shock. We'll see."

"Have fun with the interview." Jules settled in at her desk and pulled up her camera feeds. She scanned through different shots.

"Cliffy said he was going to talk to you, too. This will be fun. Maybe I should talk Jane the Pain into doing a podcast for Fern Valley. She's missing out on a hot opportunity to get on the bandwagon."

"My aunt and Jane, podcasters. You could dig up all kinds of dirt. You'd keep Elaine fretting for weeks," Jules said.

Roxanne smiled and moseyed into the store when the bells jangled. "Oh, the possibilities."

Jules continued to scan hours of footage from different angles at high speed. She paused when she caught movement near the tiny houses. Slowing down for a frame-by-frame view, she let out a gasp when she spotted two men in black creeping along the tree line near the tiny houses last night. The first one made a hand motion, and the other one disappeared behind the Harry Potter house. Both guys watched the Baum house for about fifteen minutes. Then they disappeared into the trees. She checked the other feeds and spotted the pair walking around the black trucks in the parking lot about twenty minutes earlier.

Scrolling through all the feeds, Jules didn't spot any other sightings of the pair. She sent the clips to the sheriff and watched more of the previous day's footage.

The store's door banged open, and the bells jangled wildly. Jules pushed her chair back and hurried to the front.

"Sorry," Roxanne said. "I didn't know my own strength. I was reading a text from Matt and wasn't paying attention. Cliffy said he'll meet you over at the amphitheater." She held up a black T-shirt covered in neon green and the ECP logo. "Maybe you'll get some swag too."

"Do I need to change clothes?" Jules looked down at her peach camp shirt and jeans.

"You look fine. He's only recording audio. And he can edit out any stutters, uhs, or repeats." Roxanne winked and headed to the back. "I might wear this shirt for my dinner with Matt. He'll be so jealous."

"I'm going to head out to see Cliffy. I'll be back in plenty of time to get Bijou before you leave."

"See ya," Roxanne called from the back.

Jules slipped out the front and walked across the field to the amphitheater that was normally used for weddings, concerts, and summer movie nights. *And the memorial service last fall for the TV writer who was murdered.* Memories of what happened to Sorbonne danced around her head, and Jules mentally made a list of all the murders she had a hand in solving. *Definitely more than four. Amateur sleuth doesn't sound so bad.*

When she crested the hill where the rows of the benches started, she saw Cliffy sitting down at the bottom, surrounded by a lot of equipment on the slightly elevated stage. He waved as she made her way down the incline.

"Hi. Roxanne said she had a lot of fun," Jules said as she approached. "And she loved the T-shirt."

"She was great, and she knew a lot of local ghost stories. I can listen to her and that accent all day." Cliffy blushed and fiddled with a microphone. "Okay, I'm almost ready to go here. This is casual. Don't worry if you mess up. I can edit this later. You'll sound awesome in the final version. Just take a few breaths to relax. Sit down right here." He patted the wooden platform next to him.

"Don't be nervous," he continued. "Like I told you before, this is for the episode that we're doing about finding the body and the kidnapping victim. It'll be released and billed as containing behind-the-scenes information when the documentary airs. The first few questions will be easy. Tell us about yourself stuff, and then I'll ask you some more in-depth ones." He pulled out his notebook and flipped through several pages. "You ready?"

Jules nodded and took a deep breath, and exhaled slowly. "I'm good. Thanks for inviting me."

He held up one hand and counted down silently from three with his beefy fingers.

After about what felt like a two-minute introduction, Cliffy finally paused and said, "My guest today is Julia 'Jules' Keene from the Fern Valley Camping Resort. Jules owns a resort full of tiny houses, upscaled vintage trailers, and the cool treehouse that we featured in our documentary, *The Haunts of the Blue Ridge*. Check it out. She has some amazing places to stay during your visit to the western part of Virginia, and I highly recommend it. So, Jules, how did you end up the owner of this great resort?"

"My parents bought the campground in the seventies. Back then, they offered cabins and spaces for campers during the summer months. I grew up here, except for a short stint during and after college. I returned home about six years ago, and my dad and I decided to save some beautiful vintage trailers from the scrap heap. He and our maintenance guy Jake…"

"Who is also her boyfriend?" Cliffy interrupted.

"Yes, that Jake. Anyway, we gutted and upcycled close to forty trailers. I used my interior design background from James Madison University, Go Dukes, to theme and decorate each one. We have ones that showcase James Dean, Lucille Ball, Elvis, Virginia's wildlife, Barbie, and Area 51."

"Too cool. I'll have to come back and stay in the alien one. Though the treehouse with its wrap-around deck is awesome. That one is themed for author A. A. Milne and his famous Winnie the Pooh characters. And here's a bit of trivia I learned from Jules. The famous Winnie the Pooh author also wrote a mystery for his father. It's *The Red House Mystery*, and it's pretty good, so check it out. I've been reading the book from the treehouse's little library. Speaking of mysteries. You've got quite the reputation around these parts as an amateur true crime aficionado. Tell us about the cases that you've helped the local police solve."

"Well, last summer, we had a long-term guest who was here to finish a book, and two bird watchers found him dead in the woods in only a red satin thong."

Cliffy's eyebrows rose, but he didn't say anything.

Not sure what to do next, Jules continued, "It turns out that things weren't as they seemed, and I needed to poke around to make sure this didn't damage my business. And then a reporter who was following a lead ended up dead in town. I was fortunate to be able to put a bunch of the puzzle pieces together to find out the real killer."

"Well, then, they filmed episodes of *Fatal Impression* here. I binged them when I found out, and you can see Jules's resort and the town in a bunch of last season's episodes. Check it out. Tell us about what happened there."

"The production crew filmed here for about a month. All was well until Sorbonne, the head writer, was murdered." Jules paused, wishing she had brought a drink with her.

"And the director and producer said in multiple interviews that I read online that you solved the crimes and saved the star Chavis Ratner when he was kidnapped. He raved about you on several interviews." Cliffy winked at her. "And if that's not enough, you figured out who killed a vendor at your town's Christmas festival, and you solved the murder of romance author Cinnamon Moon. You're basically a legend. I'm sure true crime followers out there have heard of some of these cases. Jules, you have an incredible track record. And you were with us when we found a body in one of our investigations. That was a first for me. Tell us about your background and how you're able to solve all of these cases."

Jules paused as she felt the heat rising on her cheeks. "I, uh, have no formal training. I read a lot of mysteries and thrillers. I've been a fan of the genre since I was little, and I probably binge-watch way too many true crime shows. The first murders happened on or near my resort, and I had to find out what happened to my guests. Fern Valley is really a peaceful little town in the Blue Ridge. All of the local businesses depend on tourist dollars, so I had to get to the bottom of what happened before people stopped visiting." Jules hoped that her response sounded sincere as she meant it.

"It's cool how you're able to uncover clues and find things out. You were able to help the police and capture the bad guys," Cliffy said.

Jules smiled. "We're a friendly bunch here, and people like to talk. I've been fortunate that I've been able to put disparate facts together and slowly piece together solutions."

"So, who are your favorite sleuths or crime fighters?" Cliffy asked.

"Nancy Drew, the Three Investigators, and Scooby-Doo were my early favorites. They got me hooked, and I moved on to Agatha Christie and her awesome sleuths."

Cliffy laughed. "Those were your gateway books. All great choices. Who else? Who do you read?"

"I love to read when I have the time. Sometimes, running the resort is a full-time job and then some. Some of my many favorites are Virginians John Grisham and David Baldacci. And I love Louise Penny, Janet Evanovich, Nevada Barr, and so many more that you don't have time for me to name them all. All of our tiny houses are themed for authors, and each one has a reading nook or a library for our guests."

"I've mentioned some of the murders that you had a hand in solving and bringing the bad actors to justice. When you were knee-deep in these cases, did you know you were going to always be able to solve them?" Cliffy paused and stared at her.

"Not really. I wanted to find out what happened. I'm a small business owner, and I couldn't afford to let the crimes damage what we've worked so hard to build here. I was asking questions and collecting lots of facts. I never really thought of myself as a sleuth, but I guess I am."

"How do you keep track of all the clues you uncover? Do you have a strategy?" he asked.

A quiet laugh slipped out, and Jules smiled. "I take a lot of notes, and I usually keep a spreadsheet of what I know, and of course, it helps me create a timeline of the events. A visual always helps me put things into perspective."

"Sounds like a pro to me, folks. She's focused, and she uses data to find killers. We need to wrap this up, but I think we have time for one more question. You're sure you don't have any special gifts that lead you to all these solutions? You know, like ESP or that little voice inside your head."

Jules shook her head and then remembered she was being recorded. "No. Not really. I think it's a lot of research and looking for every little snippet of information. It really is like solving a giant puzzle. At first, there are so many details, but when you start looking closely at them, things fall into place, and you're able to discard others."

"Okay, tell our listeners. Do you keep a murder board? And what does it look like?"

Jules laughed. "Not per se. Like I said, I usually create a spreadsheet and lists of everything I know, and everyone involved. I don't have pictures on a wall or anything. But I do post my sticky notes, so I can see all of them at once."

"No murder wall yet, she said," Cliffy said with a smile. "Do you share what you find with your local police?"

"We're a tight-knit community here in the valley. Most of the families have lived here for generations. Everybody knows everyone, and we're really fortunate to have a skilled sheriff and his team. They're always willing to listen to suggestions and ideas. Fern Valley is a great place to live and to visit. And I always share what I find, especially if it will help an investigation."

"And there you have it, listeners. The sleuthing process of another armchair detective. Thanks, Jules, for your time. Your resort is lovely. I'm going to put links to our videos and website, along with other information about the Blue Ridge Mountains and Shenandoah Valley, so people can check it out. If you haven't been here yet, it's time to put it on your bucket list. Make sure you check them out and come by for a visit. It's spring now, but I'm sure this area is great in every season."

"It was so nice to meet you all. And thanks for all the information on paranormal investigations. We really enjoyed watching your team in action," she said.

"And cut," said Cliffy. "We're done. I'll go back and edit and add a longer intro and closing and all our music and credits. I'll make sure links to your socials are included. This was fun. Thanks. And before I forget, these are for you and Jake. Eliot and I wanted you to have some ECP swag, so you won't forget us."

"Thank you. I really did enjoy learning about what you all do." She rose and picked up the gift bags.

"Cool. I'll send you a link when it airs, so that you can share it with everyone. See ya around." Cliffy stood and started to pack his equipment.

Jules slowly climbed the hill. *I hope the interview doesn't make the resort or the town sound like a place full of murderers with danger lurking around every corner. My intent was to share that I tried to help bring justice in my own little way.*

Chapter Eighteen

Friday Morning

Jules patted Bijou on the head and picked up her purse, bag, and to-go cup. "I'll be back as soon as I can." Pulling the door behind her, she jiggled the knob to ensure that it was locked.

The pinks and reds of the early morning sun peeked over the eastern ridge. Elaine wanted all the volunteers at the high school in place and ready to go before seven thirty. They hoped that hundreds of visitors would descend on Fern Valley today for the Teddy Bear Extravaganza.

Jules yawned and slid into the Wrangler's front seat. She motored down the main road through the tranquil landscape. Other than a few guests headed to the lodge for breakfast, the resort looked like a ghost town. Even the birds were unusually quiet this morning.

After a quick ride to the edge of town, Jules pulled into the school lot and pulled up alongside Jocelyn Mercer, owner of the Grateful Bread, who waved the two orange traffic flags.

Jules rolled down the window. "Good morning, Jocelyn. Round back?"

"Yep. Elaine wants all the volunteers in the teachers' lot. Just follow this road around. If you see tennis courts, you've gone too far. The side entrance near the shop rooms is open for you all, and there's coffee and treats in the teachers' lounge. We're going to have a great day."

"Thanks so much for keeping us well fed. See you in a bit." Jules headed off in search of a parking spot.

Once inside, Jules followed the line of people to the lounge and waited her turn to sign in and pick up her assignment, along with a refill on coffee and a croissant that was still warm and oozed butter.

"Good morning," Kim Lacy said. "Hey, Jules. Here's your name tag. Elaine has you and me at the information table by the cafeteria. It'll give us time to catch up, and Darlene and Jocelyn will spell us at lunch."

"Sounds good. Need any help here?" Jules asked.

Kim shook her head and turned to greet the next set of volunteers. "Oh, wait. I forgot to give you your volunteer T-shirt." She rummaged through a box under the table and handed Jules a hot pink, bear festival shirt with "Volunteer" in giant letters across the back.

"Thanks. I'll go change and meet you at the table." Jules ducked in the restroom and swapped shirts. Stuffing her original shirt in her purse, she did a quick mirror check. After a swipe of pink lipstick, she fluffed her curls and made her way to the information table.

"I'm so glad you're here," Elaine said, rushing toward Jules. "We're going to let the vendors in at eight on the dot. They're gathering at the doors and getting a little restless. Kim should be here to help you. I'm sure you're going to get flooded with questions. All of the vendors got their name tags and packets yesterday. There are extras in that box. Just write down who didn't remember to bring theirs." Elaine made a pickle face and peered over her glasses. When Jules didn't say anything, Elaine continued, "The schedules are on the table, and your lunch break will be at noon. The food is for volunteers only and will be in the teachers' lounge. The vendors know that they have to provide or get their own lunches. Any questions?"

"I don't think so. We should be good," Jules said, straightening the fliers on the table.

"I'll have Darlene or Mitch drop off a walkie-talkie for you all. If you think of anything you need, reach out. Hopefully, it will be a calm, profitable day. Ta-ta." Elaine turned and waddled down the hall.

As soon as Kim slid into the seat next to her, Elaine returned and set a radio on the table. "This is for emergencies only," Elaine said. "Do you all have any questions?" Before Kim or Jules could respond, she continued,

"Time to open the doors. Get ready for an exciting day, ladies."

Vendors flowed through the doors and made their way inside and down the hallways. Kim and Jules looked at each other as the sellers walked with a purpose to their booths. Some pushed carts and trollies full of boxes. No one stopped for questions or information.

The noise level in the nearby hallways increased as the booths and tables filled with sellers who were putting finishing touches on their displays.

"They weren't kidding. There are thousands of stuffed animals in here. This is perfect for early holiday shopping," Kim said, watching people carry bears in all shapes and sizes down the hall. "We can take turns checking out stuff when Elaine isn't looking." Kim winked and smiled as the vendors continued to stream through the glass doors. "And make sure you only use that walkie-talkie for emergencies." She waggled her finger like Elaine and laughed.

"For official business only." Jules read the schedule and list of sellers. Two hundred booths were scattered throughout the building. The place was buzzing, but so far, no one had any questions or needed a name tag. She checked her email and snapped several pictures.

The public address system crackled, and Elaine's voice boomed from every direction. "Good morning, vendors, and welcome to Fern Valley's inaugural Teddy Bear Extravaganza. We are going to open the doors at nine on the dot, so get ready. Your shoppers are already lined up outside, raring to go. I hope you have a fantastic day, and don't forget to stop by the information booth and pick up fliers on our upcoming events. Everyone, have a beary good day."

Kim groaned slightly as Mitch Hill saluted and opened the doors to the public. Bodies poured in and crowded the halls. A few folks stopped by to chat or to pick up a flier, but for most of the morning, Kim and Jules entertained themselves and chatted with each other.

The afternoon consisted of more quiet with lots of breaks, some stretches behind the table, and a little on-the-sly shopping. Elaine hustled by and stopped suddenly in front of the pair. "Have you had dinner yet?"

Kim and Jules shook their head, and Elaine continued, "The Good Thyme

Bistro dropped off boxed meals and drinks. Go get yours, and I'll cover the table."

Kim and Jules dodged shoppers on their way down the hall to the teachers' lounge. Long tables covered in brightly colored boxes lined two of the walls.

"Yum," Kim said. "These are nice sandwiches and sides. And look at all the choices. It'll be hard to decide." She walked down the length of the table and then picked up an aqua box and a peach tea.

Jules selected a veggie pita and a raspberry tea. "This looks really good. They fed us well today." She nodded at Elizabeth and Darlene and followed Kim back to the information table.

"There you both are. I hope you enjoy your dinners. I need to go check on Mitch and the deputies." Elaine stood behind the table, aligning all the fliers horizontally and vertically.

When she was out of earshot, Kim giggled. "You could lay a ruler down, and all of these piles would be exactly two inches apart. She definitely minds every little detail."

Jules nodded and dug through her box to check out the gourmet pasta salad, tropical fruit cup, and the gooey caramel brownie. "That's why she's the perfect organizer."

"She's definitely good at what she does, but she works herself into a frenzy when things don't go as she planned. I think she needs to take up yoga or something." Kim opened her fancy potato salad and dug in.

The clock's hands inched toward eight o'clock as the crowds started to wane, and the vendors started to pack their wares. The noise level shifted from chatter to the deconstruction of the booths. Jules suppressed a yawn and stood to ward off the kinks in her back. It had been a long day without that much information to dispense.

"It was busy for the vendors, but not so much for us," Kim Lacy said. "But by all accounts, I think the business council can chalk it up as another successful and well-attended event. Are you doing any of the other events?"

Jules nodded. "Jake and I signed up to help with the Teddy Bear Run tomorrow."

"That one starts at oh'dark-thirty. Make sure to bring coffee and probably a jacket. We've been having crazy weather with chilly mornings and scorching afternoons." Kim stacked the piles of fliers on the table.

Before they could continue their conversation, Elaine shuffled by with her clipboard and walkie-talkie. "Ladies, the crowds are thinning out. Whew. What a day. I need to go home and pour myself a hot tea, and put my feet up. Jules, I'd like for you to come with me to help clear out folks and help any vendors speed up their exit. Kim, keep staffing the table. All these fliers go in the folders with color-coded labels in that red bin. Mitch will go through and cordon off empty hallways and start locking doors. We hope to have everyone out of here by nine."

Jules followed Elaine, who toddled down the hall, nodding approvingly at the vendors who were almost finished packing their items. Jules held the door for one couple and helped another woman take down her large banner. Other than that, she served as Elaine's posse as she made the rounds of the halls several times. Elaine had mastered the stern look that meant pick up the pace and move along.

On their third trip down the science hall, Mitch Hill waved as he approached. "Everyone's out of the gym. I locked all the doors on that side. Now I'm working my way down this hall. Marco's covering the auditorium and the front hall. One more loop through, and all the doors should be locked. Do you want us to break down any of the tables or stack the chairs?"

"Nope. We paid the maintenance crew overtime. They'll be in at ten to do that, clean, and take care of the trash. Looking good and we're doing well on time." Elaine tapped her watch with her index finger.

After another two loops around the school, Elaine finally dismissed the volunteers, and Jules made a beeline for the parking lot. She waved to Mitch and Kim and sank into her Wrangler's seat. *What a long day. All I want to do is get home to a warm bath and some reading time. I'll probably be asleep before I even get the book open.*

Jules sped home on the empty back roads and dragged herself inside her cabin. *All I really want is to fall into bed.* Bijou had other plans for the evening. She was ready for a long walk, and she let Jules know when she rushed her at the front door.

"Okay, puppy. I know it's been a long day. I'm worn out too. I'm glad Jake came by to play outside with you and to get your dinner. Let's see if a vigorous jaunt in the cool night air will be refreshing." Jules leashed up Bijou, and the pair headed out through the garage toward the barn. Bijou sniffed everything she encountered along the path, and she was in no hurry to turn in for the evening.

After several gentle tugs on the lead, Bijou trotted to the cabin's front porch. Jules admired the warm glow from her living room and how it served as a tiny beacon that brought back a flood of memories from her childhood.

Jules, anxious to get settled for the evening, climbed the stairs behind the little terrier. Something on the left porch post caught her eye, and she paused in mid-stride. Grabbing the post, she let out a squeak.

"What in the world?" Jules fished out her phone from her back pocket and focused the flashlight app on her porch. "Oh, Bijou. What is this?"

The little dog yipped and danced around the porch like she wanted to play.

The pink bear that Jake had given her was split down the back and mounted to the post like a hunting trophy. A gnarly hunting knife stuck out of the center of the little toy. Stuffing and a slip of white paper fluttered in the breeze.

Jules let out a sigh and moved in closer to read the note without touching it. "Butt out. Mind your own business, or you'll be sorry." A chill raced through her entire body, and her knees felt wobbly. Sitting down on the top step, she dashed off quick texts to Jake and the sheriff.

Jake responded in an instant. I'm at Mike's place. Be there as soon as I can.

Then Sheriff Hobbs replied, On my way. Are you safe?

I'm fine. Bijou and I are at my cabin.

Lock the door. I'll be there in a few, the sheriff replied.

Jules hurried Bijou inside and slammed the door. She scrolled through the resort's camera feeds. At first glance, nothing looked out of place. Occasional guests walked to and from the parking lot. No marauding kidnappers with knives and mauled teddy bears. *This is getting personal.*

At about the time her heart stopped racing, she heard footsteps on the porch, and Bijou kicked into security mode.

A quick peek out the window revealed Sheriff Hobbs standing on the top step. Jules opened the door and gently nudged Bijou back inside. Pulling the door behind her, she said, "Hi, Sheriff. I was hoping for a nice, quiet night at home, but Bijou and I found this."

"Another one of those bears. You didn't touch it, did you?"

Jules shook her head as he pulled out a pair of gloves from his utility belt. "You definitely have someone's attention. Maybe you should dial back some of the questioning."

Feeling slightly deflated, Jules took a deep breath. "Maybe. But now we have two knives and two warnings. But no pills this time."

"I'll let the task force know. The lab tests on the blood on the first one came back as from an animal. They're both hunting knives. We'll test this one too, but it's probably like the first one. Maybe we'll get lucky and find a print."

"Task force?" she asked.

"We're combining resources. The state police are taking the lead on the murder, Nelson County has the so-called kidnapping, and we have the drugs."

"Those bears were all over the Hogge's stand for a couple of days, and then they were gone suddenly. Simone and Vee Jay acted like it was business as usual, and that the empty display was no big deal," Jules said.

"Either someone outside of that family was using the bears to smuggle pills, or someone in Vern's clan is involved, and it could be more than one of them. We're checking out every lead. From now on, I want you to lie low and fly under the radar. This person is dangerous. Let us do the investigating." He snapped several pictures from different angles and bagged the bear, knife, note, and his rubber gloves.

Jules let out a long sigh; she hoped he didn't notice. Usually, she was pretty good at uncovering information. *The notes are definitely directed at me.* "I've got to figure out who I set off. Thanks for coming over so quickly. I'll tone down the questioning."

"Not a problem. Let me know if you encounter anything else." He picked up the evidence bags and headed across the field.

Shutting the door and making sure it was locked, she leaned her back on the door as Bijou rushed over to play. "Hey, there. Did you see who put that bear up? Maybe it's time I put cameras up around the cabins. I heard what the sheriff said, but no one is going to scare me on my own property."

Several heavy footsteps and a loud rap on the door caused Jules and Bijou to jump.

"Hey, thanks for coming over," she said, pulling Jake inside. Not to be left out, Bijou danced around his feet until he patted her on the head.

"What happened?" Jake said, kissing her.

"I came home and found my pink bear gutted and stuck with a knife to my post."

"Nothing was on the porch when I stopped in to feed Bijou around four," he said.

"I think I'm going to have to order more cameras," she said.

"Any more pills?" he asked.

"No. But there was another note warning me to mind my own business." Her eyes filled, and she wiped away the tears before they spilled down her cheeks.

"What did the sheriff say?" Jake asked, rubbing her shoulders gently.

Jules wrinkled her nose. "He told me to lie low and stop snooping."

"Maybe it's good advice. We have one more week of this festival, and hopefully, they'll figure out who her killer is before everyone goes home. Can I get you anything?" Jake asked.

"I should be asking you that. Elaine and the company fed us well. Can I get you something to eat or drink?" she asked.

"Nah. I'm good. Mike had a cooler at the site, and he ordered pizza for dinner. We finished all the plumbing, wiring, and drywall today. When we go back this weekend, we'll do the mudding and sealing. Then it's painting, final touches, and move in," Jake said.

"Perfect for his camping and fishing excursions," Jules said. "The paranormal team is loving the treehouse, and it's booked through the fall. You may have to think about building another one before too long."

"You've got plenty of trees around. That won't be a problem. You okay by yourself here tonight?" Jake looked at her with those dark green eyes.

"I'll be fine. I have my attack dog and a baseball bat. I'm worn out from the Teddy Bear Extravaganza. Elaine had us hopping all day."

He leaned in again, and the long, gentle kiss sent a charge down her spine. "Okay, then," he finally said. "I'll see you tomorrow bright and early for the fun run. Call me if anything else happens around here."

"Will do. Get some sleep. You look like you put in a full day, too. Elaine said that they'd have breakfast goodies for the volunteers."

He smiled, and the stubble on his chin gave him a casual, sexy look. Jules kissed him again before closing the door behind him.

"Come on, Bijou. I need a long, hot shower."

After toweling off, Jules slipped into her fuzzy pink pajamas and fluffy robe and padded into the living room. *If I do some internet searches, that's not really investigating. I'm just looking at what other people posted.* Jules settled on the couch with no idea where to even start a search for Vick and Petey. Maybe on Simone's page since she's such the influencer.

Chapter Nineteen

Very Early Saturday Morning

After looking through hours of video on Simone and Vee Jay's TikTok accounts and what seemed like thousands of photos on their Instagram sites, Jules closed her laptop. "No sign of Vick or Petey anywhere. Maybe they're not friends or folks they party with. Drug dealers? I know that there's got to be a connection," Jules said aloud.

Bijou opened one eye and then closed it again when she realized nothing interesting was going on.

"I'm about ready to pack it in, too. We have to be bright-eyed and bushy-tailed at the starting line for the races before the sun fully rises. I'm probably going to look like a raccoon with major dark circles that no amount of concealer will cover. I guess I should have gone to bed earlier, but I wanted to follow the Vick and Petey lead. Somehow, they're all tied into this Simone Vee Jay thing. Could one of them be another of her boyfriends? They looked too old for her, but who knows?"

Still not interested, Bijou followed her down the hallway to the bedroom.

When the alarm blasted through her room and the sound bounced off the walls, Jules fumbled around for her phone to stop the noise. Bijou gave her a side-eye and rolled over.

"I know. It's still dark out, but I have to get a move on to meet Jake," Jules muttered. Hopping out of bed, she headed straight to the kitchen for a strong mug of coffee to ward off the headache that was forming behind her eyes.

The caffeine and sugar started to course through her veins, and Jules hurried to get ready. Thoughts of Simone, Vee Jay, Vick, and Petey swirled around her head as the warm water from the shower pulsated. *How do I find out more about Vick and Petey? I've hit a brick wall. Think, girl.*

After toweling and a quick round with the hair dryer, Jules slid on her jeans and the bright teal Fun Run volunteer T-shirt. She added a couple of swipes of lip gloss and mascara and pocketed her keys and phone. "Okay, Bijou, let's go for a walk, and then your breakfast will be served."

The pair raced down the porch steps, and Bijou won by a wet nose. The knife indents in the posts were the only evidence of the creepy warnings. Jules shuddered in the early morning coolness. Too dark to look around for footprints.

Giving up on the sleuthing, she took Bijou inside and filled her water and food bowls. "There you go," she said as she saw Jake crossing the yard. "Be back this afternoon."

"Good morning. Climb in," Jules said, opening the Jeep's door. "All ready for whatever adventures Elaine has planned for us today?"

Jake kissed her. "Yep. All set as long as she doesn't make me run any of the races. I kinda gave that up after I left the army."

She pulled out and zoomed toward town. When Bubba waved her behind one of the barriers, she found a parking spot on a side street. She and Jake hiked to the large race banner that spanned the width of Main Street. Runners, volunteers, and spectators milled around in brightly colored outfits and congregated around the food trucks that outlined one lane of the town's main route.

"Hey, Jules. Hey, Jake," Darlene Denunzio waved a handful of lanyards. "Coffee and yummies from the Grateful Bread are over there." She pointed to the back of the information tent.

"Thanks. Coffee first, and then we'll come and see you," Jake said, heading for the table full of pastries and coffee urns.

Jules stirred the heavy dose of creamer in her to-go cup. "Hi, Darlene. What would you like us to do?"

"How are y'all on this fine day?" She picked up a clipboard and ran down a list with her finger. "Let's see. Jake, you're with Mitch, Kim, and Marco at the starting line. Head over that way, and they'll show you what to do. Jules, you're with me here at the registration tent."

Jules gave Jake a slight finger wave as he trotted off toward Mitch and Marco. Settling in the empty chair behind the table, Jules looked at all the boxes.

"All the lanyards for the volunteers are in there." Darlene pointed to a blue cardboard box. "Each race is labeled. There's a welcome packet for everyone who registered. If they didn't sign up, they can do it this morning and pay the fee. Check or cash only. Let's see what else. We'll probably get a million questions, and it'll be busy before each race. The first race is the 5K. Then there's the kiddie race. That should be fun. Then we wrap it up with the fun run. Folks will be in costumes for that one. The awards ceremony will be in front of the stage about one o'clock. That's about it. You know the drill. Big smiles and talk about all the great things Fern Valley has to offer."

Jules laughed. "I'm used to that. How have things been?"

"I should ask you that," Darlene said. "I heard you all were there when they found the body and when his son escaped from his kidnappers. You always have something going on."

"Jake and I went with some of our guests to watch a paranormal investigation." Jules wanted to say more about the fake kidnapping, but she didn't know if the police had made that public knowledge yet.

"Ooooh. That sounds like fun. Spooky, but fun. I mean the paranormal stuff. Not the body stuff." Before Darlene could continue, a steady stream of runners in all kinds of brightly colored outfits queued up at the table. Darlene and Jules took turns registering guests and answering questions.

A sharp crack caused everyone to freeze and look around.

"Starter pistol," Darlene said with a nervous giggle. "It's time for the festivities to begin."

Jules took a deep breath and tried not to be so jumpy, but there were a lot of crazy things going on around here lately.

When the crowd finally thinned out, Jules and Darlene had enough time to grab coffee refills before the next wave of kiddos and their parents arrived.

When this race's box was empty of registration packets, Jules sank back in her chair.

"Whew. We get about a forty-five-minute break if we want to stretch our legs or get food or something," Darlene said.

"Sounds good. Do you want to go first?" Jules asked.

"I need more caffeine." Darlene headed off to the food trucks, where scents of sizzling bacon and sausage tempted passersby.

Jules watched spectators line the sidewalks and cheer on the tiny runners until Darlene returned with a stuffed breakfast burrito and a large soft drink. "Breakfast of champions. I'm back if you want to head out for food or shopping. The food trucks are on this side near the stage, and the vendors are further down the street."

Jules rose and did a quick scan of the food trucks. The smells were enticing. Her stomach growled, reminding her that her breakfast wouldn't stave off the hunger pangs until lunch.

She walked down the row of multicolored trucks that specialized in everything from burritos to "doughnuts as big as your face." The lime green smoothie truck caught her attention, and Jules spent her time in line looking at the hundreds of possible combinations.

When it was her turn at the window, she decided on a chocolate banana smoothie. Deciding to stretch her legs a bit more before returning to the information tent, she walked down the sidewalk to the vendor area.

Vern's giant banner fluttered in the breeze at the corner tent on the other side of the street. She snagged a spot on a bench and settled in to snoop for a few minutes. Vern's crew seemed to be at the hub of everything lately.

Jules reached for her phone as Travis barreled down the street with a dolly full of boxes. The tall guy glanced over his shoulder and disappeared down a nearby alley. *Do I follow him or hang out and see what the others do?*

Jules moved closer to where Simone worked the crowd in front of the cash register. Vee Jay sat nearby and surfed on his phone. When nothing happened except a few sales, Jules chided herself for not following Travis.

On the walk back to meet Darlene, Jules blended in with the crowds on the sidewalk. A sharp jolt on her arm caused her to glance around to see who bumped into her.

A bald guy in a tight black shirt, who looked like a bodybuilder, pushed his way through the throngs ahead of her. The shirt stretched past its tensile strength across his shoulders. Petey or Vick? It's one of them. A bolt of excitement arced through her.

Jules inched closer for a better look. He turned suddenly, and she ducked behind the nearest booth. It was hard to read her quarry's face from the side, especially with his mirrored sunglasses that blocked his eyes.

She pretended to scroll on her phone and snapped a clandestine photo of the guy chewing on a toothpick. He nodded slightly at a woman who walked past him and smiled. That was the only move he made in what felt like forever. Then he turned and disappeared down the same alley Travis used.

Before Jules could make up her mind to follow, she noticed Simone darting across the street to the same alley. Jules strolled to the intersection between the two buildings and pretended to look at her phone to get a better view of the action. Simone stood with her back to Jules about midway down the alley near a blue dumpster. She waved her arms and stomped her foot occasionally. The dumpster blocked most of her view of the guy in black.

Jules recorded the scene even though it was too far away to pick up any audio.

Simone shrieked and planted both hands on her hips. She shook her head furiously, and Jules continued to record. The guy must have said something to her because she paused when a black SUV pulled up to the other end of the alley, and the man jogged around and climbed into the passenger seat. In less than a blink of an eye, the vehicle sped away, and Simone stomped down the alley toward Jules.

With no easy escape in sight, Jules watched a beet-faced Simone with her tousled hair approach. "Hey, Simone. How are you? It looks like a big turn-out."

"Just fine. Just freakin' peachy. She blew out a long breath as she paused on the sidewalk.

"Are you okay?" Jules stepped closer.

"I'm perfectly fine. Just slightly annoyed that I'm saddled with stupid and lazy, and I'm the only one keeping this business afloat." She rolled her eyes.

"Hey, I forgot to ask you. Did you all get any more of those rainbow bears? I'm planning a party at the resort, and they'd be perfect for my guests," Jules said as Simone turned away.

"Uh, no. The ones we had were all spoken for. Here," she said, handing her a card from her back pocket. "Email me next week, and we'll see if we can work something out."

"Sounds like a plan," Jules said. "I saw your friend go by a few minutes ago. You know the big, biker-looking dude. I talked to him and his friend briefly when they stopped by the resort, asking for you."

Simone planted one hand on her hip and whirled to face Jules. "They're not my friends." Simone made a face and stomped off toward Vern's tent.

Jules dismissed Simone's abrupt departure and hustled back to the information tent. *Friends or not, the biker twins and the Hogge crew keep flocking to the same places.*

"Sorry, that took so long," Jules said, sliding into the chair beside Darlene. "I got sidetracked. Did I miss anything?"

"No worries. The fun run people are starting to arrive, and the costumes are hysterical. I hope someone's taking pictures. I saw a pair of T-rexes a minute ago. I have no idea how they're going to run in those suits, but they ought to get an award for creativity."

The pair spent the rest of the morning registering runners dressed as every kind of bear imaginable. Lots of Winnie the Poohs and Paddingtons.

"Wow, these costumes are so amazing. I feel underdressed," Darlene said.

Jules picked up the empty box. "Everyone who registered picked up packets."

"And we had about twenty folks sign up this morning. Hopefully, they're all having fun and spending a ton of money in town."

Before Jules could comment, Elaine bustled over. "Great job, ladies. As soon as the Fun Run is over, the festivities will start over by the stage. After we pack everything in the boxes, why don't you all take a lunch break?"

"Sounds good," Darlene said, stacking the empty boxes next to a cooler.

"Great. Enjoy lunch. See you over at the festivities. Toodle loo." Elaine waved over her shoulder.

Jules picked up the fliers and put them in folders, and added them to a plastic tub with the lost and found items, clipboards, and an assortment of pens.

"I think that's it," Darlene dusted her hands off on her jeans.

Whatcha doing? Elaine gave us a lunch break. Jules texted Jake.

Mitch and I are wrapping up race stuff. It'll probably be an hour or so before we're done. Meet you at the stage area when I can, Jake replied.

Need me to bring you lunch? She asked.

No, thanks. They've been feeding us all morning. Love ya.

She followed up with a string of heart emojis.

"I'm going to go find lunch and come back here to eat since we have a table and shade. Wanna join me?" Darlene asked.

"Sound good. Especially the shade part. It's getting warm out here. Meet you here in a few," Jules said. Scents of grilled onions and peppers at the lavender taco truck drew her like a magnet toward the row of food trucks. When it was her turn, she ordered two chicken tacos with a side of guac and a large peach iced tea.

Making her way through the throngs of people, she ducked behind a row of tents to avoid the foot traffic. Behind a green tent full of racing supplies and gifts, someone bellowed, "Let go of me!"

Darting around the corner for a better view, she spotted one of the biker guys with Travis. "I said don't touch me," Travis yelled, putting his hands up to block the other guy. "I don't know what you're talking about. Vee Jay handles all the business. I don't make deals. I help with the inventory and logistics. I don't know what you want."

"But you have that little twinkie's ear. You need to convince her or her other boyfriend that she needs to be loyal to her business partners," the biker guy snarled. Travis cringed, and his cheeks flushed.

"Huh? Vee Jay owns the shop now. And she doesn't love him anymore. Vee Jay can do whatever he wants with the stuff. Deal with him. We're getting out and moving on." Travis glared at the other man.

"Nobody's going anywhere until Vick and I get a bigger cut of the action. If you know what's good for you, you'll use whatever influence you have to make her understand." The biker guy poked Travis's chest with his sausage-sized finger.

The other bald biker slipped around the corner and stepped closer to Travis. "I'd listen to him if I were you. Or you could have an unfortunate accident and maybe disappear."

Jules's heartbeat pounded in her ears. Side-stepping a pile of boxes, she hurried around the corner, hoping none of the men noticed her.

"Come on, Petey," Vick said, loud enough for Jules to hear. "It's getting hot out here, and I don't want to hang out here all day. And you, make sure Vee Jay and your honey get the message and make the right decision."

Jules held her breath and peeked around the corner. The two men who looked almost like mirror images of each other disappeared around the other side of the tent. Jules counted to fifty, hoping Vick or Petey were gone before she stepped out and walked briskly to the information tent.

"You look like someone stepped on your grave. You okay?" Darlene asked.

"I'm fine. Lots of folks out and about. Glad it's lunchtime. What did you get?" Jules asked.

"I found a barbeque truck with all the fixin's and sweet tea. Mmmmm." Darlene wiped some stray sauce off her chin with a paper napkin.

"Smells good," Jules said.

"Yours does too." Darlene pointed to the paper bag that Jules clutched. "I may have to grab dinner on the way home." Darlene turned and said, "Hi, may I help you?" as a shadow crossed over them and the table.

Vick and Petey seemed to block out the sun and take up most of the space at the front of the tent. As usual, both were dressed in all black with thick chains from their belts to their wallets. Their tight T-shirts accentuated their bodybuilder physiques. Jules sucked in a little gasp of air and tried to quell the jitters.

"Good afternoon. We're looking for a master schedule for the rest of the festival," the one on the left said. "One that shows the vendors and food trucks." Part of a bird with talons tattoo peeked out from under his sleeve.

"Sure thing. We have those." Darlene set her sandwich down on the wrapper and rummaged through one of the plastic bins. "Here you go. One for each of you."

"Thanks. You ladies, have a fantastic day. And stay safe," the other one said. The biker twins disappeared into the crowd as quickly as they appeared.

Chapter Twenty

Saturday Afternoon

Jules took several deep breaths to get her heart rate back to normal. Who were these guys? *I really need more than just their first names.*

"You okay? You really do look like you've seen a ghost," Darlene said.

"I don't know about you, but I'm ready for a nap. It's been a long couple of days." Jules scanned the crowd to see if there was any sign of the dynamic biker duo. "I stayed up too late last night."

"I think we're done with the race stuff. Elaine said to leave all the bins under the table. I'm going to grab some dinner to take home and head out. I'm sure my husband and cats think I've abandoned them this week. See ya around." Darlene picked up her purse and waved.

Jules rose too. I'm going to walk around the vendor tents. No rush. Just wanted you to know where I was, she texted Jake.

Wrapping up race stuff. I'll come and find you in about an hour. He added a few heart emojis.

Tucking her phone in her pocket, she wandered toward the teddy bear tents. *Maybe I can do some research while I wait.* Jules wandered by the wrought iron fence around the Good Thyme Bistro's patio. The staff buzzed around filling take-out orders at a table near the sidewalk. It was nice to see all the tables full.

Runners, still in a variety of costumes, and spectators mingled on the street and sidewalks. The crowd seemed to double as she approached the rows of teddy bears and toy tents.

After browsing in several booths, she bought a pair of dangly bear earrings and a grizzly bear T-shirt for Jake. Picking up her bags, she crossed the street. Vern's red teddy bear banner drew her like a magnet.

Simone, Vee Jay, and Travis stood around with almost no shoppers at the purple tent. Diagonally across the street, the red tent was jammed with visitors who crowded around a woman with a headset microphone. The woman stood in a chair and waved her arms. "And just what do I have for you this fine afternoon? Teddy bear kitchen utensils and dishes. This is what every fan and collector needs. For nineteen ninety-nine, you get this teddy bear picnic set." Jules tuned out the spiel as the woman emptied the box and held up each of the contents.

Movement back at Vern's tent caught Jules's attention. She slipped through the crowd and caught her breath as Deputy Caswell and Trooper Isaacs ducked under the canopy. Jules weaved her way through the bystanders and found a spot outside the tent where she could spy.

A shrill scream, loud enough to make the teddy bear dish lady pause, echoed from Vern's tent. Jules stuck her head inside for a better look. Vee Jay resisted as Deputy Caswell cuffed him. He twisted and turned behind him like he was break dancing. Trooper Isaacs stopped talking and grabbed his shoulders, and said something that Jules couldn't hear. The red-faced Vee Jay grimaced and shook his head.

As they led Vee Jay to the street, he continued to shriek like a twelve-year-old girl. People nearby stopped and stared as he writhed and kicked as the deputies half-dragged him to a side street. A couple of spectators recorded the escapade on their phones. Jules tried not to roll her eyes when she thought about how Elaine would react.

When the police and Vee Jay disappeared, and there was no other drama nearby, the fickle audience returned to see what the dish lady had to offer. Jules looked up and down the street and zipped into Vern's tent.

Travis leaned on a stack of boxes, reading something on his phone. Simone filed one of her long pink nails and yawned.

"Oh, hi," Jules said. "Is everything okay?"

"Why wouldn't it be?" Simone asked with a smile that resembled a sneer. *That's odd after the hysterics that happened moments ago.*

"I saw two police officers drag Vee Jay away in handcuffs. What happened?"

Simone shrugged. "Who knows with him. He's always got some scheme going. One of them must have caught up with him."

"What did the police say? They had to accuse him of something." Jules prodded, hoping to get more information from the pair.

"Not much," Travis said. His voice boomed in the tent. "They said he faked the kidnapping as part of his plot to kill his father."

Jules's eyes widened. "Do you think he did it?"

"Who knows. He hated being under his dad's thumb," Simone said. "I wouldn't put the kidnapping stunt past him. He was always trying to stir stuff up. Vern was constantly yelling at him about falling for every get-rich-quick scheme that came along, like looking for cheap distributors or knockoffs that cost less than the toys Vern carried."

"The kidnapping was a stunt," Travis said. "He thought it would get him on TV, and he could talk about the store. He was always looking for ways to get free publicity." Jules's eyebrows shot up behind her bangs.

"Did you tell the police?" Jules stared at Travis until he looked down at his phone.

"They didn't ask," he replied.

"I hope they don't come back for you as an accessory. That will leave me here with all this junk and no help." Simone waved her hand dismissively.

"They won't. Vee Jay won't rat me out," Travis said without looking up from his phone.

"Are you going to see if he can make bail?" Jules asked, still probing for answers.

"He's a big boy," Simone said. "Vee Jay can call his own lawyer. We need to keep things going here. Plus, it's almost dinner time." *What caring friends.*

"If it's a murder charge, he'll be there for a while. Simone's right. We'll take care of things here if we want to keep our jobs," Travis said.

"If I can help with anything, let me know," Jules said, curious about their nonchalant attitudes.

As she backtracked through the tall displays, she stepped out in the sunshine and blinked several times for her eyes to adjust. She spotted a bald guy in all black on the phone. Dodging people on the sidewalk, she inched closer to him. *Maybe I can overhear something that will give me a clue as to who these two are.*

She moved slowly, trying not to attract attention, until she could hear his side of the conversation, which was mostly a series of grunts.

Jules jumped when he said loudly and waved his arm. "No. The statie and a local hauled one of the boyfriends out…Nah, the dead guy's son. I'm going to swing by for a chat. Not sure he'll make bail. Pick me up. I'm still near the food trucks. I was watching her and the tall one. They're still in the tent selling bears." After a pause, he continued, "Nah. No more of the special ones. Come and get me. I'm at the end of that same alley. I'll be looking for you."

He disconnected the call and glanced over at Vern's tent. Jules hid behind a tall rack and pretended to look at bear hats.

The biker guy's phone trilled, and he fumbled in his pocket for a second phone. "Pete Green here."

A tingle of excitement jolted through Jules. Finally, a full name, and he had two phones.

Petey said something quietly and jammed the phone in the front pocket of his black jeans. He turned and strode down the alley between the travel agency and an art gallery. Jules followed him around the corner. She blended in behind a group of twenty-somethings who laughed and snapped pictures of their souvenirs as they cut through the alley.

Trying not to lose Petey or Pete Green, she found a spot on the sidewalk at the next corner when he stopped and rifled through his pockets.

A black SUV squealed tires and blocked the alley, causing pedestrians to walk around it. Petey jumped into the passenger side. Taking a chance that they might spot her, she stepped into the street for a look at the back plate. It looked like a Virginia plate, and it ended in 1048. Disappointed that she couldn't get the full number, she typed a quick text to Pixel with Petey's name. She added a photo for good measure. Maybe her friend would be able to find out who these guys really were.

Hey, still here with Mitch and the gang. It could be a couple more hours before we're done. I can catch a ride with them if you have stuff to do.

You sure? She replied to Jake.

I'll text you when I leave in case you want me to bring dinner.

Deal, she replied. See you back at home base.

Jules hustled to the Wrangler. On a whim, she drove to the sheriff's office. *It wouldn't hurt to see what I can dig up on Vee Jay's arrest before heading home.*

Space at the government center was at a premium. It looks like folks were using it for overflow parking. Making her own spot in the grassy field near the side of the sheriff's office, she fluffed her hair and climbed out.

The same black SUV with tinted windows crawled past the complex. The driver turned around and drove slowly back like he was on the prowl for something. Jules's heart rate played a staccato rhythm in her temples. *It can't be a coincidence.*

Before she could decide what to do, Petey jogged out the side door of the sheriff's office and waited on the curb as the SUV inched closer. The driver floored it before Petey barely got the passenger door shut.

Jules double-timed it across the grass and into the sheriff's office, where a blast of cold air and antiseptic smell greeted her.

"Hey, Jules. I haven't seen you in a month of Sundays. What brings you by?" Millie Jackson, the receptionist for as long as Jules could remember, pulled a pen from her blond bouffant.

"Hey, Millie. It's good to see you. Is the Sheriff around?" Jules asked, looking at all the occupied plastic seats in the waiting room. The orange and beige décor looked like it hadn't been updated much since Pet Rocks and bellbottoms were in style.

"He's on the phone. You wanna wait? It's been a zoo here. Lost kids, a stolen wallet, a domestic, and countless complaints about parking tickets."

"Thanks. You've got your hands full. I'll wait over there if he has a few minutes after the call."

Jules stood next to the wall and scrolled through the local news. Changing her mind after what felt like hours, she waved. "Thanks, Millie. I'll talk to him later."

She nodded and picked up the jangling phone.

Jules walked toward her Wrangler. Holding the Jeep's door open to let out some of the heat, she tapped a quick text to the sheriff.

Before she climbed inside to head home, he responded. It's been insanely crazy. Marco and the trooper are questioning Vee Jay. We got this.

Jules rolled her eyes and pocketed her phone. "You've got Vee Jay, but there are still two biker guys popping up all over town, and something hinky's going on, especially since one of them visited your office," she muttered. Climbing inside, she blasted the air conditioning.

Vee Jay probably faked his kidnapping, but did he kill his father? And what about Vick and Petey, the two muscle-bound guys who were interested in Simone? And how did they all relate to the pill smuggling?

Jules hurried back home to do some more digging.

Chapter Twenty-one

Saturday Evening

Jules's phone binged as she sat at her dining room table. The alert didn't phase Bijou, who snored loudly from her spot under the chair.

Have you eaten?

Nope, whatcha thinking? She replied to Jake.

There's a BBQ truck with a 100 different combos. They all look good.

Yum, she tapped into her phone. Do they have pulled pork?

I'm on it. I'll bring dessert and hush puppies, too. See you in a few.

Perfect. No cole slaw. XXOO, she replied.

Jules picked up the living room and dragged out two TV trays. Then she rummaged around the fridge for drinks. "Bijou, I think it's about time to get groceries." She made a pitcher of tea and set it beside the almost-empty half-gallon of milk.

So far, her search had revealed nothing new on Pete Green or Vick. *Am I losing my touch? Usually, I can at least find something.*

Jules crossed her arms and rested her head. *Maybe I should leave this one to Sheriff Hobbs's team.* Jules's phone vibrated across the table.

"Hi, Pixel. What are you up to this evening?"

"I've got the night off, so it's game night. I found something interesting, so I decided to call you before I log on. The plate you sent was a Virginia one?"

"Yep. I think so. It was white with navy numbers."

"There were fifteen plates in Virginia ending in that series of numbers."

Pixel took a swig of something.

Jules let out a long puff of air. "Hmm. I wish I could have gotten all the numbers, but I only had a couple of seconds and a quick glance."

"It was weird. All fifteen of those Virginia plates are blocked in the system I checked."

"Blocked?" Jules asked, staring at her spreadsheet.

"That usually indicates some kind of law enforcement, either state or federal. You said it was a black Suburban? That could fit. They don't want random searches of plate databases to call out vehicles registered to police, especially if they're used in undercover work."

"Yep. Definitely a black Suburban. Law enforcement? But these are two biker types," Jules said, tapping her pen on her stack of papers.

"I'll see if I can dig up anything else. Maybe they're from another state. With all the specialty plates, it could be from somewhere else."

"Would there be any other reason a plate is blocked in the system?" Jules asked.

"I don't think so. It's to protect law enforcement." Pixel's voice faded.

"Interesting. Thanks for checking on it. Vern's brood is from New Jersey. I saw a sticker on one of their vehicles for a biker bar in Philadelphia. I'm not sure how a law enforcement plate on the big black SUV fits in, and maybe it doesn't. I'll keep it as a fun fact in case I need it."

"And I'll keep at it too. I didn't find anything on a Pete Green or a Peter Green either. There are 23,420 Peter Greens on the East Coast. Maybe it's one of them, or maybe it's an alias." Music blared in the background. "Sorry about that. I didn't realize the volume was up so high on my TV. Not every search yields gold. I'll poke some more later."

"Thanks, Pixel. You're my best source for info that mere mortals can't access. Have fun with game night."

"We need to have dinner soon. Call me. Lately, I'm usually available on Sundays. Not the most hopping day for girls' night, but we can still have fun."

"Sounds good. See ya," Jules disconnected and stared at her spreadsheet. "Partial plate, blocked license identification, possible wrong state, and nothing on his name. This is so full of dead ends and brick walls." Jules sighed and stacked her notes neatly by her laptop. "Bijou, somehow, I know the Hogges are doing more than selling teddy bears. I need to figure out who the smugglers are. Was it Vern? Or was it one of his relatives? Vern's death is somehow linked to this. *I just have to prove it.* She tapped her finger on the table.

Bijou looked up and yawned.

"Okay, here's my working theory. In my head, someone in Vern's crew is smuggling drugs in the bears. I don't think all three are involved. Maybe someone put the rainbow bears on display by mistake. Why else would they disappear so quickly? Someone stole my pink bear off my desk. It had to be one of the Hogge gang or someone here on the property. And someone also killed Vern. Did he find out about the smuggling, or did he cheat someone, or did someone want him out of the picture to take over his sweet deal? Vee Jay faked his own kidnapping. Did Vee Jay kill Vern to get the business or for revenge, or to keep the smuggling a secret? Or what about Simone and Travis? They always seem to be plotting. Lots of possibilities. Not a solid, working theory at all. Just a bunch of questions that sounded better in my head."

While waiting for Jake, she taped several sheets of copy paper together and drew out scenarios. Some of her ideas implicated one person, while others involved some partners in crime. "And Vick and Petey are either the dealers or the buyers. I think it makes the most sense for Vee Jay to be the culprit. Simone keeps talking about his get-rich-quick schemes. What if Vern found out and Vee Jay killed him, either on purpose or accidentally? But the biker bar sticker is on Travis's truck. And why was the truck and trailer hidden in the woods? It was also the truck spotted at the Afton site."

Bijou yipped her response as she darted toward the door and the footsteps on the other side.

"Hey, you," Jules said to Jake after she opened the door. "Elaine must have put you on the work crew. I don't think I saw you all day."

He kissed her and followed her to the den. "It's all good. I had fun. Mitch said to tell you hi. I also ran into Sally Evers. She's back from her trip to

CHAPTER TWENTY-ONE

Florida."

"That reminds me, I need to call her about partnering with Wine O'Clock for a wine tasting for a family reunion that's coming to the resort in August," Jules added a note with a reminder on her phone. Setting her phone on the table, she asked, "Is iced tea okay?"

"Sounds good. I got pulled BBQ with lots of sides. I'm starved. How was your day?"

The pair settled on the couch and spread the food out on the TV tables.

"It was good. Darlene and I stayed busy with tons of questions. I guess the most exciting part was when Mario and the state trooper arrested Vee Jay," she said.

"What for?" he asked, biting into his sandwich. Cole slaw and sauce oozed out, and he reached for a paper napkin.

"His dad's murder. They're sure he faked the whole kidnapping thing. The sheriff and his team are going to be busy for a while."

"What were you working on when I got here?" He wiped more sauce off of his stubbled chin.

Jules popped up and grabbed her latest diagram. When she returned, she held it out for him to see. "I'm working on my murder theories. I think the big, buff biker guys are either getting or receiving the smuggled pills from the teddy bears. I've caught the two of them several times watching the Hogge gang. Vee Jay seems to be the obvious culprit, but the more I think about it, something's bothering me about his arrest. I think it might be too obvious. Simone and Travis said he faked his kidnapping for publicity. He's not the brightest bulb, and he's always dodging work. Simone has quite the collection of fancy clothes and jewelry. For a store clerk, she's always dressed to the nines. What if she's supplementing her income with something illegal?"

"Possibly, but didn't you say she was a social media influencer. Maybe she makes money that way?"

"Maybe, but Pixel said that her following didn't put her in the big league. And then there is quiet Travis. Why was his truck with that biker bar sticker hidden in the woods? That was suspicious. Why not park it in the lot with the rest of their vehicles?" she asked.

"They could have been trying to keep it under wraps after the kidnapping. Or maybe there was something hidden in it."

Jules hopped up again and retrieved her phone. "Is it still in the woods?"

Jake nodded. "Yep. The contract security checks on it each night. According to Tony, it was there last night."

She tapped a quick text to the sheriff about the truck. "Maybe Sheriff Hobbs's folks will want to take a look at it, especially if it has secrets inside."

Before she could continue, her phone beeped with the sheriff's response. Near the road behind your place?

Yep. In the clearing. A red truck with a tarp over the trailer. The windows are tinted. I think it belongs to Travis.

Thanks. I'll send a deputy by to check on it. It's abandoned on your property, right? he asked.

Yep. Jake said the night security has been watching it for the last few nights, she replied.

Steer clear. My guys will check on it. Jules held up her phone so Jake could read the conversation.

"I'll let the security guy know," Jake said, raising one eyebrow.

Jules tapped her lip with her index finger. "Maybe Travis and Simone are involved, too."

Jake laughed. "I know you. You're going to keep poking until all your questions are answered. Just be careful."

She nodded, as possible motives and suspects swirled around in her head.

Chapter Twenty-Two

Sunday Morning

Jules woke when the sun streamed in through her curtains. Rolling over, she rubbed her eyes and realized she hadn't set her alarm. "Come on, Bijou. We've got to get a move on. We have some check-outs this morning."

After a shower and coffee, Jules threw on a resort golf shirt and jeans. Corralling her wild curls into a ponytail, she added some eyeliner, blush, and lip gloss. "Let's get the office open, and then we'll get some breakfast. Mel and Crystal probably have something fabulous on tap for Sunday brunch."

Jules gathered her things, and Bijou tried to drag out the walk to stay outside for as long as possible. Jules eventually won the tug of war, and the pair headed for the office.

Jules buzzed around the office and store, following her opening routine while Bijou watched from the comfort of her bed. After Jake left last night, she had pored over her motive diagram and notes for hours with no a-ha moments.

"Hey, what's shaking?" Roxanne asked, breezing in and dropping her belongings on the other desk. "You okay?"

"I stayed up too late last night looking for a motive." Jules rubbed her eyes and stretched.

"Sheriff Matt did too. He called me on his way home from the office last night. It was well after twelve-thirty. The trooper arrested that Vee Jay guy for his father's murder. The son had a rap sheet as long as my arm, but it always seemed that his dad's lawyer bailed him out each time. This time will be different if the murder charge sticks."

"Does the sheriff have his doubts?" Jules asked. A tingle of excitement pulsed at the thought.

"You know him. He never likes to make an arrest unless it's an iron-clad case. I think he's running down some ideas to make sure he followed every lead."

Interesting. Thoughts that it's not Vee Jay keep tickling the back of my brain. Something doesn't fit.

"You wanna get breakfast? Jules asked.

"Nah. I had oatmeal at home. I'm good. What's the plan for today?" Roxanne asked.

"We have ten check-outs and ten new groups this afternoon. Turn-over day. I'm going to grab some food. I'll be right back."

Her aunt finger-waved and picked up Bijou.

Jules slipped out the front door. The sun, birds, and the mountain view made it a scene worthy of a movie. As she passed the two black Hogge trucks, she heard an angry voice. So much for a peaceful morning.

"No, you shut up!" The outburst was followed by some mumbled swearing.

Jules strained to hear more. She inched around the pull-behind trailer.

"I don't see why you're getting so upset. It was just an idea. I'll leave it where it is," came from the other side of the teddy bear trailer.

"It's now or never," she whispered to herself. "Hi, Travis," Jules said louder than she meant to, making the tall guy jump.

"Oh, hey." He shook his head and pocketed his phone.

"Anything I can help you with?" Jules asked.

"Nah. Simone and I are getting ready to head to town. She's running late as usual. She called with more excuses. I'll probably get a sunburn out here waiting for her."

"Any word from Vee Jay?" Jules asked, hoping to keep him talking.

"Nothing since he called and told me to reach out to Uncle Vern's lawyer for him."

"Do you really think he killed his dad?" Jules probed.

Travis shook his head. His longish hair jiggled and returned to its rumpled look. "It doesn't make sense. Uncle Vern was grumpy, but he was good to us. I learned a lot from him about toys. Vee Jay's not interested in the business. He wants to be a professional poker player."

"Then what happens to the bear business?" she asked.

"Who knows. I hope I still have a job, but I guess it depends on what happens with Vee Jay. For now, Simone and I will keep it going. She said we have an obligation to our customers. If Vee Jay sells it, I guess I'll be looking for another job." The big guy shifted his weight from one motorcycle boot to another.

"I'm curious about something. Maybe you could help me out. Was Vee Jay really kidnapped that day up at the spooky motel?" She batted her eyelashes for effect.

He continued to fidget. "I guess it's okay to tell. Heck, he's in jail now. What's he going to do but yell? No. That was one of Vee Jay's schemes. He got paranoid with all that cop's questioning him when Uncle Vern died. He was super paranoid that he was going to get arrested." Travis paused and looked over his shoulder. "He thought if everyone saw him as a victim that it would create more sympathy for him. I told him it was stupid, but he insisted. I'm sure the cops have figured it out by now."

"Was Simone part of that plan?" Jules asked.

Travis shook his head vigorously. "She would have told him it was a dumb idea."

"Is the red truck in the woods yours?" she asked.

A sheepish look crossed his face. "Yep." He nodded. "That was another one of Vee Jay's bright ideas. And what Simone's ticked about." *Interesting. He didn't even ask how I knew about the other truck.*

Jules stared up at Travis and waited.

When the long silence seemed to bother him, he said, "I went to get my truck out of the woods, and she threw a hissy about it. She wants me to leave it where it is and not touch it. Fine. Whatever. I don't see why she even cares. She had nothing to do with the kidnapping scheme."

"Can I ask you a personal question?" Jules asked, trying to keep him talking. "What's up with you and Simone?"

Travis rammed his hands in his front pockets. "We're friends. We've been hanging out a lot."

"I've seen you two together, and it looks like more than friends." Jules cocked one of her eyebrows and continued to stare at him.

A smile danced across his lips, and he suddenly looked like an overgrown teenager. "I dunno. It kinda just happened. It started out as talking. She needed someone to listen. She said Vee Jay is too wrapped up in himself and doesn't treat her right."

"Why not leave and make a clean break if you both want to get away?" Jules asked.

A pink flush covered his cheeks. "She said she can't leave. She likes being around me, but we have to keep it on the down low. She told me I make everything bearable." He snickered at his own joke. "But she's not ready to take off and start over. She said she doesn't want to settle down."

"Well, I hope you all get things worked out," Jules said.

Travis chuckled again. "It's been calm and quiet since Vee Jay's been gone. Maybe I can convince her we're better without him." He saluted with two fingers and walked toward the tiny houses.

Jules whipped out her phone and tapped a note to the sheriff. He probably already knew what she had learned from Travis.

After no response from Sheriff Hobbs, she continued on her breakfast mission. Mel and Crystal had a bountiful buffet set out. Jules filled a to-go box with pancakes, turkey bacon, and a dab of fruity teddy bear salad. She smiled when she spotted the teddy bear toast next to the oatmeal topping station. The gals had used banana slices and raisins to make the faces.

Sidling up next to Simone at the coffee station, she said, "Good morning. Are you getting enough pictures around here for your social sites?"

"Huh," Simone said, turning to see who was behind her. "I guess. I've been kinda busy lately. I haven't posted much since we've been here."

"I was hoping you could give me some pointers. I'm working to expand my reach for the resort's accounts. I heard from Vee Jay that you're an influencer." Jules hoped her smile didn't look plastic.

A pained look crossed Simone's face as she reached for the creamer. "My best advice is to have an interesting life to post about. Have adventures and hang with cool people. People know if you're faking it."

Jules nodded like it was sage advice. "Thanks. I ran into Travis earlier. He said you all were heading to town."

"We have a few more days here. Might as well make the best of it. Who knows what will happen with Vee Jay?" She stirred her coffee with enough force to create a whirlpool in her mug.

"Do you really think he did it?" she whispered.

"Probably," Simone smirked. "I wouldn't put it past him. "If you excuse me, Travis is waiting for me."

Jules nodded as Simone walked to the nearest door. She gave her a head start and then followed.

With no cover in the field, Jules pretended to look at her phone as she picked her way across the grass to the parking lot. Simone leaned into Travis's truck and put her to-go cup in the drink holder. Then she hoisted one leg up and pulled herself into the mammoth black vehicle. She barely had the door closed before Travis revved the engine and floored it, and the truck and trailer rumbled down the resort's maintenance road, leaving a cloud of gray smoke in its wake.

Jules hustled back to the office for breakfast and another look at her notes. Simone seemed uncaring and put upon, while Travis seemed genuine.

"What's good over there?" Roxanne asked, looking up from the registration computer.

"Pancakes, oatmeal, and fun teddy bear things. How's it been here?"

"Checkouts have been steady and smooth. Only waiting on four more. Go ahead and eat your breakfast before it gets cold. I'll go check it out for a refill on a latte when you're done," her aunt said.

"Thanks. I'll be back to take over the registration desk." Bijou followed Jules and her breakfast container to the workroom. As she swished syrup over pancakes, Jules looked at her spreadsheet and added a few Travis and Simone updates.

"Well, hey there, stranger. I didn't think we'd see you around for days," Roxanne said as the front door shut, and the bells jangled. Bijou tore off to the dividing door and started a barking jag. Jules slipped into the store. "Hi, Sheriff. How are things?"

"I was on my way to town and decided to swing by. I got your text," he said, turning toward Jules.

"Is it really the son?" Roxanne asked.

Sheriff Hobbs pursed his lips and then replied, "There was enough evidence to arrest him. I'm not sure if it'll hold in court if he gets a good defense attorney. But that doesn't mean for you to go off snooping." He stared at Jules.

"I'm not snooping. Just talking to my guests. Vern's death and Vee Jay's arrest don't seem to completely jive. Plus, we haven't tied up all the mysteries like who keeps leaving me love letters with knives."

"I don't think it was Vee Jay. He seemed surprised when I asked him about it," he said. "So far, not much has come back from the lab. The prints were smudged. They did confirm it was animal blood, so neither seem to have human blood on them."

"And anything else on the pill smuggling scheme?" Jules asked.

The sheriff shook his head. "The state and their task force are taking lead on that. Seen any more of those bears around?"

"Nope. I told Simone and Vee Jay that I wanted to order some more. They both said they didn't have any. Have the bears and their contents turned up anywhere else?"

He frowned slightly and shook his head. "Not that we know of."

Roxanne interrupted with, "I was going to head over and see what's on the brunch menu. You hungry?"

"Thanks. I've got to get back for a task force meeting. Wanna try for dinner tonight?"

"Sounds like a plan. What about you come over about six? And I'll keep everything warm if you get waylaid," Roxanne said as she followed him out the front door.

About a half hour later, Roxanne blew into the back door with breakfast and a large iced coffee. "Everything was yummy, so I helped myself. This'll either be my second Hobbit breakfast or lunch. Did I miss anything?"

"Nope. It's been quiet."

"Then why don't you head to town and see what else you can find before all these folks pack up and head home. I looked at the schedule. There's a teddy bear picnic in the field next to the library and a concert this afternoon with the teddy bear street fair." Roxanne winked at her niece.

"You know me too well." Jules smiled.

"I can tell when there's a bee in your bonnet. Just fill me in on all the details that you find. Bijou and I will greet all the new folks." Roxanne took a bite of her slice of teddy bear toast and shooed her niece out the door.

Chapter Twenty-Three

Sunday Morning

Jules zipped to town and used her commute to think more about Vee Jay's arrest. The threats, drug smuggling, and the murder had to be related. Those were too many things happening around here to be random. *And I don't believe in coincidences. But was Vee Jay responsible for all of it?*

He didn't seem motivated or organized enough to plot and implement a smuggling operation without help, especially with his work ethic and the way he ran the legitimate business. The police believe that Vee Jay didn't like his overbearing, controlling father, and he killed him to get the business. *But isn't he the obvious suspect? And that kidnapping ruse was the best he could do to throw suspicion off of himself?*

The mysterious biker duo knew Simone, and she acted nonchalant about them. It stands to reason that they could be in cahoots. They've been in town quite a bit lately, to be a coincidence either. And she leads the other men in her life, Vee Jay and Travis, around by their noses. Travis admitted to helping Vee Jay with the kidnapping scheme, and he's having a dalliance with his cousin's girlfriend. Lots of suspicious people and lots of possible motives.

Jules found parking a few blocks from the festivities and hiked to Main Street.

Before she could enter Vern's tent, Simone flew out. Her head was almost inside of her designer bag as she rummaged for something.

"Hey, there. Just stopped by to check on some bears," Jules said.

Simone looked up and scowled. "Ask Travis. I'm busy right now. But you may want to give up on those bears. It's doubtful we'll get any in soon." Simone speed-walked in her stilettos toward the food trucks.

Jules dismissed her curtness and headed for the cash register. "Hi, again," Jules said, stepping toward the counter where Travis stared at his phone.

Travis looked up, and a pained expression crossed his face.

"I was in town, so I decided to stop by to see if you all had any more small bears for party favors."

"Oh, yeah. You said you were planning a party. All of our rainbow bears are gone, and we didn't bring any more with us. Email the website, and we can see if we have any back at the warehouse. If that doesn't work, look around and see if you can find any substitutes."

"Thanks. If not, I may have to come up with another theme. These are cute." Jules fingered a fuzzy teddy bear key chain.

Travis continued to stare at her.

"I thought of something else that I wanted to ask you." She tapped on her phone and scrolled to the knife pictures. "We found these on the property, and I was wondering if they look like they belong to Vee Jay." She held up her phone for him to see.

He moved closer, his ruddy face paled. He squinted and leaned forward more.

"Or what about this one?" Jules scrolled to the one of the knife sticking out of the pink bear.

"Uh, no. Those are hunting knives. Vee Jay wouldn't be interested in anything like that. He doesn't go outside unless he has to," Travis said quietly.

"I'm guessing they're not Simone's either."

He shook his head. "Nope. This is probably the first time she's been outside in years, too. They do a lot of computer work."

"Are the knives yours?" Jules said in almost a whisper.

Another pained look settled on his face. He stalled by looking closer at the pictures on her phone again. "Uh, no. My hunting knives are in New Jersey.

Why would I bring them here? I didn't expect to go hunting or fishing. I came here to work. You run a campsite. It could have been any one of your guests."

"Well, thanks. Just thought I'd ask. I'm checking with my guests to see if they recognize them. And thanks for the info on the bears. See you around."

Jules hurried out of the tent and kept walking until she was near the stage. The sound crew tested the microphones and speakers for the afternoon concert. Sound checks and counting bounced off the food trucks and almost drowned out her thoughts.

Her heartbeat faster as blood swooshed in her ears. *Travis knew something about those knives. He's a terrible actor. He also admitted that he had hunting knives. Did he leave me the warnings?*

Before she could think more about the ominous messages, Simone zipped by on the nearby sidewalk. Jules followed from a few steps behind, trying to use the crowd as cover. For someone in heels, Simone moved at a good clip. She managed to speed along and dodge pedestrians without any effort or collisions.

Simone paused for a beat and kicked off her shoes. She scooped them up and cut across the grassy area near the stage where sound checks still blasted from large, black speakers. Heading to the back of the stage, Simone stopped suddenly and pulled her phone from her oversized purse.

Jules moved a few feet back and blended in with a small crowd near a gelato truck. Simone alternated between tapping on her phone and glancing over her shoulder every few minutes. She wiped her brow with the back of her hand and checked her phone again.

At about the time, Jules's legs started to cramp, Simone waved and hopped up and down in her bare feet.

Jules sucked in a mouthful of air when she saw Vick and Petey, in their signature black outfits, approach the stage. Jules played Frogger, hiding behind different groupings of people on the grassy area to get a better view and to try to pick up some of the trio's conversation.

Simone did most of the talking, waving her arms around as she spoke. The biker guys nodded occasionally as she continued her animated talk.

Vick leaned closer to Simone and said something in her ear. Her shoulders slumped forward, and she didn't reply. Petey said something and frowned at her. Then the two men jogged away from the stage toward the other end of Main Street.

Deciding who to follow, Jules did some mental gymnastics and chose Simone, who stopped suddenly near the sidewalk to slip on her shoes. She wiped her eyes with the back of her hand and hustled across the street to the Good Thyme Bistro. Skipping the outdoor seating, she headed for the door and disappeared inside.

A few minutes later, Simone reappeared and slid her fancy sunglasses in place. She said something to the hostess, whose face scrunched up. The hostess yelled something to Simone's back. *Still winning friends wherever she goes.* Simone clomped down the sidewalk, pushing her way through the crowd.

Jules followed for several blocks and stopped when her quarry approached the curb and paused. Before Jules could catch her breath, Simone was off again.

Simone swooped into Vern's tent, and Jules crept around the edge, hoping the boxes and displays blocked the view of her from the people inside. She inched around the corner and down the side in the tiny space between tents. She had to pick her way over chords and navigate around discarded boxes. Getting as close as she could to the edge where Vern's counter was, she leaned in, trying not to be spotted.

"Did you get lunch without me?" Simone demanded more than asked.

"I was hungry, and you disappeared again," Travis mumbled. "You didn't say how long you would be gone."

"Didn't you think I might want something?" Simone tapped her foot and planted both hands on her hips.

"You want me to get you something?" he asked.

"One of those cherry slushie drinks," Simone snapped. "And two chicken tacos with extra guac. And some of that yummy Mexican corn."

Travis took one last bite of his burger and wiped his hands on his jeans. He ambled out of the tent.

When he was out of sight, Simone pulled out her phone and sent a series of texts.

Her phone rang, and she let out a string of obscenities. "What do you want? I told you I can't talk. Travis will be back any minute."

Jules held her breath. The voice on the other end was loud enough to hear through the tinny speaker. "Did you hear what I said earlier? You need to produce something soon or else. This is your one and only warning," a gruff voice said.

"Understood." Simone jammed the disconnect button with her pink nail. She stomped her foot and growled.

Before Jules could move, Travis lumbered back in and handed her a large paper cup and a greasy bag.

"Just put it over there." She pointed to the counter. "I'll be back in a minute."

She exited the tent, and Jules had a moment of panic. *Did Simone notice her?*

Jules held her breath as Simone walked around the tent. Jules had enough time to duck around the corner. She lapped the tent and took a peek down the narrow space between tents. Simone lit a cigarette and scrolled through something on her phone. The younger woman's face turned bright red, and then she dissolved into a flood of tears and sobs.

Not sure what to do, Jules watched for a few minutes as Simone calmed down and wiped her cheeks with the back of her hands. She clicked on a contact and took a deep breath.

"What?" a male answered.

"I don't know where your stuff is," Simone said in a whiny voice.

"Not my problem," the guy snapped.

"Come on. Give me a day or two to find it. I know I can. Please. It's not my fault. I'm trying to help you."

"That's all you get. I don't like to wait."

Simone disconnected and wiped several tears that ran down her cheeks.

Chapter Twenty-Four

When Simone wandered away from the tent, Jules let out a long stream of air. Her insides felt like a mouthful of Pop Rocks. Not taking any more chances, she speed-walked down the nearest side street and headed for the Jeep.

All of her energy leaked out when she slid into the Wrangler's seat. Exhaustion flooded over her. *Simone is the center of all of this.* Thoughts of Vee Jay, Travis, and Simone bounced around and crashed into each other in her head. They all seemed guilty of something, and everyone was sneaking around.

Jules parked outside her cabin and jogged to the back of the office, where Bijou waited by the door. She picked up the brown and white bundle of energy and nuzzled her neck. "Hey, baby. I missed you. There was way too much excitement this morning."

The dog yipped at the voices drifting in from the store. Jules kissed Bijou and put her in her bed.

Roxanne handed a woman a welcome packet. "Let me know if you need any ideas for meals or for things to do."

"Thanks," the woman said. "We're looking forward to our stay here, and these two are excited about the bear festival." She held a rosy-cheeked toddler who clapped her hands.

A curly-headed brunette who held her father's hand said, "I love bears. I have so many at home. And dad said he would buy us a new one here."

"Then you all are in luck," Roxanne said. "You all are staying in our 1959 Airstream that has a woodland theme. Look carefully around the trailer. You'll see deer, foxes, bears, turtles, and a whole bunch of other animals in the decorations."

The little girl clapped her hands and pulled her dad toward the door. "Let's go see."

When the family waved and headed to their accommodations, Roxanne said, "Hey, there. What did you find? You know something. You have that twinkle in your eyes."

"First, how's it been here? Sorry to have abandoned you if it got busy," Jules said.

"Nope. All's well. Bijou and I took care of everything. I did have to send Jake over to the Area 51 trailer. The new folks thought there was a leak, but he said someone didn't close the door all the way, and it was condensation. All's well. He said to tell you he's over at Mike Cooley's place working on the tiny house this afternoon."

"Oh, good. Glad everything is running smoothly. I had a chance to eavesdrop on Simone and Travis. She keeps having phone conversations with someone about handing over something, and she keeps claiming that she doesn't have whatever it is. The biker boys keep hounding her, and she's dodgy. She seemed really upset, and I'm going to make an educated guess and say it's the drugs. So, either Vee Jay had a deal that went bad, and now Simone is on the hook, or she's smack dab in the middle of something she created and can't deliver. Simone did a lot of yelling and crying. Not sure if she's playing the drama queen or whether she is a victim in all of this."

"With her hot temper and sharp tongue, it's hard to see her as the victim. She's been lashing out since she got here," Roxanne said. "And of that bunch, she's definitely the brains of the operation."

"Then there's quiet and creepy Travis. I think he's madly in love with Simone and will do anything she says. But that could all be a front, too, for his drug smuggling scheme to use Vern and Vee Jay's business as a way to transport things." Jules let out a long puff of air that wiggled her bangs.

"Lots to think about it. I talked to Sheriff Matt last night. I don't get the sense that he's convinced the killer is Vee Jay. But you didn't hear any of this from me. They found some DNA on Vern's clothes and cell phone that belonged to his son, but that could be explained since they lived and worked together. Matt's nervous that there's no other physical evidence that links the son to his dad's murder. And this part is hush-hush. Keep this to yourself." Roxanne paused and looked around the empty store. "He said that there is a federal team that is investigating the drugs you found. So, this is really complicated with all the jurisdictions and investigations. Matt's got his hands full."

"That makes it sound like they're watching the Hogges. I wonder how the biker guys fit into all of this," Jules whispered.

"Why are we whispering? Bijou won't tell our secrets." Roxanne laughed.

Jules giggled too. "I don't know. You said to keep it on the down low." Jules drummed her fingers on the counter. "So that makes it sound like the pill smuggling isn't a one-time thing and that somebody has been using the bears as part of their distribution efforts for a while."

Roxanne raised one perfectly manicured eyebrow. "It may be an easy way to move things across borders. I'm assuming that most of these toys are imported from somewhere else. It's less risky. Nobody has to be the mule."

"Maybe you're right. So, is Vern or Simone the mastermind behind this? We kinda ruled out the other two," Jules said.

"Dunno. We need to be careful and watch what goes on around here. Someone's already left you two warnings," her aunt said. "I don't want you to put yourself in any danger."

Jules hoped her expression looked braver than she felt. "I think that was to scare me. I don't think they were real threats, just scare tactics."

Roxanne patted her arm. "Be vigilant anyway. There are a lot of kooks out there. Let's talk about something more pleasant. Do you have any exciting plans for tonight?"

"Nah. Jake will probably want to work late with Mike Cooley. They're so close to finishing his house. Mike's days off are limited since he's on-call at the sheriff's office. He's trying to cut costs by helping out with the labor on his tiny house build. It's probably movie night. Bijou and I will find something good to stream."

Roxanne winked. "And I'm sure you're going to work on your murder timeline. If you find anything good, make sure to let Sheriff Matt know. I'd really like to get this thing solved, so he can stop being the phantom boyfriend."

Jules smiled. "I'm sure he and his guys would like to catch up on some sleep, too. I can imagine the overtime that they've been putting in on this."

"Yep, every time there's a task force, they are swamped with interviews and research and their regular day jobs," her aunt said.

"What about you? Any plans?" Jules asked.

"Tonight's book club, and it's at my house. So, I'll be the hostess with the mostess. As long as there's wine, we're good. And we may even talk a little about the book. I'm going to head out and start getting some things set out. And I need to swing by Wine O'Clock and pick up my order. You need me to do anything before I skedaddle?"

"Nope. Have fun. If you have any good appetizer recipes, let me know. I need to work on the summer newsletter. Hey, you want to do an article on what your book club is reading?"

"Or drinking." Roxanne winked. "Maybe I could pair my summer reading choices with an appropriate adult beverage. See y'all later. And hurry up and solve that murder. I want the sheriff back." Roxanne picked up her bag and lunch container.

"Bye," Jules said as Bijou scampered to the door for a kiss or a chance to go with her.

Jules settled in her chair and booted up her laptop. Not seeing any snacks or trips in her future, Bijou darted toward her bed and settled in for her pre-dinner nap.

Jules pulled out her make-shift timeline. She used a red marker to draw links between the players and added hearts for romantic links. Unfortunately, there were no neon arrows pointing to a killer. She pulled up a blank Word file and listed each name in a chart. Then she created a bulleted list of the reasons each could have killed Vern. The most used reasons included greed, anger, preservation of a drug smuggling business, and jealousy. Then she copied the chart and changed it to who would smuggle drugs. The major motivators turned out to be a lust for money and power. Still no clear suspects.

Jules hopped up for a jolt of caffeine and grabbed a can of Coke from the fridge. "Okay, Bijou. I thought mapping this out was going to help me, but I can argue that all the motives in my list apply to the players in the love triangle. What am I missing?" She tapped her forehead with the end of a pen.

"Let's try this from another angle." Bijou opened one eye to see if that theory would work.

"What if one or more of the Hogges are the transporters and not the dealers? Could that be one of Vee Jay's get-rich schemes? It would explain why the dynamic biker duo keeps asking Simone for what's theirs, or could Vern have been on this, and it got him killed? Did one of the three younger employees get the bright idea to steal from the dealers? If so, that could be deadly. I've got to find out who Vick and Petey really are."

Chapter Twenty-Five

Monday Morning

Jules tossed and turned all night. Her thoughts of drug deals, murders, and kidnappings mixed into a scary dream. When she couldn't fall back to sleep, she took a hot shower. Afterward, she made an espresso to work on the groggies. "Come on, Bijou, let's get a start on this day."

The Jack Russell zipped around the living room and waited impatiently at the door for Jules to catch up. She needed no sugar or caffeine for her energy bursts.

After her extra-large coffee, Jules buzzed around the office following her opening routine with Bijou hot on her heels. Everything was a game to the little terrier.

Settling in at her desk, Jules watched the purply pink of the sky turn lighter. She thought about their busy season that now included the fall. The end of summer, always melancholic for Jules, signaled the end to freedom and fun. Though Labor Day weekend was no longer a sad end of the season ever since she kept the resort open year-round. Things used to get packed away and boarded up. The campground in winter used to look like a ghost town. Jules smiled. Her gamble to keep the resort open year-round paid off.

Before she could dive into her administrative tasks, the front door opened hard enough for it to slam into the door jamb and for the bells to make a screechy sound.

Jules got the jump on Bijou and made it through the Dutch door before the little dog had a chance to escape. Lately, she had been a Houdini when it came to sneaking into the store.

"Is everything okay? May I help you?" Jules asked a disheveled Travis. His clothes looked like he had slept in them, and his bedhead added to the look.

"I can't find my truck." Travis's gaze darted around the store. "It's missing."

"One of the ones parked out there?" Jules asked, mentally flipping through her memories, trying to remember if both of them were in the lot when she arrived. "I can check my cameras."

"No, it's my red truck, and it had a pull-behind with it. The black ones belong to Vernon, well, Vee Jay."

"I don't remember seeing a red one." Jules tried to pump him for more details.

"No. Over near the field." He paused and stared at Jules. "I figured we were taking up too much space, so I moved it out of the way. And now it's gone."

"When did you last see it?" she asked.

"A couple of days ago. We've been using the black ones since you know, what happened to Uncle Vern and Vee Jay." The tall man wiped his hands on his jeans and shoved them in the front pockets. He stood jingling his change. "I don't know what I'm going to do. This place is cursed. We've had way too many bad things happen. The only thing that made this whole trip worthwhile were the good sales. I'm ready to go home. Uh, no offense."

Before Jules could speak, Travis rocked back on his feet and looked at his hand. Then he ran his hands through his unruly hair. "First, we can't get them to release Uncle Vern, so we can give him a proper funeral, and now we have no idea how long they're going to keep Vee Jay. I don't know how we're even going to get all our trucks and our equipment home. We've run out of people." He laughed a strange little chortle that almost sounded like a sob.

"I'm so sorry that you all have had a horrible experience here. Let me contact our sheriff to see if he has any recommendations about your truck." She pulled out her phone and pushed Sheriff Hobbs's contact.

After three rings and a, "Good morning, Jules. What's up this early in the morning?"

"Hi, Sheriff. I have Travis…. What's your last name?" she whispered to the tall guy who fidgeted on the other side of the counter.

"Bates," he whispered.

"Sheriff, I have Travis Bates here. He's Vernon Hogge's nephew. He came into the office this morning to ask about his missing red truck and trailer. It was parked in the field on the other side of the woods."

"Umm-huh. Tell him I'll be over in a bit to take his statement. Can he wait there?" Sheriff Hobbs asked.

Pulling the phone away from her mouth, she asked Travis, "Can you hang around here a bit for the sheriff to come by and take a report?"

"Uh-huh. I guess. Simone wants to go into town, but she can go ahead. I'll meet her at the booth when I can." He pulled out his phone and sent a text.

"He'll be here," Jules said to the sheriff.

"Good. See you soon." Sheriff Hobbs disconnected.

"Thanks," Jules said to dead air. "He's on his way. Can I get you something to drink while you wait?"

Travis continued to stare at his phone.

"Sheesh. That girl. She can yell and curse in a text just as well as she can in person. Uh, no. I'm good. I'll wait on your porch if you don't mind. I like the peacefulness of this place. I don't get too much quiet time. Your place looks like it's good for tent camping and fishing."

Before Jules could respond, he plodded out the front door, closing it more gently this time.

Jules made another strong coffee and settled in at her desk to check the resort's social media sites. By the time she made it to her email, she heard voices on the porch. She clicked on the store's outdoor camera feed and spotted Sheriff Hobbs leaning on the porch railing, talking to Travis.

Now it was Jules's turn to fidget. She was dying to hear the discussion on the porch. "I know Bijou. I want to hear what they are talking about, too." She moved to the laptop at the front counter, and Bijou followed along, plopping down by the front door and whining to go out.

About a half hour later, Bijou let out a yip that sounded almost like a siren as the front door opened. She danced around the sheriff until he reached down and patted her.

"Hey, there. Good morning," Sheriff Hobbs said, closing the door behind him.

"Thanks for coming over so quickly," Jules said. "Can I get you some coffee?"

"I'm good. Thanks. Just wanted to give you an update before I take off. I took Mr. Bates's report on his missing truck."

"The one in the field that had the tarp on the trailer?" Jules looked up at the sheriff and paused, waiting for him to continue. She hoped she had her poker face on, but it probably looked like her skeptical face.

"Yep, that one. I'll have an update for him as soon as I can. Any idea why he parked on the other side of the woods and tried to cover the trailer?"

"When we talked, he said he felt like they were taking up too much of the parking lot with the two behemoth black trucks and trailers." Jules shrugged a shoulder. "My team didn't ask him to move it."

"I'll let him know something when I can. If any of them come in asking about it, tell them to contact the sheriff's office. It may take a few days to get it sorted out."

"Okey dokey. Didn't your guys tow it?" She asked.

He held up his index finger to his lips before he slipped out the door.

After a busy day that included booking a family reunion, a ninetieth birthday party, and a ladies' wine-tasting retreat, Jules and Bijou trudged home for dinner. "Hey," she said, stopping suddenly beside her Jeep. "Since Jake's still at Mike's working on the tiny house, why don't you and I grab some dinner in town?"

Bijou waited for her to open the passenger door. Once settled in for the ride, the pair drove to town. Most of the crowds had cleared out, and all the roads were open except Main Street. They found parking on a side street and strolled to the Good Thyme Bistro's patio.

"Good evening to you both. Aren't you such a cutie?" the hostess cooed at Bijou. "What can I do for you all?"

"Dinner on the patio, please," Jules said, following the svelte twenty-something to a table near the wrought iron fencing.

"Here you go. Your server will be right with you."

Jules scanned the menu and picked out her choice by the time the lanky waiter with the long bangs approached. "Good evening. What can I get you for dinner?" he asked, setting down water and utensils. "The pink sheet in the menu has all our teddy bear specials," he added.

"I'll have the grilled chicken Caesar salad with an unsweetened iced tea."

"Very good. Be back in a sec with your drink."

Jules scrolled through her phone, looking at the Instagram posts from this week's events. If you don't count all the problems with the Hogges, it looked like everyone was having a good time.

"Here you go," the waiter said, setting Jules's tea on the table and a water bowl down for Bijou. "Your dinner will be out in a few."

Jules and Bijou people watched until dinner arrived. Bijou plopped down at Jules's feet, waiting for any chicken or crumbs to fall her way.

As twilight settled on Fern Valley, Jules paid for dinner, and the pair headed down the sidewalk where the crowds had thinned considerably. Jules rounded the corner near where she left the Jeep and got a glimpse of a large guy in black in her peripheral vision. Her pulse raced, and she glanced around to see if it was one of the biker twins.

False alarm. She willed her heart rate to ease back to its normal level. Jules scooped up Bijou and hurried to the Jeep. Letting out a long breath once the doors snapped locked, she sat behind the wheel for a few seconds and scanned the area around the Wrangler.

Jules drove to the resort with a purpose. She couldn't shake the creepy feeling that someone was watching her. *Get a grip. Your imagination is running wild.*

When she skidded to a stop in her driveway, she cut the engine and rested both palms on the steering wheel. Her heart was still pounding out its staccato beat. "Okay, get it together. You saw someone in black, and now your thoughts are bouncing around like ping pong balls in a lottery drawing. You jumped from someone wearing black to a stalker to drug smugglers in less than ten seconds. Deep breaths. Just focus." She closed her eyes and took several cleansing breaths.

Bijou hopped up on the console and licked Jules's nose. She laughed and hugged the little dog. "Let's go for a walk before night-night."

When Jules held open the door, Bijou jumped out of the Jeep and took off toward the lodge. Jules couldn't convince her to slow down until they got to the edge of the woods. Darkness had settled, and the woodland noises sounded spookier than normal. Jules tried to push thoughts of being watched out of her mind.

She guided the brown and white dynamo back toward the cabin. "Come on. That's enough excitement for one evening. Let's go see what's on the DVR."

Bijou acquiesced and trotted toward home and the possibility of a treat.

Before they could climb the porch steps, loud footsteps echoed in the darkness. Jules reached for her phone and dropped it as a hand grabbed her shoulder.

She let out a shrill squeal and scrambled for her phone.

"Uh, sorry. I didn't mean to scare you. I saw you out here, and I wanted to see if you'd heard anything on my truck. I kinda need it back," Travis said, taking several steps back and displaying his empty hands.

"You startled me. Uh, no. I haven't heard anything else from the sheriff. Did you call him?" Jules tried not to sputter.

"No. I don't want to be a pest, but I need some of my stuff," he whined. "I mean, if it was stolen, I need to call my insurance company. You'd think the police would be out looking for it or something."

Didn't the Sheriff tell him they towed it?

"Why don't you give them a call and see what they're doing. If the sheriff isn't there, they can get a message to him. At least, you would know what to do about your stuff," Jules said, trying to quell her racing heartbeat.

"I guess you're right." He let out a heavy sigh. "I'm kinda over it. But if the truck's been stolen, that'll cause more delays. Simone is going to freak over this." He paused and shifted his weight to his other leg. Then, without a sound, Travis disappeared into the darkness.

Jules nudged Bijou, but the little dog changed her mind about ending their outdoor time. She lunged after a toad, and the race around the cabin was on. Then a rabbit skittered out of the bushes, and Jules let out a squeal. The dog gave chase to the edge of the woods.

When Bijou stopped for a rest, Jules guided her to the cabin and shut and locked the door behind them. She let out a long breath as her heart pounded in her rib cage.

Chapter Twenty-Six

Tuesday Morning

Jules and Bijou strolled to the office the next morning. A calm, much different than how last night felt, spread over her like a cozy blanket. "Come on, puppy. It's a brand-new day. I hope Travis got an update on his truck."

Bijou was more interested in a June bug than Travis's problems. It took Jules a few moments to get her headed in the direction of the office. There were too many bugs and interesting scents that captured her attention.

After she started the coffee brewing, Jules checked the voicemails from the night attendant. *Time to get a move on.*

Roxanne moseyed in while Jules jotted down a contact number for a reservation. Her aunt waved and picked up Bijou for a squeeze.

When Jules hung up, her aunt said, "Good morning. How's everyone doing? I do believe that things might be getting back to normal. I have a dinner date with our sheriff. Maybe we'll really have a meal together. It'll be the first time in weeks he hasn't had to work late or cancel on me."

"I hope things are settling down. I booked some good-sized group reservations this morning, and I'm going to call this gal back. She wants to arrange a leaf peepers' getaway for her book club in October."

Jules grabbed her mug and settled in at her desk. Seven thirty-eight. Too early to call a potential guest. Jules skimmed email and waited for a more reasonable hour to return the call.

Footsteps in the store caused Bijou to dart toward the dividing door. She barked like a marauding mob was invading. Jules dodged the Tasmanian devil and headed for the front.

"Oh, I'm so glad you're open. I need your help," Simone waved both arms and pointed to the door. "Can you come with me?" Simone's shirt hung untucked on one side, and her eyeliner had smudged into large, panda circles around her eyes.

"What's the problem?" Jules asked. "Are you okay?"

"Just come with me, please! I don't have time to explain it. And yes, I'm okay." The woman's voice rose two octaves as she grabbed Jules's arm. "I need your help. This is really important. I need you to look at something." She tugged again, almost knocking Jules off balance.

Jules nodded to Roxanne. "I'll be right back."

"Let me know if you need me to call anyone." A concerned look crossed her aunt's face as the two women hurried out on the porch. Roxanne followed the pair and stood at one of the front windows as Simone rushed Jules off the porch.

"This way." Simone pointed to the parking area. "Please hurry. I don't know what to do."

"What is it?" Jules asked.

"I told you I don't have time to explain. Just come with me." Simone pulled on Jules's arm and led her to the edge of the parking lot, where one of Vern's big black trucks sat with its driver and passenger doors open. The unconnected trailer leaned on the pavement. The hitch was still attached to the truck's bumper.

Jules looked around. Nobody else was around. "What's up?" Jules asked. "Why is your truck wide open?"

She felt something hard poke her in the spine. "Ouch." Jules tried to turn and swat at Simone, but the woman grabbed her around her neck and squeezed.

"Get in and shut up," Simone hissed. "I'm not messing around anymore. I've had enough of you sticking your nose where it doesn't belong. So, if you're going to act all helpful, you're going to actually help me. Get in and don't try anything, or I will shoot you." Simone let go and shoved Jules forward.

Catching herself on the truck's front seat, Jules turned to look at her attacker. Simone's face flushed with rage as she waved a silver gun around. "I'm a Jersey girl, so you may want to get in, shut up, and fasten your seatbelt. I know how to use this." She let out a high-pitched giggle that sounded more like a cackle as she pointed to the inside of the truck with the gun barrel. "Move!"

Jules put up both hands and leaned inside the giant truck that resembled a dumpster. Litter covered every inch of the floorboard and seat. The fast-food wrappers and discarded snack bags left a stale, greasy smell that made Jules gag.

Jules slipped a couple of times on the debris as she tried to get her footing and climb into the oversized truck.

"Get in and don't let me have to say it another time. I have had enough. I am over all of this. I want my life back. Nothing has gone right since we've been here." Simone poked her again in the side with the barrel. "Close that door and no funny business, or I won't hesitate to use this."

A jolt of panic flooded through Jules. No one knew where they were going, and she couldn't pull out her phone without Simone noticing. She took several calming breaths and tried to work out an escape plan. *Please let Roxanne realize that something is wrong.*

Simone flew around the truck and jumped into the driver's seat. Much to Jules's relief, she stopped waving the gun around and set it in her lap. It took Simone a moment or two to adjust the seat and mirrors. "Travis is such a pig. And he took the good truck and left me with this disaster. I don't know why I expect better. I'm never going to get anything but whining and stupidity from this bunch." Her lips curled into a sneer. "Idiots. All of them. And he better find his other truck if he knows what's good for him," she growled. "Sometimes, he's so stupid."

Simone had a crazed look in her eyes as she floored the accelerator and zoomed out of the parking lot. She drove faster than what she should on the narrow back roads. Jules hoped Bubba had one of his speed traps up this morning.

The two women drove for several miles past town and down a winding country road. No other cars in sight. Jules let out a sigh that she hoped didn't sound like a whimper. *I have to stay calm. Just breathe and look for an opportunity to get out of this truck. Maybe there will be another car I can signal.*

Simone sped up when she saw signs for the interstate. "Which way?" she demanded, staring at the map on the screen.

"What? How should I know where you're going?" Jules snapped.

"To that crappy old motel. I want to go back where this all started and show you something. Now, which way?" Simone screeched.

"Go west and look for the Rockfish Gap exit."

"The what?" Simone poked the map on the screen. "I don't see it. I don't see anything named for a stupid fish. How am I supposed to find roads in this po-dunky town? I swear, half the roads don't even have mile markers. What kind of place is this?"

"Slow down, or you'll miss the turn. I mean it. You'll never be able to make that sharp curve going this fast. You need to slow down!" Jules glared at Simone, who didn't seem to notice.

"Don't tell me what to do. Everyone tries to tell me what to do. I am over it. I want out. I am smart enough to make my own decisions." A tear leaked from the corner of Simone's eye. She pressed the pedal, and the truck sped forward on the acceleration ramp to the highway. *I hope she yields to oncoming traffic.*

Jules stiffened and tried to brace herself in case Simone hit the guardrail or crashed into someone. *What is wrong with this woman? Maybe I'll have a chance to get away if she does wreck this thing.*

Somehow, Simone managed to merge without flipping the truck or crashing. Jules let out a long breath through her gritted teeth and tried to calm herself. The blood swooshed around her head, and it sounded like rushing water. Jules felt light-headed and queasy.

"Where now?" Simone demanded. "And be quick about it. No stalling. And don't think about giving me bum directions."

"Slow down. Take the turn and follow this road until you see the old Inn at Afton signs. You'll turn on that road and follow it up to the top of the hill." *I wish I had given her directions to the sheriff's office. I just didn't think of it quick enough.*

"You better not be lying," Simone hissed.

"Why don't you pull over and let me out. I'm queasy, and there's nothing really I can help you with. I can walk back, and you can go on about your business."

"Shut up. I need some time to think. Everything has been crashing down on me. And I didn't sign up for any of this crap." Simone struggled to keep the truck in its lane on this part of Skyline Drive. "I mean. I wanted to do my own thing and be an influencer. I didn't realize what I'd gotten myself into until it was too late. Now it's all a big, hairy mess. And I will kill you if you throw up in here. It's already a stinking mess."

"I'm sure we can find someone to help you work whatever it is out," Jules said softly.

"No. I'm not ready for that. I can fix this. And you're going to help me. So shut up about all your rainbows and unicorns. And your stupid teddy bears."

"What? How is this my fault?" Jules asked.

"You fell in love with those stupid bears. You couldn't let it go. I mean, how many times did you come in and ask about them? Couldn't you let it drop?" Simone asked, taking her eyes off the road to stare at the map on the GPS. "How much further? I swear, I can't wait to get away from this place. I have had enough of the mountains and your little town ways."

"It's about three miles or so," Jules said. "The site is at the top of this ridge. And what was up with those bears?" Jules asked, hoping Simone would reveal more information.

"Bears, bears, bears. I've had enough. I want to work in fashion. I gave up my modeling career for Vee Jay. How stupid was I? All it got me was a lot of work and no money. Vee Jay leans on me to do everything he can't or won't do. I'm sick of it. And he can sit and rot in that jail for all I care. I want out, even if this isn't the right time. And you're going to help me make that happen."

The pair rode in silence up the mountain.

"Oooh, there it is," Simone squealed like a schoolgirl, turning the steering wheel sharply to head up the road to the abandoned motel. "This place is creepy. I'm glad the Ghostbuster guys told us about it. It's the perfect setting. I can get some good shots up here."

Simone drove into the empty lot by the burned-out cabins and former gas station. She parked near the rusted water tower and pulled several makeup bags and a brush from her oversized purse.

Jules watched as the younger woman scrubbed her face with a wipe. She climbed out of the truck and used the seat as a counter while she did her makeup and hair.

She dragged me all the way out here by gunpoint to help her with a photo shoot. Is she for real? I've got to figure out a way to get away from this wackadoodle.

"Stay in the truck," Simone demanded. "Don't even think about running. I don't feel like chasing you. I'll shoot you." She flipped her head forward and teased her long, dark hair. Flipping it back and standing up, she said, "There. Just a little touch-up on the lips, and I'll be ready. Oh, wait. I forgot the hairspray." She let loose with a cloud from an econo-sized can that filled the cab of the truck and made Jules cough.

Putting her gun in her purse, Simone pulled out her phone. When it connected, she said, "Where are you? And what's taking you two so long?"

"Huh? What? I can't hear you," Simone said louder. "What are you doing at the police station. You didn't get freakin' arrested, did you?"

After a long pause, she snapped, "Quit whining. I heard you. I know you keep saying this is not your fault. But you better figure it out and get my stuff back, or we're both dead meat. Call me the minute you know something. Wait a minute. I changed my mind. Get up here now! Meet me in the room we went to before. You know, at that old, abandoned motel." Simone disconnected and slammed the phone down on the seat. "Idiot. I have got to get away from these cavemen who think they're tough guys and soooo smart."

Turning to Jules, she pulled out her gun and phone again and said, "Come on. Let's get some shots while the sun is bright." She pointed with her gun to the overgrown area near the dilapidated gas station. "Here, take some of me here. I like the urban decay look in the background. It makes me look edgy."

Simone posed like Annie Oakley with her gun for several shots. "Now I want some in front of that rusty water tower. Those will look good."

After a few more shots, where she held the gun like one of Charlie's Angels, Simone said, "I need a minute to do a video. Sit down. Sit down now and put your hands on your head where I can see them. And give me that." She snatched the phone out of Jules's hands.

"What?" Jules asked. *I have to figure a way out of here.*

"Move. Now." Simone pointed to the cracked asphalt with her gun. "Now! And hands where I can see them. Be quiet, and don't ruin my video." Simone fluffed her hair and pointed the phone at herself. "Hey, all. I'm still in this god-forsaken place, but I wanted you to get a chance to see my new outfit. I'll show you my chichi bag later. I'm here at this old, abandoned site on top of this lonely mountain. I heard it was haunted. I like the creepy vibe here and all the decay. So, I had to show it to you. What do you think?" Simone moved the camera around and turned it back to herself. "My love life is a hot mess right now. Girls, I may need some help. Make sure you like this video and leave me a comment. I'm trying to decide if I want to be with either of these guys. One's in jail right now. I mean, for real. What's a girl like me to do? Tune in tomorrow to see what happens." Simone stared at the camera and blew several kisses.

Chapter Twenty-Seven

Tuesday Morning

Simone licked her lips and smiled. "There. All done with today's post. It's fabulous, and I already have thirty likes. They're going to love seeing what happens next live. Now all I have to do is get some true crime or fashion show producer to pick it up. This is my ticket out of this stink hole." She looked down and checked her phone. Her giddiness faded as she stared at the screen. Her phone binged in her hand.

"I told you to fix it. Just fix it!" She angrily typed. "Sheesh."

"What?" Jules asked.

"None of your business. Get back in the truck and no funny business." Jules climbed as slowly as she could into the truck. She tried to stretch out each second until Simone yelled, "Enough! Just get in."

Simone hopped in behind the wheel and moved her purse on top of the middle console. She rammed the transmission in reverse and sped out of the parking lot before Jules could get the door closed or her seat belt fastened.

As Jules got herself situated, Simone slammed on the brakes and parked outside the old restaurant and lobby entrance. "Get out."

Jules tried to stall. She inched her way out of the truck and walked at a snail's pace.

"Pick it up," Simone demanded, jamming the gun in her back again. "I don't have all day. Go through there."

They stepped over trash and discarded motel furniture on their way through the lobby that still sported some of its sixties' décor behind stacks of old furniture and piles of debris. For a moment, Jules tried to imagine the lobby and restaurant in its heyday. Even with all the trash and decay, the view of the Blue Ridge Parkway was stunning. Too bad all of this was rotting away.

"Get a move on and quit dragging your butt," Simone ordered, poking at Jules again with the gun.

"Okay, okay," she said. "I'm moving as fast as I can across this war zone. You don't have to keep waving that gun at me. I'm doing what you ask."

"I am in charge here!" Simone yelled. "And don't you forget it. Turn down that hall and keep walking. And quit dragging your feet, sister."

The pair walked down a long, dark hallway. Simone screamed and waved the gun around when a rat skittered by. Jules hoped she wouldn't shoot her accidentally.

Several minutes later, Simone stopped screaming and waving the gun, but she stomped to her feet as they moved down the corridor.

"That one. No, it's the next one. Go through that doorway. The one with the pentagram on it," Simone ordered.

Jules stepped into a room that had been trashed by a marauding horde. Afraid to touch any of the soiled mattresses and bedding, Jules tiptoed inside next to a credenza covered in beer and wine bottles and drug paraphernalia. *I need a steaming hot shower, or at least some hand sanitizer, or maybe a tetanus shot.*

Jules opened her mouth to ask a question, but closed it again when Simone swung around with her gun. "And now we wait," Simone said.

"For what? I'm still not clear what you need help with," Jules said.

Before Simone could respond, a scraping sound came from the broken slider door that led to what was the pool. *It's probably just another rat.* Jules took a deep breath to calm the anxiety.

The noise outside got louder, and Simone waved the gun at the large opening in the wall.

Panic jolted through Jules's body like a shock of electricity. Every one of her nerves felt like firecrackers going off. *I have to get control of this if I'm going to get out of this mess and away from this place.*

The noise outside got closer and louder. Travis stumbled through the opening in the wall and looked as surprised as Jules felt.

"What are you doing? I almost shot you?" Simone yelled. "I thought you were going to text me when you got here."

"Uh, I assumed we'd go to the same room last time. Remember, we joked that this was our special room. And thank you for not shooting me. Put that away. What are you doing?" He stepped inside, trying to avoid the broken glass.

"I had to make her come with me," Simone said, widening both of her eyes like she was trying to send him some telepathic message.

"Why is she even here?" Travis asked, looking back and forth between the two women.

"You said you thought she knew where your truck is. We need to find that stuff you lost. We're running out of time." Simone gritted her teeth and made a face. Turning to Jules, she said, "Sit down in that chair. Right there."

"Listen. Y'all work out whatever it is between you two. I can walk from here." Jules started toward the opening.

"Stop her! And make her sit in that chair. Tie her up. You will stay put until I can figure out what to do." Simone barked orders like she was part drill sergeant.

"With what. You didn't say bring anything with me," Travis said.

"Do I have to think of everything? Be creative. Use that chord off those broken blinds." Simone planted one hand on her hip and glared.

"Because we all know how smart you are, because you tell us every chance you get," Travis muttered.

"What?" Simone asked.

"Nothing. I can use this." He cut the ties off the blinds with a large hunting knife and wrapped them around Jules's ankles and the chair.

"Make sure she can't get away," Simone said, looking at her phone.

Travis rummaged through another pile and found some more blinds. He wrapped the cord loosely around Jules's hands, that were pulled behind the chair.

"Okay," Simone said. "Where is the red truck and all our stuff?" She glared at Jules.

"The sheriff's office gave me the run-around and the copy of some dumb report," Travis said. "But no truck."

"Where is it?" Simone tapped one of her feet on the broken glass and other garbage.

"In the truck," Travis said sheepishly. "Do you want me to get the papers?"

"I was talking to her." Simone glared at him. "And no, I don't want to see your stupid papers," she said in a sing-songy voice. "I want to see your stupid truck." Simone stamped her foot. "I need my stuff."

"I don't think it says anything about your stuff," Travis said quietly.

Simone stomped her foot again and stepped toward Travis. "Where is the truck?"

The large guy took several steps back like she was going to attack him. "I told you I dunno. They were all real nice and stuff, but no one at the police station could tell me much of anything," Travis whined.

Jules realized how loose the hand restraint was. She wiggled her wrists. Maybe she could free herself, but she had to make sure Simone and Travis didn't notice. *Hang tight, girl. Look for an opportunity and make your break.*

"Where is the truck? Who has it?" Simone stomped like a three-year-old throwing a tantrum. "I. Need. My. Stuff." She took a deep breath and let out a growl that almost sounded like a wounded animal. "I don't get paid without it. And I lose everything. We have no job and no money."

Simone sucked in air and wiped her eye with the back of her hand. "This is deadly serious, and we're all going to pay. I had four aqua tubs filled with something valuable in them. And now they are missing along with the truck. And it's all because stupid Vern got a burst of energy and unpacked it and sold some before I found out. It's all his fault. We've got to get it back. I'm running out of time and patience." She took several breaths and shook her head slightly.

"I don't know what to tell you," Travis said, wiping his brow with the back of his hand. "I can't give you what I don't have. And what is so important to get you this upset? I put those tubs in the truck."

"Yes, Travis. You put the tubs in the red truck, and now they're missing. Do you see the problem here?" Simone balled her hand into a fist and swung it in the air.

"I don't know what you want me to do. I can't make any of it magically appear. Guess I should have put them in the other truck." Travis slid his foot back and forth, moving debris on the ratty carpet. A puzzled look crossed his face. "Those were the tubs with the rainbow bears?"

"Yes, those were the rainbow bears. No thanks to you or Vern." Simone turned to Jules. "You're friends with the sheriff. You talk to him. We need our stuff like now. I mean, how many stolen trucks can there be in this god-forsaken place? And why can't they find it? This place is like Mayberry. You can't have gangs and syndicated crime here running car theft rings."

Travis punched something on the screen. "Hey, this is Travis Bates again. Can I talk to someone about my stolen truck? Preferably, the sheriff. I have a friend of his here who has some information for him."

Simone's overly stylized eyebrows formed a giant "V" in the middle of her face. "What are you doing?" she mouthed to Travis.

Ignoring her, he continued to wait for an answer from whoever was on the other end of the line. He clicked on some buttons. I'm going to put this on the speaker. He held up a finger to his lips.

"Sheriff Hobbs. What can I do for you?"

Jules felt a wave of relief wash over her.

"Uh, hello. Is this the sheriff?" Travis asked.

The sheriff made a slight grunt and replied, "Yes."

"Good. I have Jules here. She has some information for you. You're on speaker, so let me know if you can't hear her. Say something to him. Oh, and tell him what you know." He held the phone closer to her as Simone waved the gun as a reminder.

"Uh, hi, sheriff. This is Juliette Keene. How are you?"

"You okay?" he asked, crunching on something.

"Just peachy. I'm hanging out with Travis and Simone here at the HoJo. And they're still looking for their red truck. I told them that I'd check to see if you had any more updates for them. They're really concerned about getting their truck back. It seems they had some personal belongings in it that they really needed. They let me know several times that they really need to get them back."

After a pause and what sounded like a laugh, he replied, "Nope. Still missing. We've got bulletins out all over the area. We're hoping that it's not in some chop shop by now. Just so you know, we'll be out in full force on this. It's definitely on our radar. We've got a couple of roadblocks going on today. Hopefully, we'll be able to find it. If not, they'll have to get in contact with their insurance company. I don't know what to tell them about their personal stuff. I guess they'll have to wait and see if it turns up."

Simone let out a squeal. "I need my stuff!"

"Tell her we're doing our best. We're going to put it out on the Crime Stoppers alert today. Hopefully, we'll get some leads from the public. Anything else I can do for you? I gotta run to a meeting. Hey, come by the office later. I have a business council folder for you."

"I can't today. I'm a little tied up," Jules said, trying not to smirk. "But you've been helpful. Can you let Travis know the minute you hear something about his truck? And send my love. You know, hugs and kisses to Bubba for me," Jules said.

Travis disconnected the call and pocketed the phone. "What do we do now? Just wait? Who has time to wait for leads from the public?"

"I'm thinking. I have to meet the guys soon. We don't have much time. I need to be able to tell them something." Simone twisted a long strand of her hair around her finger. "I've been stalling too long. They want to get out of town with their stuff. If they don't get it, I don't know what they'll do."

"Maybe we should go back to the campground and wait," Travis said. "At least we can find food there and a place to sit down without getting some horrible disease. And I'm kinda getting hungry."

"We could go back to the resort," Jules suggested. "We have plenty of food at the lodge. You can have whatever you want."

Simone snapped, "Shut up," and Travis's grin faded. "We're not going anywhere. We don't have time to think about food. I need time to come up with a plan. Maybe I can buy us some time with the guys. Am I the only one who sees the severity of this?" Simone pulled out her phone and stepped out of the room into the old motel's former hallway. She spoke in low tones, and Jules strained to hear Simone's side of the call. Only catching a few of the words, Jules assumed she was talking to Vick or Petey.

A shriek and stomping noises rang out. Travis bumbled through the doorway, slipping on garbage as he braced himself on the door frame.

Jules wiggled out of her hand restraints and untied her ankles. Before she could escape from the room. A dark shadow crossed the gaping hole in the wall where the sliding glass doors once stood.

Jules sucked in a mouthful of air.

Chapter Twenty-Eight

Later Tuesday

Jules tried to keep the bats that were floating around in her stomach at bay as two shadows that turned into Vick and Petey slipped in through the opening near the patio.

Her eyes widened, and she wondered if she could outrun both of them. Each sported a large gun that matched their black outfits.

Before she had a chance to move, Petey lowered his gun and put his index finger to his lips. He held up the corner of his black T-shirt to reveal a gold badge.

Jules was sure her eyes bugged out as the realization hit her. *So, the law enforcement thing was real. Pixel was right.*

Vick leaned over and whispered in her ear. "It'll be okay. Where did they go? And just play along."

Jules nodded and pointed down the hall as Simone stormed back in. "What are you all doing here? I thought we were going to talk on the phone. I tried to call you to plan something for later today. I was leaving you a voicemail. The police still don't have any word on his truck."

"Simone, we're here to have a nice, friendly chat," Vick said. "Put down the gun. I don't like it when my friends point guns at me."

"You scared me the last time we talked. A girl has to protect herself." Simone looked wildly at the biker guys and Travis, who was slowly backing out of the room.

"Simone, Simone. And you. Stop moving," Vick said to Travis. "We told you we wanted our stuff, and you continue to stall. Petey here and I are beginning to think that you've found another buyer at a better price and cut us out. We don't like it when our friends aren't trustworthy. And why the heck is she here?" He pointed at Jules, who was trying to fly under the radar in hopes that Travis and Simone didn't notice that she was no longer tied to the chair.

"We were hoping she could help us find the truck. It was on her property. Plus, she kept nosing around and asking about our products. I still think she knows more than she's letting on," Simone said.

"Her?" Petey said, pointing to Jules. "I think she bought some of the bears that you all stupidly sold. Which one of you bungled a good plan? Vick and I don't like it when our friends don't follow the plan."

"It was all an accident. I can't watch everyone twenty-four seven. One of the idiots set up the display." Simone glared at Travis.

"It was all her idea," Travis sputtered. "This isn't my deal. I only did what she told me." He pointed at Simone, who frowned. "And it wasn't me. Vern set up that part of the booth."

"Come on, guys. We're all pals here. If you're trying to tell me you want to end the relationship, then that's a different story. We're all still on the same team, right?" Petey asked.

"Of course. But I don't have what you want. I need more time to get our stuff back," Simone whined. "You've got to believe me. We're not trying to get out of anything or cheat you. We like working with you guys. This is much smoother than our last distributor." Simone paused as her voice quivered. "I can't help it if I work with lazy incompetents. If they hadn't got in the way, everything would have been fine. And then she started sticking her nose where it didn't belong. Asking stupid questions." Fire flashed in Simone's eyes as she sneered at Jules.

"What did I have to do with it? I tried to help you," Jules said, trying to keep her voice calm.

"I tried to warn you. I thought you'd take a hint, but nooooo. You're too nosy for your own good," Simone said, waving the gun in an arc.

"You left the notes and the knives?" Jules asked.

"You stole my knives," Travis whined.

"Shut up. I tried to scare you off, but you couldn't take a hint. I had a great thing going until Vern started nosing around. And then Vee Jay messed everything up. I should have known they'd screw it up. It was the perfect storm." She pointed her finger at Jules and continued to wave the gun around. "And now the stuff's missing."

"Let's put the gun down," Vick said, stepping closer.

"No. Leave me alone. Get away from me. Don't come any closer. You two don't scare me."

A sudden scraping sound made everyone turn toward the interior door. Travis lunged forward and flew out into the hallway, slipping and sliding as he poured on the speed.

"I got 'em," Petey said, giving chase.

Vick stepped closer to Simone.

"Get away from me," Simone shrieked. She grabbed the gun with two hands and pointed it at Vick.

Everything seemed like it was in slow motion as Jules watched from the sidelines.

Vick sprang forward, and the retort from Simone's gun echoed in the small space. The ringing in Jules's ears made her head hurt, and everything looked like Vick and Simone were moving in slow motion.

The big man fell backward. Simone screamed, dropped the gun, and ran toward the pool.

Jules hurried over to Vick. "I'm fine. She got my leg. It'll be okay. See if you can see where she went."

Trying not to get tangled in all the blind cords, Jules stumbled outside and blinked several times to get her eyes to adjust. She saw movement out of the corner of her eye, and Simone bolted toward one of the other motel rooms.

Jules gave chase. Simone paused and then darted in the other direction toward the building. She skidded to a stop and looked at the row of rooms with busted doors and broken windows. They were midway between the motel's two wings, so it was several hundred yards in either direction to get to the side of the building and the parking lot.

Simone turned and fled toward the overgrown shrubbery. She wobbled and fell forward into the dirt and weeds at the edge of the cracked cement.

Jules launched herself forward and landed on the other woman's back with a loud oompf. The two wrestled in the dirt and debris. Jules hoped there weren't needles or broken glass in the weeds.

"Get off of me," Simone ordered. "We both need to get out of here if we know what's good for us. Those dealers will kill us in a heartbeat. They probably already have Travis. And when he can't tell them anything, they'll kill him. They'll throw us all over the side of the mountain and go on with their lives like nothing happened. You've got to believe me."

Simone used the conversation as a distraction and tried to wiggle free from Jules's grasp. Jules pulled herself forward and grabbed at the woman's legs. Simone kicked wildly, and Jules tried to subdue her and protect her own face from the flailing limbs.

The younger woman got in one good kick before Jules leaned forward and punched her in the nose.

"Oww," she screamed. "I think you broke my nose. And now there's blood all over my new shirt. Look what you've done." She deflated like a leaky beach ball onto the dirt and dead grass. "We need to get out of here," she sobbed.

Jules took advantage of the moment to catch her breath.

Then Simone started wiggling. "Come on. We've got to get out of here before we're killed. They are going to come after us. We can make it to the truck. You're going to have to trust me if we're going to make it out of here alive." Simone tried to raise one of her legs. Wincing in pain, she sank back down on the ground, grabbing her ankle. "Crap. I think I sprained my ankle when I fell. We need a plan. And I'm bleeding all over the place."

"How long have you been using Vern's toys as a way to smuggle drugs?" Jules asked as she relaxed her grip on the other woman's arm.

"A few years." Simone wiped the blood from her nose on the back of her hand. "I used my marketing training. The prof said to look for new revenue streams. I wasn't getting anywhere with Vern, and he kept pushing me to marry his stupid son. I hooked up with some guys I met at a bar and figured out a way to get the product into the bears and ship them. It worked well until Vee Jay started asking questions."

Jules stared at her. Simone's face reddened, and she balled her hands into fists. "At first, he kept threatening to turn me in. He was shocked that I would use his pop's business for a crime. Then the idiot wanted a cut. He wanted to take over and expand my thing. Oooooh." Simone's voice cracked. She cleared her throat and continued, "This was my thing, and I was doing well. Why couldn't everyone just butt out? Then he told his dad after he sold some. Then Vern decided he wanted a cut, or he was going to call the cops. I flew into a rage.

That was my money," Simone whined.

"So, what else happened?" Jules prodded, hoping to get her to admit more.

"Wasn't that enough? I'd already had to find new partners when my plan fell apart. One got killed, and the other got arrested. I wasn't sure what to do. In one weekend, I lost my contacts and my supply chain, but then these two biker dudes appeared out of nowhere, and they said we could help each other. A win-win for me. I didn't have to shut down or find other sources. I thought my problems were over until all the screw ups on this end, and Vern started hounding me for his cut."

"Keep going," Jules said when Simone paused again. She looked around. No one in sight. She let out a long breath, calming down slightly.

"And then we got set up for this stupid festival, and you already know that Vern found my special boxes and made a rainbow display. He'd sold a ton of them before I could do anything. I mean, sheesh. It could have blown my whole operation if someone found the stuff. And my expensive product was going out the door with no way to retrieve it. I told Travis that they were recalled, and we had to pull down the display. He has a good heart. He may not be the brightest bulb, but he is sweet."

"But why the hidden truck?"

"We used it when I got rid of Vern. Travis hid it for me. I guess, in his mind, it made sense to put the recalled toys in there, too. He was always afraid of getting in trouble. And now they've been stolen. I can't cover the cost of the pills. I've got to get that truck back and my stuff."

"So, you lured Vern up here, and then you killed him," Jules said. "What did you do with his vehicle?"

"He rode up here with me. And it wasn't like that. I thought we could talk it out and come up with an agreement. He was so pig-headed. There was no reasoning with him. He lost his temper and threatened me. Then I lost mine, and I must have flown into a rage when he said he was going to turn me in if he didn't get what he wanted." Simone paused, and her gaze darted around the motel.

"What did you do with the murder weapon?" Jules's thoughts bounced from throwing it in one of the piles of rubbish here or dumping it somewhere along the route back to the resort.

Simone let out a screechy laugh. "I put it back in Travis's stuff. It was probably the knife he used on those blinds earlier."

"But why kidnap Vee Jay?"

Simone sat up and laughed. "That was my fault, too. And it shows you how self-centered and stupid Vee Jay really is. I was young and stupid when I met him. I thought he'd be a way out of the neighborhood. Instead, he was something else to hold me back." She cackled again. "After his dad's murder, I told him the police would be looking for him since he was the prime suspect. The idiot posted all the time on Facebook that he couldn't wait to take over the business. With the murder, I convinced him that the police would think his posts were premeditated and that he had a strong motive to want his dad dead. He and Travis concocted the stupid kidnapping to make him seem like another victim. That dummy thought that one of his competitors was targeting his business for a hostile takeover."

Footsteps crunched nearby. Vick limped slightly and pointed a gun at them.

Simone squealed and tried to scrabble to her feet. "I told you he was going to kill us. We've got to get out of here."

He cuffed Simone's arms behind her back and read her her rights. Then he helped Jules to her feet.

"What? You can't fake arrest me. I know you're a street dealer and fancy yourself some tough biker guy. What is going on here?" Simone screeched.

"I'm Special Agent Vick Davis with the DEA. Our task force has been watching you for a while. And thanks to what Ms. Keene found, we were able to focus in on your operation." He turned to Jules, "You okay?"

Jules nodded.

"Huh? You said you wanted in on the action when Ronnie got killed. You said you and Petey wanted to be part of my quality operation. You said I had a lot of potential! You can't be arresting me. There is no way you're a federal agent. I saw you do all kinds of shady stuff," Simone wailed.

"We say a lot of stuff when we're undercover. But the DEA part is true. We've had a sting operation in the greater Pennsylvania and New Jersey area going for quite a while. And this teddy bear festival provided the right time to shut down your racket."

"I want to see some ID. I don't believe you. I'm not going anywhere with you." Simone's face paled, and she looked around for a possible escape route. "Plus, I'm injured. I need an ambulance."

He pulled out a billfold and offered his identification to Simone and Jules.

"I still don't believe it," Simone said, turning her head.

"Let's go," Vick commanded.

"Be careful," she whimpered. "She broke my nose. I'm really sore, and I don't think I can walk on this ankle."

"Stay there," he said sternly. "We'll have someone check you out."

"Are you okay?" Jules asked, pointing to his thigh.

"The bullet grazed me. I'm glad she wasn't a better shot," Vick said.

Simone opened her mouth and then closed it again as Petey guided Travis around the bushes.

"Everything okay?" Petey asked.

Vick nodded. "Backup is on the way. I called for an ambulance to check her out. He okay?" He nodded toward Travis, who hung his head.

"Yep. He gave me a good run, but I caught him when he slipped on some trash." Petey pulled out his phone and tapped a text. "I let them know we're around back."

"I can't believe you two lied to me. You tricked me," Simone whined as a caravan of emergency vehicles zoomed up the road with sirens blaring.

198

Chapter Twenty-Nine

Still Tuesday

Jules sat on the bumper of one of the ambulances, sipping from a bottle of water. Someone had draped a light blanket over her shoulders. A combination of excitement and exhaustion battled inside of her.

Sheriff Hobbs sat next to her. "You doing okay? You look like you wrestled a pig or something?"

"Nope, just a drug smuggler." Jules smiled. "You should have seen my opponent."

"I'm sure you neutralized her. What you found was a turning point in this investigation," he said quietly. "It kicked this investigation into high gear. When we put it in the system, we found out about Agents Davis and Green and their investigation. The truck you reported had the mother load of those bears in it. We were waiting for the right time to move in, but Simone seems to have messed up the plan. Rox called me when you went outside with her and didn't come back. And your call with Travis was perfect. I knew you were under duress and exactly where you were. Good thinking."

"I'm glad everything came together. It was touch-and-go for a while," Jules said. "I was trying to figure a way out."

The sheriff looked down at his rough hands. "I tried to warn you. Next time, I'll try to be clearer in the future about key information."

Jules smiled. *He said next time. He does appreciate my help.*

"Your intel was good. The feds were able to shut down Simone. The bear you found full of pills and Travis's truck, filled with the others, was the evidence the task force needed. They moved in on Simone, and it tied directly to our murder investigation. Roxanne is going to kill me when she sees you." The corners of his mouth inched up just a bit.

"Everything but the stolen bear got wrapped up, it seems," Jules said with a wry smile.

"Actually, that was either Simone or Travis, too. We found it in one of the bins with the drug-filled teddies. Not sure why they took it, but I'm sure the insurance company and Vee Jay will be interested in the story," the sheriff said.

"It all worked out," Jules said, patting his arm. "I'm glad it's over. I want to get home and into some clean clothes. I've had enough adventures for a while."

The sheriff grinned. "When they're done with us here, I'll take you back. Not sure if they're taking Travis and Simone to Nelson County or back to Fern Valley. Stay here. I'll be back in a minute. We need to get some details sorted out."

A tall EMT poked his head around the ambulance. "You doing okay back here? Need anything? No pain or new symptoms?"

"I'm fine. Thanks for all of your help." Jules slid out from under the blanket. She folded it and set it on the back of the ambulance.

"If you feel dizzy or nauseated, get checked out," the EMT said. "And take it easy for a couple of days. You're going to be sore from the bruises and cuts."

"Thanks. Hopefully, a hot shower and a quiet night are in my near future."

He smiled and moved on to check on Travis, who was handcuffed in the back of an unmarked car. Simone sullenly sat in the back of another ambulance across the parking lot.

"You ready to go home?" Sheriff Hobbs asked as he approached. "I'll drop you off and then head over to the station to the war room. It's going to be another long night, but at least we're heading toward a resolution."

"I appreciate it. But if you have to go, I can call Jake," she said.

"No problem. Roxanne'll have my head if I don't get you home safe and sound." He winked and pointed toward his vehicle.

Jules stared out the window during the ride down the mountain. "It's funny," she said over the chatter of his radio. "I would always make up stories about this place when I was little. I never imagined that I would spend so much time up here. Hopefully, someone will do something to improve this place. It's sad to waste such a great view." The sheriff nodded and listened to the radio chatter.

About thirty minutes later, the sheriff pulled into the resort, and Roxanne and Jake hurried out of the office with Bijou leading the parade.

Before Jules could get out of the vehicle, they bombarded her with questions, and Bijou vied for kisses.

The sheriff let out a whistle, and everyone froze. "Okay, give her a moment. Let her get settled, and she'll tell you the whole story. How about some coffee or hot tea for her? She's had quite the ordeal."

"Of course," her aunt said, taking her niece's elbow and guiding her toward the office. Jake picked up the wiggly Bijou.

"I've got to head back to the office. It's going to be another long night. Rox, you okay with pushing dinner to tomorrow night?"

"No problem. Be careful," Roxanne said, giving him a peck on the cheek. "And for you, missy, let's get you settled, so you can fill us in on all the details. All of them. Start at the beginning. We don't want to miss anything."

After Roxanne fixed her a mug of hot tea, filled with honey and lemon, the three settled in at the workroom table. Bijou, not to be left out, curled up at Jake's feet.

"I knew something was up when you didn't come back after Simone's outburst." Roxanne clutched her pearls. "I had no idea where you went. It's not like you to disappear into thin air and not tell any of us where you're going."

"We spotted you and that gal's truck on the camera feed and let the sheriff know," Jake said. His kind eyes clouded with concern.

"I'm fine." Jules patted his hands. "Simone didn't make much sense. She rambled a lot, but I figured out that she had killed Vern when he wanted a cut of her business. She was using the toys as a way to move drugs, and that was her major source of income. The two biker guys were undercover agents. It seems they've had her under surveillance for a while."

"The sheriff said that your find helped connect the dots," Roxanne said, patting Jules's shoulder. "Another big case solved. Good job. You're getting quite the reputation around here as the Fern Valley sleuth. And as much as Matt fusses about you getting involved, he really does appreciate your help. You have a knack for finding stuff. So, what's next?"

Jules took a deep breath. "First, a shower and some clean clothes."

"How about dinner later at Pop's?" Jake asked. "You too, Roxanne. I'm not sure when any of us ate last. We could all use some good ole comfort food."

"Sound good. Let me give Bijou a good walk. I'll be back as soon as I get cleaned up. And as far as what's on the horizon. I think I want a couple of weeks of quiet before Elaine and the council plan any more events," Jules said with a wink.

Chapter Thirty

Wednesday Morning

The door to the camp store flew open, and Jules looked up from her computer. Eliot and Noah trudged in, followed by Cliffy, who was trying to balance an oversized backpack and large rolling suitcase. "Good morning," Jules said. "All ready to head out to your next adventure?"

"It was awesome here. We were trying to figure out how we could move into your treehouse. That's my new bucket list item. I want one now for my office and our home base. Too bad, I won't have the view that you do," Eliot said, pulling out a black and neon green folder from his messenger bag.

"I hope you all enjoyed your stay," Jules said. "How did the investigations go?"

"Out of this world," Cliffy interrupted. "That old sanatorium in Staunton was the perfect place. I think we got enough footage for a whole series. The whole trip, well, maybe except at the abandoned motel, was a treasure trove of activity."

"Hey," Noah said, "But we did get the murder and a sort of kidnapping at that place, so there's enough material for a weird stuff we uncover segment. I'd say the whole trip was a success."

"Here are the keys. And this is our broadcast schedule in case you want to tune in," Eliot said, sliding the folder across the counter.

"Of course. I'll share the links on our site. It was so nice to meet you all."

"Oh, we'll be back," Cliffy said, with a wink. "Suz and Drew are planning a wedding, and she fell in love with the area. We'll definitely be back for the ECP wedding."

"Please let me know how we can help. We've hosted a couple of weddings here throughout the years." Jules handed him several of her business cards.

"Thanks again. We've gotta hit the road," Noah said.

"Safe travels." Jules waved as the trio made their way to the parking lot.

Jules settled in at the counter to check on reservations this week. Bookings were solid for the rest of the summer and most of the fall. The council didn't have another event planned until the end of August. They planned to showcase the cideries, local craft beers, and wineries with a two-week festival, and she would open the meadow to trailer campers to accommodate more guests.

Before she could work on her other tasks, the bells on the door jingled. The door opened almost in slow motion as Vee Jay Hogge stepped inside.

"Hi," Jules said. Her voice seemed to echo through the store, and it seemed to startle the toy seller.

He recovered a few seconds later and said, "Uh, hi. Just wanted to drop off the keys. I packed Simone's things and Travis's. I've got a buddy coming in this morning to help me get the other truck and trailer back to New Jersey. Not sure about Travis's truck. He'll have to work that out on his own."

"It's good to see you. I know you've been through an ordeal," Jules said. The normally bombastic toy seller looked subdued.

He let out a sigh. "They finally released Dad, so I guess I'll be planning his funeral by myself. Then I have a lot to sort out. You know things happen. This may be an opportunity for me to figure out what I really want to do."

"Any word on Travis or Simone?" Jules asked.

He shook his head and set the keys on the counter. "I'm still shocked and angry and disappointed. But I guess I should have seen the signs. Hey, but I have a long drive home to do some thinking and decide what to do next. They're both looking at a long list of charges. And they brought it on themselves."

"Be safe, and please let me know if we can do anything for you."

Vee Jay nodded and slipped out the door as the phone rang.

"Good morning. Fern Valley Luxury Camping Resort. How may I help you?"

"Hi, this is Dave Rogers. I'm the events coordinator for the Virginia British Motor Club," and I'd like to talk to you about hosting a meet up for us."

"Sounds like fun. How many in your party? And when would you like to do this?"

"I heard from some friends that you have an area for campers and trailers. We haven't done sign-ups yet, but the last event like this, we had about a hundred participants."

"Sounds good. We definitely have trailer and tiny house accommodations, and we can open the meadow for those in your group with campers and tents, and depending on when you want to do this, I can connect you with our business council's event coordinator if you all wanted to do a parade or other events in town."

"That would be great. Can you let me know some dates next spring or fall and some pricing? And I'd definitely like to talk about events. We've done a poker run, parades, and lots of car shows. That would be nice to open it up to the locals, so they can come and see our restored beauties."

"I can definitely send you some package ideas and get you that business council information." Jules jotted down his information and started a quote.

No sooner had she hung up than the phone rang again. Before she was able to do her introduction, a male voice interrupted with, "Hey, this is Russ, and I've heard some great things about your resort. I have about ten folks who'd like to make a reservation for some time in August. Could you tell me what you have available? We'd need individual accommodations for three couples and one group of four. We heard you had some cabins for larger parties."

Jules explained what her facility offered and provided some available dates.

"Oh, good. I like the week of August tenth. Could you hold the three trailers and one tiny house? That would be perfect. We heard about your place from the East Coast Paranormal guys. We're hunters of sorts, too. We've done searches in North Carolina and Georgia, and now it's time to follow up on some sightings of Bigfoot in Virginia."

"Interesting," Jules said, trying not to sound surprised. "We'd love to hear about what you uncover."

"We're looking forward to it. Can't wait to see you and whatever is hiding up there in your mountains in August," Russ said as the line went dead.

Acknowledgments

Many thanks to my family and friends who are always there with a hug and something caffeinated. Stan Weidner, thanks for traveling on this writing journey with me, my parents who instilled in me a lifelong love of reading, Cortney Cain for everything you do, Meagan Van Laeken and Jocelyn Cain, my subject matter experts on all things generational, and Bill Cain for always keeping everyone entertained. And I appreciate all the encouragement from my Bethia UMC family.

A huge thank you to Shawn Reilly Simmons and everyone at Level Best Books for letting me share the fun of glamping and the mayhem in Fern Valley.

I treasure my talented Sisters in Crime, Guppy, Writers Who Kill, and James River Writer friends. Your support is invaluable! Many thanks to Jackie Layton and Sue Minix for all your critiques and advice!

A shout to James Burnette and his team at RSVP Paranormal for the great presentation that they did for the SinC Chessie chapter. And thanks to Meezan Hassan Ford for suggesting the fairy forest theme for one of Jules's trailers!

To all the readers, podcasters, bloggers, and reviewers. Thank you for helping me spread the word about Jules, Bijou, Roxanne, Jake, and the rest of the gang.

Fruity Teddy Bear Salad

Ingredients:

- 1 package of vanilla instant pudding
- 1 ¼ cups buttermilk
- 1 container of Cool Whip (16 oz.)
- 1 can of mandarin oranges (drained)
- 1 can of crushed pineapple (drained)
- 1 cup Teddy Bear Graham Cracker Cookies (Save some for garnish.)
- Shredded coconut (optional)

Instructions:

1. Mix the pudding and buttermilk together and let it stand for about 10 minutes. Then stir in the rest of the ingredients. Mix well.
2. Refrigerate for about three hours.
3. Decorate the salad with the teddy bear cookies and shredded coconut (if desired).

Teddy Bear Triple Layers

Ingredients:

For the Crust

- ½ cup of unsalted butter
- ½ cup of light brown sugar
- 5 tablespoons of white chocolate powder
- 1 egg (beaten)
- 10 ounces of Honey Teddy Grahams (chopped)
- ¼ cup of slivered almonds

For the Middle Layer

- ½ cup of unsalted butter
- 2 ½ tablespoons of heavy whipping cream
- 1 box of chocolate pudding mix
- 2 cups of confectioners' sugar

For the Top Layer

- 4 ounces of milk chocolate
- 2 tablespoons of heavy whipping cream
- 3 cups mini marshmallows
- 24 Honey Teddy Graham cookies

Instructions:

1. Line an 8x8 inch pan with foil.
2. Melt the unsalted butter, sugar, and white chocolate powder in a double boiler. Then add egg and stir. Remove from heat and stir in the chopped cookies and almonds.
3. Let the crust cool slightly and press mixture firmly in the foil-lined pan and set aside.
4. Then in a bowl, mix the butter, heavy cream, chocolate pudding mix, and sugar. Spread mixture over the cookie layer.
5. For the topping, melt the milk chocolate and heavy cream in a double boiler. After it is fully melted, remove from heat and allow to cool. Then pour the mixture over the previous layer. Chill your dessert overnight.
6. Before serving your dessert, top with the mini marshmallows and teddy bear cookies.

Teddy Bear Hot Tub Time Machines

Ingredients:

- 1 chocolate cake mix
- ½ cup of melted butter
- 1 egg
- 24 Rolo chocolates (unwrapped)
- 2 cups miniature marshmallows
- 40-50 Teddy Graham Cracker Cookies
- Cooking spray
- Muffin tin liners

Instructions:

1. Spray muffin tins with cooking spray and add the paper liners. Preheat the oven to 350 degrees F.
2. In a medium bowl, mix the cake mix, melted butter, and egg. Measure out a spoonful of dough and roll it into a small ball. Push the dough into the muffin tin. Push a Rolo candy in the center of the chocolate dough. Bake for 10 minutes.
3. Remove muffin tins from the oven and add 4-5 marshmallows to the top. Then put two teddy bear cookies in the marshmallows. Bake for 2 minutes.

Lula Belle's Teddy Bear Oatmeal Cookies

Ingredients:

- 1 cup unsalted butter
- 1 ¼ cup light brown sugar
- ¾ cup granulated sugar
- 2 large eggs
- 2 teaspoons of vanilla extract
- 2 ¼ cups of all-purpose flour
- 1 teaspoon of kosher salt
- 2 teaspoons of baking soda
- ½ teaspoon of baking powder
- 2 cups of old-fashioned oats
- 1 teaspoon cinnamon
- Baking sheet
- Parchment paper
- Brown M&Ms
- Mini chocolate chips

Instructions:

1. Preheat the oven to 350 degrees F. Line a baking sheet with parchment paper. In a large bowl, mix the butter and sugars. Add the eggs and vanilla. Mix well. Then add the flour, salt, baking soda, baking powder, and cinnamon. Combine all the ingredients. Add the oats.
2. Use a cookie scoop to drop the batter on your baking sheet. This is for the bear's head. Flatten the ball with a glass. Then roll three smaller

balls (about a ½ inch) for the ears and nose. Place the nose in the center of the face and flatten carefully. Then put the ears at the top (attached to the head). Flatten these carefully too.

3. Bake cookies for 8-10 minutes or until the edges are golden. Let the cookies cool for 2 minutes and then move them to a cooling rack.
4. Add an M&M for the nose. Use two chocolate chips for the eyes. Move the cookies to a cooling rack.

Honeybee Sippers

Ingredients:

- 1 cup water
- 1/3 cup honey
- 3 tablespoons of granulated sugar
- 8 sage leaves (for garnish)
- 1 orange, cut into 8 pieces
- Apple Cider
- Bourbon

Instructions:

1. In a medium skillet, heat water, honey sugar, sage, and 2 orange slices on high. Heat to boiling and then turn the heat back and let it simmer for 3-4 minutes. Make sure all the sugar has dissolved.
2. Cool the mixture to room temperature. Fill your glasses with ice and add a shot of bourbon. Then add your honey mixture. Garnish each glass with sage leaves and orange slices.
3. For a sweet, nonalcoholic version, skip the bourbon.

Teddy Bear Trail Mix

Ingredients:

- 1 cup Teddy Grahams (chocolate)
- 1 cup honey-roasted peanuts
- 1 cup raisins
- 2 cups Honey Nut Cheerios
- Large Plastic Bowl with Lid
- ½ cup mini pretzels
- ½ cup of mini chocolate morsels
- ½ cup of mini marshmallows (Colorful ones are fun.)

Instructions:

1. In a plastic bowl, add all the ingredients. Put on the top and shake vigorously to mix all the ingredients.

Crystal's Teddy Bear Toast

Ingredients:

- 2 slices of white or wheat bread
- 2 teaspoons peanut butter (or chocolate or Nutella spread)
- 6 banana slices
- 6 raisins (You can substitute brown M&Ms if desired.)

Instructions:

1. Toast the bread. Cover one side of each slice with the peanut butter or other spread. Add banana slices for the ears and nose (two at the top and one in the center).
2. Add a raisin or a piece of candy to the center of each banana slice.

Mel's Teddy Bear Pizza

Ingredients for 12 Pizzas:

- 6 English muffins, each divided
- 18 slices of pepperoni, cut in half
- 12 black olives, cut in half
- 6 whole mushrooms sliced (or 12 sliced mushrooms)
- 1 jar of pizza or tomato sauce
- 2 cups mozzarella cheese (grated)

Instructions:

1. Preheat the oven to 350 degrees F. Divide the English muffins in half and place them on a cookie sheet.
2. Cover each muffin with the pizza or tomato sauce. Place the grated mozzarella on the sauce.
3. Put two of the half-pepperoni slices on the top of each muffin for ears. Then put one half-slice on each bear for a mouth. Use the black olives to add two eyes to each, and then add a mushroom to each pizza for the nose.
4. Bake the pizzas for 7-10 minutes until the English muffin is toasted and the cheese has melted.

About the Author

Through the years, Heather Weidner has been a cop's kid, technical writer, editor, college professor, software tester, and IT manager. She writes the Pearly Girls Mysteries, the Jules Keene Glamping Mysteries, the Mermaid Bay Christmas Shoppe Mysteries, and the Delanie Fitzgerald Mysteries.

Her short stories appear in the *Virginia is for Mysteries* series, *50 Shades of Cabernet*, *Deadly Southern Charm*, *Murder by the* Glass, *First Comes Love, Then Comes Murder*, and *Crimes in the Old Dominion,* and she has non-fiction pieces in *Promophobia* and *The Secret Ingredient: A Mystery Writers' Cookbook*.

She is a member of Sisters in Crime: National, Central Virginia, Chessie, Guppies, and Grand Canyon Writers, International Thriller Writers, and James River Writers, and she blogs regularly with the Writers Who Kill.

Originally from Virginia Beach, Heather has been a mystery fan since Scooby-Doo and Nancy Drew. She lives in Central Virginia with her husband and a crazy Mini Aussie Shepherd.

AUTHOR WEBSITE:

http://HeatherWeidner.com

SOCIAL MEDIA HANDLES:

Blog: http://www.heatherweidner.com/Blog

Facebook: https://www.facebook.com/HeatherWeidnerAuthor

Threads: https://www.threads.net/@heather_mystery_writer

BlueSky: Heather Weidner (@heatherweidner.bsky.social) — Bluesky

TikTok: https://www.tiktok.com/@heather_weidner_author

Instagram: https://www.instagram.com/heather_mystery_writer/

Goodreads: https://www.goodreads.com/author/show/8121854.Heather_Weidner

Amazon Authors: http://www.amazon.com/-/e/B00HOYR0MQ

Pinterest: https://www.pinterest.com/HeatherBWeidner/

LinkedIn: https://www.linkedin.com/in/heather-weidner-0064b233?trk=hp-identity-name

BookBub: https://www.bookbub.com/authors/heather-weidner-d6430278-c5c9-4b10-b911-340828fc7003

YouTube: https://www.youtube.com/channel/UCyBjyB0zz-M1DaM-rU1bXGA?view_as=subscriber

Twitter/X: https://twitter.com/HeatherWeidner1

Also by Heather Weidner

The Jules Keene Glamping Mysteries
Vintage Trailers and Black Mailers
Film Crews and Rendezvous
Christmas Lights and Cat Fights
Deadlines and Valentines

The Mermaid Bay Christmas Shoppe Mysteries
Sticks and Stones and a Bag of Bones
Twinkle Twinkle Au Revoir
A Tisket A Tasket Not Another Casket

The Pearly Girls Mysteries
Murder Strikes a Chord
Murder Plays Second Fiddle

The Delanie Fitzgerald Mysteries
Secret Lives and Private Eyes
The Tulip Shirt Murders
Glitter, Glam, and Contraband
Male Revues and Subterfuge

Nonfiction
Promophobia
The Secret Ingredient